Heart of the Bear

Book 2 In the Bearwalker Series

Other Books by Lori K. Johnson

People of the Bear

Heart of the Bear

Book 2 In the Bearwalker Series

Lori K. Johnson

Mundania Press

A Mundania Press Production
Mundania Press LLC
6470A Glenway Avenue, #109
Cincinnati, Ohio 45211-5222

To order additional copies of this book, contact:
books@mundania.com
www.mundania.com

Cover Art © 2009 by Skyla Dawn Cameron
Edited By: Cheryl A. Wilson-Bonner

Trade Paperback ISBN: 978-1-59426-116-9
eBook ISBN: 978-1-59426-115-2

First Edition • May 2009

Production by Mundania Press LLC
Printed in the United States of America
10 9 8 7 6 5 4 3 2 1

To Mom and Dad
with love and gratitude

Prologue

Lindy Anderson stared at the wooden medallion dangling from the string in her fingers. The ancient wood was burnished from the touch of innumerable hands over the years, but the image it bore was still as sharp and clear as the day it had been carved. Her eyes followed the outline of the tiny image—tracing four legs, a head with rounded ears and a stocky body. A tiny, perfect bear. It was an image that reminded her not only of the Bearwalkers she was sworn to protect, but of how her life had changed since the day she'd found the naked shapeshifter on her icy porch steps. Mostly, though, it reminded her of her love for their Guardian, who was neither wholly man nor wholly bear, but lost somewhere in-between.

Even now, she sometimes had trouble accepting the fact that the shapeshifters were real. They were folklore come to life, literally, on her family room floor. Gareth had proven that to her when he'd shifted during his sleep, changing from a gunshot-wounded man to a cinnamon-colored bear. Once she knew his secret, his clan had been forced to either accept her or kill her, and luckily for her, they had chosen the former.

She had never dreamed that she would be welcomed into a clan of shapeshifters, let alone end up rescuing them from the humans who had discovered their existence. It had been so easy to turn against people of her own species that it scared her. But then, that's how it is when you're in love, she figured. You'll do anything for those you care about.

So when Marin had offered her the wooden medallion, the ancient symbol of the human Protectors who vowed to safeguard the clan, she'd gladly accepted. She had willingly taken on the burden of protecting creatures so rare that few even knew of their existence. And for a woman who had recently sworn off men, she'd fallen for Marin faster and harder than a building falling to dynamite.

The bear man was incredible. He had the body of a god and the courage of a hero, but a heart seriously in need of repair. His strength was obvious just by looking at his six-foot-four, 230-pound body of muscle. When he walked through the forest in his human skin, his olive-gold hue glistened as though a bronze statue of a Greek god had come to life and was strolling in the sunlight of Olympia. His jet hair was so black it shimmered with a bluish cast in the light and perfectly matched the dark depths of his penetrating eyes. And oh, when those eyes gazed at her they penetrated right to her soul.

When he assumed his bear form, he was still imposing. Moving with speed and agility that seemed impossible for a bruin his size, Marin took down anything that threatened his clan. Born of the Guardian line, he had dedicated his forty years to protecting his bear kin from the humans that constantly threatened their safety. Only once had he failed. That mistake had cost him the life of his beloved mate and had changed him forever.

Lindy put the string around her neck and let the medallion slide down inside her shirt. It rested in its usual spot. She laid her hand over it and pressed it close to her heart, knowing that this is where the precious symbol would remain for the rest of her life. She gazed out the kitchen window toward the forest where they lived, her shoulder pressed against the woodwork for support, and let her memory slip back to the day she'd learned Marin's agonizing secret.

In her memory, the daylight faded to darkness so cold and biting it took her breath away. She followed the he-bears of the clan as they pursued Marin's kidnappers through the forest that night, hoping and praying that he was still alive. Then the silence was shattered by a terrifying howl of agony and they all knew that there was still time to save him.

They had burst into the kidnappers's camp and found their Guardian beaten and helplessly chained to a tree. The humans had narrowly escaped into the darkness. The bears charged after them, leaving her to care for Marin. In the little time she had known him, he'd scared her so badly that she wished it was one of the other Bearwalkers she'd come to rescue instead of him. Marin had damn near killed her the first time he saw her with Gareth, guaranteeing himself a place of terror in her heart. Still, he was the most gorgeous and exciting man she'd ever seen and he toyed with her as though the feeling might be mutual. It gave her hope that someday she might break down the defensive wall that he had built around himself.

In her mind, she saw him chained to the tree, naked, beaten and freezing to death in the bitter cold of the night. She knew she had to save him, knew that the only way was to share her body heat with him, so she'd passed the night with her bare skin pressed against the flesh of the man who had almost killed her. Her heart thumped wildly even now at the memory of his heart beating next to hers, of his muscular chest so hard and strong against her body. She knew then that she wanted him more than any man she'd ever wanted in her life.

In a moment of weakness uncharacteristic of him, he'd told her how the hunters took the life of his mate and how much he'd grown to hate humans because of it. For the first time, she understood the reason for the depth of his hatred, even though she knew she must be included in that hatred. But then he had turned her world upside-down with the admission that he wanted and needed her the way he had his own mate. He'd set her soul on fire that night.

When he was finally freed, she'd taken him to her

home to heal his wounds and had ended up healing his heart, too. She remembered the way he looked lying in her bathtub, the steam rising above his bruised body, and the way his dark eyes bored into hers before he'd pulled her close for a kiss. It was the first time he'd ever been kissed, and he made her feel like it was her first time, too. To this day she could still feel the warmth of his lips on hers. How could she ever forget that?

Then he was gone. Despite the kiss and the warm words shared between them, she'd known that he must leave. His life was with the clan, among his own kind, and not with her, as much as she wished it to be. Marin would never stop being the Guardian of the Bear People. All she could do was wait for the day when the clan needed her help and protection again. Then he would come for her. Maybe by then, he would have come to terms with his humanity. Unlike the others in his clan, he was part human. The recent discovery of his shameful heritage had ripped him apart, and as much as she wanted to help him, she couldn't. He would have to work it out for himself. With a heavy heart, she'd been forced to admit that only then would the wall between them finally come down. And so she waited.

Chapter One

"Gareth! What are you doing here?" Lindy opened the door and waved the young Bearwalker in, surprised at his sudden appearance.

He smiled broadly, his honey-brown eyes sparkling beneath his mop of cinnamon- colored hair, and stepped into the kitchen. "I remember the first time I came in this door," he said, stopping his visual sweep of the room to pull her into his embrace. He hugged her hard before leaning back to gaze into her blue eyes, his heart thumping wildly at the feel of her again. "I thought I was a dead man."

"Honestly, Gar, I did, too," she said, hugging him tightly. "You looked terrible."

"How do I look now?" Raising his arms out to his sides, he spun around to show off his naked body to her.

Despite her effort to control it, Lindy felt a heated blush rise to her cheeks at the sight of him. *The curse of the fair-skinned*, she thought, hating how her embarrassment was always so obvious. It didn't seem to matter how many times she saw the Bear People in their nudity; it always made her uncomfortable. Pushing the feeling aside, she let her gaze fall across his slim, handsome body. He had gained a little weight and put on some muscle, filling out nicely in his chest and arms. Her mouth curved up in a smile at his familiar body. "You look great, Gareth, like a new bear. How's your shoulder feeling?"

He swung it toward her to show off the pink, circular scar like a badge of honor. "You can hardly even tell I was shot, can you? You did a wonderful job healing me, Lindy. I feel stronger than I've ever felt in my life."

She stood beside him for a moment and just looked at him. His hair had grown longer with the approach of winter and hung almost to his shoulders. It stuck out in shaggy swatches that gave him the look of a wild, unkempt teenager, though she knew he was a decade older than that. It wasn't hard to remember why she'd felt attracted to him when they'd first met, or why she was as grateful to him as he was to her. After all, it was through him that she'd met Marin. She turned abruptly and looked out the back door, her heart racing with hope at the thought.

"Did anyone come with you?"

His arms slumped down to his sides again, and he dropped his head to gaze at her from under lowered eyelids. "No, Marin didn't come, if that's what you mean," he said, obviously irritated. He knew it was the Guardian she wanted to see most; and no matter how many times he told himself he didn't mind that she loved Marin, it still hurt to see the look on her face when she talked about him.

"Oh," she replied simply, trying to hide her disappointment. She closed the door and took him by the arm to sit him down at the kitchen table, then took a seat on the chair next to him. "I thought you weren't supposed to come here alone."

"That was before you became our Protector," he said, helping himself to a grape from a bowl on the table. He popped it in his mouth and sucked on it for a moment while he studied her face. She was trying to act nonchalant but her disappointment was plain in her eyes. "You know, back in the days when we didn't trust anyone who didn't have fur."

She nodded with a laugh, sending her blonde hair sweeping over her shoulders. "It's nice to be trusted enough that Marin let you come here without him."

Gareth's gaze became a heated stare. "Marin didn't *let* me come here. I'm quite capable of doing things without his supervision or his permission, you know."

Lindy arched her eyebrows above her clear blue eyes at his defensiveness. He'd obviously misunderstood her meaning. "I know that, Gareth, and I didn't mean to imply that Marin didn't trust you or that you needed his permission. It was that he didn't trust *me*, and now he does. I know you don't need him to tell you what to do." She slid her hand across the table to touch his. "You know how Marin is," she continued, squeezing his hand reassuringly. "He's so overprotective. I wasn't sure that he would ever give you guys the independence you want. But I'm glad he did, because it's nice to see you again. I've missed you."

"Have you?" he asked sharply. "I'm sorry I'm not Marin, the mighty Guardian; but he said to tell you 'hello,' if that's any consolation."

"Oh Gareth," she sighed, moving to bend down beside him and wrap her arms around his shoulders. He tensed for a moment before she felt his body relax, and he returned her embrace. "I never meant to hurt you. You're the sweetest man I've ever met, and it kills me to think that something I've said or done has hurt you."

"I know," he whispered, brushing his mouth across her ear through the soft blonde strands. Even through the hurt, he could feel his heart thumping with affection for her. "You couldn't help falling in love with Marin–any more than I can help loving you."

She rubbed her cheek against his, amazed as always by the smoothness of his face from his lack of whiskers. "I'm just so sorry. I want you to know that."

He pushed her back and gazed at her beautiful face. How her foolish husband could have let her go was beyond his comprehension, because he would have taken her in a heart beat. "I know," he said, waiting until she was seated again before continuing. "I'm sorry, too. I didn't come here to make us both upset." He took another grape and swallowed it down. "I need you to do something for me."

"Anything. Name it."

"Do you still have those clothes you got me when I was here?"

Her eyes flared wide open. There was only one reason why he would need clothes and it wasn't a good one. "Yeah, I have them. Why?"

A sly smile crossed his boyish face. "I want to borrow them."

"Why?"

He angled his head away to look out of the corner of his eye. Gunther had just trotted upstairs from the basement, and Gareth still wasn't too sure about the dog. He felt safer keeping the wolf in his sight. "You're not my Guardian, Lindy."

"No," she replied, patting her leg to call Gunther to her side. "But I am your Protector now, aren't I?"

Gareth looked down at Gunther, still afraid of him even though the dog had saved his life. He hated the way the creature stared at him with those rolling brown eyes. He forced his gaze back to the woman. "Does that entitle you to know everything about me?"

Being Protector of the Bear People was the most important thing in her life now and she wasn't about to let Gareth do something stupid. "There's only one thing you'd use those clothes for, Gar, and that's to go among humans. Please don't tell me that's what you're thinking."

He leaned back in the chair and stared up at the ceiling. *Great. First Marin, now Lindy. Won't they ever stop treating me like a child?* He answered without looking at her. "What if I am?"

She jumped out of the chair, her hands shaking in front of her. "Are you crazy? After what happened to you, you want to confront humans? I won't..."

"You won't anything," he yelled, standing up to face her. "You are not my mother or my Guardian, despite what you might think. You can't stop me from doing anything I want to do."

Her shoulders trembled as she threw her hands on her

slim hips. "I'm only trying to look out for you because I care about you. Do you think I want to see you hurt again? I cleaned up your blood once, Gareth. I don't want to do it again. Maybe next time it won't be a wound that's fixable."

He sighed deeply and backed away from her, regaining his composure. "I'm disappointed in you, Lindy. Do you think I'm stupid enough to get into a confrontation with humans? You think I want to get hurt again? I really don't appreciate you trying to control me."

She remained standing and lifted her arms to cross them over her chest. She wasn't sure if she was more hurt or pissed off by his harsh words. "I'm sorry you think I'm sticking my nose in your business, but I would never forgive myself if I had a hand in something that hurt you. Not to mention that Marin would kill me. So forgive me for being such a bitch, but I will not give you those clothes without a very good explanation."

"You're not a bitch."

"That's what you make me sound like." Her voice trembled with the emotion she couldn't choke back.

For the first time, he saw what his hurtful words were doing. He stepped closer to her. "I'm sorry... I don't know why I'm acting like this." He held his arms open to her. It took a few seconds before she slipped her arms around him. He melted into her embrace. So many times since his rescue, he'd dreamed of her holding him, fantasized about her fingertips brushing lightly across his chest, and he hated himself for being so mean to her. He loved her, and despite the fact that the feeling wasn't mutual, he knew he always would.

"Please try to understand, Gar. I've almost lost you twice now and I don't want to chance a third time." Her fingers slipped beneath his hair to clench his neck and pull him tighter against her.

A groan slipped from his throat at the feel of her breasts pressing against his chest and he forced himself away. Sinking back down on the chair, he took a deep breath to calm himself. "I know, Lindy. I guess I'm just so accustomed to Marin constantly pushing me that I automatically push back, no matter who I'm talking to." Running his hand across his forehead, he swept his fingers back through his hair, unable to hide his anxiety. He had thought long and hard about the favor he needed from her, and he'd blown it. Completely blown it.

"Let's start over," he said, reaching across the table to take her hand in his again. "When you found me, you changed my life. You opened my eyes to things I never even knew existed. Lindy, try to imagine living in my world, where it's the same thing, the same place, the same people every single day. It's like being locked away in a tiny room but still being able to look out the window and see freedom waiting out there. That's what I want Lindy, to get out of that locked room and have some freedom. You gave me a taste of it, and now I want it back."

She was struck by the passion in his voice, but she couldn't push her fear aside. He had no idea what human life was like, being so sheltered the way he was, no clue to the danger awaiting someone as naïve as he. "Gareth, you're not safe out there where humans live."

"I'm not even safe in my own home," he countered, determined to wear her down until she gave in. "I got shot here in my own damn forest, you know. No place is completely safe for me. But I know one thing. I can't go through life being afraid. I'd rather die experiencing something new and exciting than die of boredom in forest home. I feel like I'm dying there, Lindy."

His words tore at her heart and she squeezed his fingers tightly in hers. She knew exactly what he meant because it was the same way she'd felt about leaving her family behind to move with her husband to New York. There was nothing she had wanted more than to assert her independence and see the world. Poor Gareth had never been more than a few miles from the place where he'd been born and raised. It was no wonder he was going stir crazy. She knew she had a hand in his longing, too, since she was the one who'd told him all about her world and shown him the amazing technological things humans had. He was like a child who'd received his first toy and now begged to go to the toy store.

She gazed into his liquid brown eyes and found them staring back at her with more determination than she'd ever seen in him. How could she deny him the one thing he longed for above all else? "How about this," she said, deciding to offer a compromise. "How about if you and I go together? I can drive you to town, show you around for a while, and then bring you back. That way you won't be alone, and I'll feel better about you being there."

A huge smile lit his face. "You'd do that for me?" He leaned so far over the table toward her that he almost fell out of his chair. "Really, would you?"

She leaned forward and kissed him on the cheek. "Yes I would. And I'll get you nicer clothes than those sweat pants, so you'll blend in with the crowd."

Sinking back down in his chair, he covered his hands with his eyes as if to cry.

"Are you okay, Gar?"

His hands fell on the table, exposing an even bigger smile. "You have no idea what this means to me. One of my dreams is finally coming true. When can we go?"

Sucking her lower lip for a moment, she paused to figure out how to break her last stipulation to him. There was no other way than to just say it. "We need to ask Marin first."

Gareth slammed his palms down on the table so hard that Gunther lifted his head from Lindy's lap and whined. "No," he groaned. "He doesn't need to know."

"Yes he does."

"No, he really doesn't."

"Gar, it's only right to ask him. It would be disrespectful not to, and anyway, he'd kick both our butts if he found out afterwards what we'd done."

"Jeez, Lind," he moaned, running his fingers through his hair again. "You know as well as I do what his answer will be."

"Yeah, but I think I know how to convince him."

Gareth's forehead wrinkled above his soft brown eyes. "How?"

She puckered her lips in a mock kiss and looked at him with a gleam in her eye. "A little romance might do the trick."

Gareth forced himself to smile, knowing that he didn't have any choice but to accept her offer. "Okay, let's go for it," he said. "Let's try to melt the great ice bear." Then he clamped his mouth shut to keep in the words he really wanted to say.

We don't have a chance in hell.

"Are you out of your mind?" Marin roared, nearly falling off the boulder on which he'd perched himself to watch the clan. He slid to the ground and stood in front of Gareth, glaring down at the younger man's face. "Absolutely not."

Gareth rolled his eyes toward Lindy to give her that *I told you so* look before he turned around and walked away. It was better to let Lindy handle this than to shoot his mouth off and completely ruin his chances.

"Marin, let me explain," she said, stepping close to the Guardian. Her gaze drifted across his long, luscious body before coming to rest on his dark eyes. It had been weeks since she'd seen him but he'd rarely been out of her thoughts all that time. Now that he stood before her, she wanted her body to melt into his. God, how she missed him.

He stood still, looking down at her with the cool expression he always wore when he wanted to exert his authority. Her golden hair was pulled back in a ponytail that showed off her delicate oval face, reminding him once again of how beautiful she was. He'd tried to push thoughts of her out of his mind during their separation, but he'd failed miserably.

A lump formed in his throat when Gareth brought her back with him just now and he swallowed it down so he could speak. "Please do," he said.

She sucked in a deep breath and licked her lips. They'd gone suddenly dry at the sound of his forceful voice when he had spoken to Gareth. No matter how much she loved and desired him, Marin could still be intimidating. She watched his eyes follow her tongue as she swept it across her lips and saw his eyelids flicker, betraying his desire. They'd only kissed a few times but she knew he wanted more–just as she did. First she needed to get through this. "This is something Gareth has dreamed about for a long time," she said.

Marin grunted and crossed his arms over his chest. "And something I have nightmares about."

She eyed his bulging biceps, savoring the way they curved in front of his broad, bare chest. He always assumed this stance when he thought he was right, so she knew she was in for a battle. "It's only a little trip to town, for God's sake. I'll drive him there in my car, show him a few things, then bring him right back. It should take a couple hours, tops, and I'll be with him every minute. I'm the Protector now, so let me do my job."

Still motionless, he dropped his gaze from her eyes to the curves of her chest. She wore a light pink, long sleeved tee shirt with the words *Wild Woman* emblazoned on it. The words were perfectly positioned over her breasts and clung to her generous curves. Marin pursed his lips and nodded down at her shirt. "Is this the motto of our new Protector?"

She didn't know what he was talking about, until she glanced down and read the words. It hadn't dawned on her what she was wearing. "Oh heavens, Marin, it's just the style," she groaned, shaking her head so her ponytail swished across her shoulders. "It doesn't mean anything." Damn, this wasn't going well at all. If she screwed up, Gareth would probably never forgive her. "Look Marin, in all your life, hasn't there ever been something you wanted to do but never had the chance? Something that you would have given anything to experience but couldn't? That's how Gareth feels about having to spend his life confined to forest home. The world has so much more to offer..."

"Like humans with shotguns?"

"People don't walk around town carrying shotguns."

"Yes, you're right. They're handguns."

Now he was starting to piss her off. He loved to push her buttons, and he was so damn good at it. She knew he would win this argument if she lost her cool. She took a deep breath and forced her sexiest smile to her face. It was time to try a new tactic. "Have you ever been to town?" she asked sweetly.

"Once."

"Did you find it interesting?"

"Not particularly."

"No? Then why did you go there?"

A devious smile lit his handsome face when he leaned forward to bring his mouth nearer hers. His voice softened to a whisper. "To rescue Gareth from the humans."

Lindy yanked herself backward. The smile vanished from her face. If she didn't love Marin so much, she would've punched him. Why did he always have to be so God-damned smug? She swung around to look over her shoulder and get away from the sight of his expression.

The hurt look on her face made his heart thump with regret at his cocky attitude. Taking her shoulders gently in his hands, he forced her around to face him again. "Lindy, don't be angry with me. I assume Gareth didn't tell you about his wandering when he was a cub. He left the forest and followed a human family into town one morning. I had to go rescue him, and we were both lucky to make it back alive."

Now she wanted to punch Gareth, too. "Yeah, he neglected to share that tidbit with me." She felt like such a fool.

He laughed softly and pulled her against him, wanting to ease her embarrassment. Resting his chin against her cheek, the scent of flowers drifted from her golden hair and filled his head in a maddening rush. It was the same scent he'd noticed the first time he got that close to her, the night she'd saved his life. It was a scent he would never forget.

Nuzzling her ear with his lips, he pressed her harder against him and wrapped her in his arms. For a moment he wondered if she would pull away from him in her anger, but she slid her arms around him and held him tightly. He felt the strong pulse of her heart racing in time with his own, making him want her more with each passing second. He closed his eyes and inhaled slowly, willing himself to keep in control.

"Why is it so important to you that he do this?" he asked.

He held her so tightly that she had to grasp his sides and push herself back to be able to look up at him. Strands of black hair had tumbled down over his face, begging for her fingers to sweep them back. She brushed her fingertips softly over his forehead to clear her view of his penetrating eyes. She could almost feel their heat as he gazed down at her.

"It's not about Gareth," she admitted with a sigh. Marin's eyes flared slightly at her words. "You have no idea how much I want to prove to you that I'm worthy of being the clan's Protector. I need to do this for me, not for him."

Taken aback by her unexpected reason, Marin raised his head to stare past her into the distance. This was something he hadn't considered, that perhaps she needed to prove her worth to him in much the same way he felt he needed to constantly prove his worth to the clan. Sometimes, she was so much like him it was startling.

"You have nothing to prove, Lindy," he said, lowering his face down to her level again. "You earned the right to be our Protector when you saved all of us from Dean. Don't you know that?"

The look in her eyes revealed the truth before she even spoke the words. "No, Marin, I want to believe it but I don't. I need to be sure, and I want *you* to be sure that I'm up to it. I know that taking Gareth to town is something I can handle. And besides..." she stopped and laid her palm gently on his cheek before she continued. "I really want to do something to make up for hurting Gareth, if you know what I mean."

He nodded without answering, knowing exactly what she meant. He'd stolen her away from the young he-bear and had claimed her for himself. If anyone needed to make amends to Gareth, it was him, not Lindy. Rubbing his face harder against her hand, he exhaled slowly and lowered his eyelids in concession. This was one argument he wasn't going to win. "I'll allow it," he said reluctantly, "*if* you allow me to accompany you."

Lindy jerked her head up to stare into his eyes, hardly daring to believe what she'd heard. Her heart raced even harder at the thought of it. "Are you serious? You'll come with us?"

Marin laughed again. He loved the way her sky blue eyes danced with emotion when she was happy. It was the most beautiful thing he'd ever seen. "Just promise me that we won't do anything risky. We don't need to be calling attention to ourselves." He gazed down at her chest again, indicating the words on her shirt.

"Don't worry," she laughed. "I won't get you a shirt that says *Wild Woman* on it."

He scowled playfully with a shake of his head. "You know what I mean."

She rose up on her toes and planted a firm kiss on his lips. His eyes widening with surprise at her passion, he grabbed her and smashed her against him. Then from the corner of his eye, he saw Gareth approach and he slowly pushed her away from him again. He growled softly to himself. Damn, if Gareth didn't have rotten timing.

Gareth's mouth drew up in a knowing smile. "I guess this means we're going to town, huh?"

Chapter Two

The bruin ambled slowly along the forest path with his nose low to the ground. Sweeping his large muzzle back and forth while he walked, he stopped to investigate the two irresistible scents he'd detected. A low growl chuffed from his throat at the discovery that two bear sows had traveled this path not long before him, and he quickened his pace.

He was a huge boar, bigger than any others of his kind. His black fur was strangely tinted with a reddish hue that made him look like he had rolled in live embers. Though it set him apart, it was a look he had grown to like. It made everyone take notice, as if his size alone didn't. He thought the look fit his personality, especially his hot, quick temper that practically sizzled when he was pissed off.

He sniffed the ground again. The scent was growing stronger the farther he followed the trail. Even though it wasn't mating season, he was more than ready for a female and the scent assailing his nose was making him crazy with desire. He'd gone without physical satisfaction for far too long, thanks to the clan's Guardian. It was a mistake he was damn sure not to repeat this time.

Winding through a huge stand of white pines, he lifted his head and saw them grazing in a meadow beyond the trees. One was a large brown sow, the other a smaller black one. Both had qualities which appealed to him—primarily the fact that they were breathing. It didn't hurt that they were alone, either. He glanced around, double checking for any sign of a male nearby, but the area was empty. Perfect.

Fire burned in his beady round eyes at the sight of them feeding contentedly on the tender grass, spurring him to move faster. Almost running, he covered the ground between them in a few steps and slid to a stop in the grass a few yards away.

Lena and Lilea raised their heads simultaneously to look at the stranger. Not only was he huge, but when the warm afternoon sun beat down on him, it cast his coat in a peculiar reddish glow that almost seemed to be radiating the light back into the air. It was the strangest thing they'd ever seen, though appealing in an exotic sort of way. Lena looked at her companion and snuffled softly, curious if she knew who the visitor was.

Lilea shook her shaggy head no. She had no idea who he was, but she was going to find out. They rarely had visitors at forest home and when they did, Marin never let them get close enough to get to know their guests. But thankfully Marin wasn't around, and she knew this might be the only chance she got to meet this handsome bear. She took a step toward him.

The bruin lowered his head to stare into her gentle dark eyes. She was a beauty, from the tip of her dark nose to her thick shapely legs. Petite, but that was okay. He couldn't be as rough when he took her. He glanced over at the other female, who stood behind her friend, watching. She was bigger, more stout. This one he could take any way he wanted and probably not hurt her. Not that he cared if he did.

He opened his mouth in a wide grin, showing his gleaming white canines. This was going to be sweet, very, very sweet. Raising his front paws off the ground, he pulled his huge body up and stood erect, stretching to his full six foot six inch height. He gazed down at the female bears, who looked back up at him with their mouths gaping.

"Afternoon, ladies," he said in man-speak, his deep voice booming. "Lucien has come calling."

Chapter Three

Lindy's stomach was in knots when she looked at the two men standing side by side in her family room. A few months ago she wouldn't have believed that shapeshifters even existed and now two of them stood in her own home, buck naked, and both of them in love with her.

Her eyes fell on Gareth first. At her own five foot seven height, he was a good nine inches shorter than Marin. He had the sleek, slim lines of a runner with thin, toned muscles. The only hair on his body was the cinnamon-colored mop on his head and between his legs. If she hadn't known his actual age, she would have thought him an athlete from the local high school track team–his face was that boyish. His eyes were a soft, honey brown that gazed at her sweetly while he waited.

Marin couldn't have been more opposite. His towering six foot four inch body was a mass of bulging muscles, from his well-defined pecs and six-pack abs right down to his sculpted calves. His dark hair and eyes complemented his olive skin, giving him a vaguely Mediterranean look that was brooding and exotic. The man was well built and definitely well hung.

Lindy forced her eyes away from Marin's handsome body and picked up two bags from the sofa. She handed one to each man and stood silently with her hands clasped in front of her while they removed the contents and examined them.

"Oh wow," Gareth said, holding a hooded sweatshirt

up in front of him. He flipped the hood a couple times, trying to figure out how it worked. "I've never seen a shirt with a top on it before."

"It's called a hood," Lindy said, trying to suppress a laugh. She walked over to him and helped him slip the shirt over his head and put the hood in place. "All the young people wear them."

Marin lifted an eyebrow as his gaze fell upon the clothes in his bag. "And what do old guys like me wear?" He was almost afraid to look, not wanting to find a shirt with some embarrassing motto printed on it.

"For you," Lindy said, lifting something out of the bag, "a practical flannel shirt." She held up a long sleeved, blue and black checked shirt that perfectly accentuated his piercing dark eyes. "All the ladies will go wild when they see you."

"Because of a shirt?" he asked doubtfully.

"No, because of this." Reaching into the bag again, she yanked out a pair of form fitting, button fly, boot cut jeans. "Believe me, these jeans are going to do your butt justice."

Gareth snorted out a laugh. "Women want to look at Marin's butt?"

"That, among other things," she sighed appreciatively, holding the jeans up to his waist. "Don't laugh, Gareth, they'll be looking at your booty, too."

"Ha," Marin grunted. Without a bit of modesty, he began to dress in front of Lindy, pulling the pant legs awkwardly up his muscular limbs.

"Uh, maybe you'll want to put these on first." She threw him a pair of briefs.

Marin took a look at them, shook his head and tossed them back to her. "One set of pants is restrictive enough, thanks." Fastening the buttons on his fly, he eased the waistband flat and straightened up to show himself to her. "How do I look?"

"Divine," she said, biting her tongue to keep from

adding *but I'd rather see you naked in my bed.* Forcing her sex drive back into neutral, she focused her attention on Gareth, who was standing there awkwardly, feeling a little neglected. "Try your jeans on, Gar."

He slipped his pair up over his slim legs and whirled for her assessment. "Well?"

"You're a god," she swooned, bringing a huge smile to his face. Then stepping back, she put her hands on her hips and looked them both over again. There was no way anyone could tell that they weren't human. Even she had a hard time believing it. "Well, are you guys ready?"

Gareth had his shoes on and was at the door before she had her purse and car keys in hand. "Let's go," he said, his voice high-pitched with excitement.

"Yes, let's go," Marin added, following behind him with a scowl. "And get this over with."

Lindy never dreamed that a car ride could be such an adventure. The three of them were jammed inside her tiny five-speed Toyota Corolla. Gareth rode in the passenger seat, and Marin sprawled across the backseat. Every time she looked in the rear view mirror, the scowl on his face was bigger as he struggled to find a comfortable position. "We'll be there soon," she called back to him, but he just growled.

Gareth acted like a four year old going through the annoying stage when kids ask one question after another. His face was plastered against the side window to get a good view of everything they passed, not wanting to miss a thing.

"What's that?" he asked, swiveling in his seat to keep a building in sight even as they zipped by it.

"That's a gas station. They sell fuel to make cars move."

"And that?" He stuck his arm in front of her face to point out her window.

"That's a bait shop, where you can buy worms and minnows for fishing." She pushed his arm back into his lap.

"And don't do that unless you want to get us killed."

"That would be merciful right about now," Marin grumbled behind her.

Lindy bit her lip to keep from laughing. It was funny how Marin had scared her for so long, but now that she knew him, she understood that he had a lot more bark than bite. He was a tough cookie with a soft, sweet center.

"Are we there yet?" Gareth asked, leaning forward to stare out the windshield.

"Oh, don't even start with that," Lindy groaned, reaching her arm out to push him back in his seat. "And sit still. We'll be there in a minute."

She said a silent prayer of thanks when they finally rolled into town. She eased the car into a parking space on the town square and turned off the ignition. "This is it," she said, turning to face Gareth. "The jumping town of Timberlake. Are you ready?"

His face was red and sweaty with anticipation. "I've been ready for this for twenty five years, Lindy. I can't believe I'm really here."

She leaned over and kissed him lightly on the cheek, delighted by the obvious joy the trip was giving him. It felt so good to make him happy after all the horrible things he'd been through. "Then let's not keep you waiting a moment longer. Let's go."

The three of them walked side by side down the sidewalk, blending in perfectly with the townspeople and the few tourists who remained this late in the season. Gareth had taken position closest to the storefronts, with Lindy next to him and Marin on her other side. At every window they passed, he pulled them to a stop and hauled them inside while he *oohed* and *aahed* at the merchandise.

He couldn't believe the variety of things available for humans to buy. Not just the necessary things they needed like clothing and food, but frivolous things that enriched their lives and helped fill their hours. The books, TVs, CD players, toys and games were endless. There was so much stuff it made his head spin. Every discovery he made, he had to show to Lindy, and she tried to respond with as much enthusiasm as if it was the first time she'd seen them, too.

Marin was less than impressed. He tagged along behind them with his hands jammed in the pockets of his jeans and a sneer on his lips, finding little need for humans' toys. The only worthwhile thing he'd gotten from the trip so far was the satisfaction of watching Lindy's rear end when he followed her. That alone was worth the trip.

After a couple hours of shopping, she grabbed both men's arms and pulled them toward a small café called the Lumber Inn. "I don't know about you guys, but I'm starved," she said.

Gareth looked at the sign taped to the café window and started reading out loud. "Daily specials: spag...hetti and meatballs, venison steak, poor-boy sandwiches..." His face screwed up with confusion and he turned to Lindy with his mouth open. "Humans eat poor children?"

"No, silly" she snorted. "It's just a weird name for a sandwich."

"What's venison?" Marin asked, shaking his head at Gareth's naivete.

Lindy grinned, as amused as he was. "It's deer meat."

He nodded disgustedly. "That's what I thought. I hope we didn't know him."

She opened her mouth to ask him what he meant, and then thinking better of it, grabbed his arm and pulled him inside the restaurant, deciding it was just better not to know some things. When they were seated, she showed them both how to order from the menu so that when the waitress came over, they wouldn't act like aliens.

A few minutes later, the waitress stalked over and yanked a pencil out of the red hair above her ear. "You all ready?" she asked bruskly, apparently having better things to do than serve customers. Her red-painted lips pursed with annoyance while she waited for them to make up their minds. Though she probably wasn't much older than Lindy, she looked like she'd seen twice the mileage.

"I'll have a cheeseburger, fries and a diet," Lindy said, showing them how it was done.

Confidently following her lead, Gareth flipped his menu open and looked over the choices again. There were so many items it was difficult to decide. "Give me pancakes with honey. Lots of honey. And onion rings. Some apple pie. Toast. Also a hot dog. Don't forget the honey." He set the menu down and flashed the waitress a proud grin.

Rolling her eyes, the waitress turned her gaze to Marin. She hadn't seen him come in the restaurant, but she saw him now. She planted her eyes firmly on his gorgeous body. Even through his clothes, his physique was obvious. "How about you, Hon?" she drawled, trying to ooze sex appeal.

"A salad," he said gruffly. "And water."

She jammed the pencil back in her hair and stared down at him, eyeing the huge thighs that filled his tight jeans. "Sweetie, you aren't going to keep up that body eating rabbit food.

How about some nice steak and potatoes?" She grinned seductively, imagining what he would look like after she'd slipped those tight jeans off him.

Marin squirmed uncomfortably beneath her stare and finally looked up at her. A low, threatening growl slipped from his throat. "How about you put your eyeballs back in your head and bring me that salad? Now."

The grin vanished from her face as she spun quickly and walked away. Lindy laughed and shook her head. "Nice going, Marin. Now we'll have to leave her a really good tip."

When they were finished eating, Lindy had one last thing to show them. Taking each of them in arm, she led them across the street and down two blocks to a decrepit looking building, tucked back from the street.

Marin looked around the dark interior as they walked in the door, feeling somewhat unsure about their safety.

"What is this place?"

"It's the Timberlake Historical Museum. A place to learn about the town's history through displays of artifacts used by people like my ancestors. We'll see all kinds of interesting old things from this area dating back to when it was first settled. There are a lot of Indian artifacts here, too."

Marin stopped abruptly, a worried expression on his face. It was the first time since his kidnapping that he'd allowed the awful thought into his mind. He was part human. The woman his great-grandsire had mated with was from this very town. Suddenly he was terrified that some part of her, some piece of her history, and *his*, would be here in the museum. If it was, he didn't want to see it. He just wasn't ready.

"What is it, Marin?" Lindy asked, stopping beside him. She'd never seen a look on his face like that before. It almost looked like fear. "Are you all right?"

"Do you suppose that... something of Emma's might be in here?"

Suddenly she realized what he was thinking and how terrified he was of confronting the human part of himself. She placed her hands firmly on his upper arms and squeezed them tight to reassure him. "No, I'm sure there's nothing of hers here." She forced herself to sound confident, though she had no way of knowing if it was the truth or not. "But if you're uncomfortable about being here, we can leave."

Marin looked past Lindy to Gareth, who stood in the hallway watching him–watching to see if his mighty Guardian walked out in fear. He couldn't stand the amused look on Gareth's face. "No, I'm fine," he said, looking back at Lindy. "Go ahead, I'll follow you."

They walked together through the building, wandering slowly through the exhibits while she explained what they were seeing. Gareth was fascinated. He wandered off on his own, oblivious to his companions lagging behind. There were too many intriguing things to look at, and Lindy and

Marin were moving way too slow to suit him.

Lindy thanked her lucky stars for the opportunity it gave her. When she was sure that Gareth was far ahead of them, she pulled Marin into a dark, dead end exhibit and backed him up against a wall. His dark eyes flared at the feel of the cool wall at his back and the heat of Lindy's body at his chest.

She leaned up against him and pressed her hands softly on each side of his head. "Now where were we?" she whispered, her breath warm on his ear.

All the emotion he'd kept penned up came crashing free and he knew that he couldn't have stopped it even if he'd wanted to. Crushing her body against him, Marin lowered his face to hers and smothered her mouth with his own, loving the hot moistness of her full lips moving beneath his. He had dreamed of this for so long.

She moved against him, wanting to feel every curve and bulge of his muscles. Her thigh slipped between his legs and pressed hard until she felt his groin tighten with desire. She needed to know that he still wanted her, desired her, the way he had the night she'd rescued him. The old familiar ache throbbed deep inside, desperate to be eased by the feel of him inside of her.

"Marin," she whispered between kisses. Her mouth moved to the corner of his mouth, across his cheek, and swept down the thick cords of his neck. She felt him shiver with delight and his arms clenched her even tighter. Unbuttoning the top of his shirt, she pulled the fabric apart to expose the top of his chest and swept her kisses over his olive-hued flesh.

The feel of her mouth on him was unbearable. He threw his head back against the wall and arched his back, raising his chest harder against her. Her hands slipped behind the small of his back to pull him even closer. His groin was hot and hard, throbbing so fiercely that he was sure she could feel his blood pulsing. A groan rumbled from deep in his throat.

"No Lindy," he begged, his voice hoarse with desire. "No more, not here." Using all the willpower he could muster, he grabbed her slender waist and pushed her away. It almost killed him to do it—now when he was so close to having her—but this was not the time or the place.

She stepped back and lowered her eyes, ashamed to look at him. How could she have been so thoughtless, jumping on him like a hormonal teenager? It was just too easy to forget that he wasn't a normal, human man. The poor guy was probably scared half to death by her aggressiveness. "I'm sorry," she whispered. "I shouldn't have done that."

He gazed down at the anguished look on her face and felt his heart break. He couldn't stand the thought that he had hurt her. "Lindy, I'm not rejecting you. Please don't be angry with me." When she finally looked up at him, he saw not anger, but affection.

"I could never be mad at you, Marin. I've just missed you so much and you feel so good." Her gaze settled on the triangle of skin showing near his collar. She reached up and rebuttoned his shirt, then dropped her hands by her sides, afraid that if she didn't, they'd be all over him again.

"I've missed you, too," he said, brushing the hair away from her face. The feel of her skin against his fingers made his heart pound again. He took a slow breath and looked past her toward the hallway. "We'd better go find Gareth before he gets into trouble."

They walked down the dark corridor, searching each exhibit as they passed. Lindy finally spotted Gareth near the exit door, laughing. She couldn't imagine anything in this musty museum that would make him laugh so loudly until she neared the end of the hallway and saw that he was standing beside a blonde woman. They were busy chatting, obviously entertained by each other, and then Gareth's hand slipped seductively around her back. The woman turned her face to the side and laughed.

"Ohhhh damn," Lindy groaned.

Marin looked down at her, alarmed by her tone of

voice. "What?"

She threw her hands on her hips and stared at the floor. "Gareth is hitting on my *sister.*"

"Gareth!" Marin roared from down the hallway.

The young man jumped and turned to look at the Guardian. The moment he saw Marin's disapproving glare, he knew he was in trouble and quickly withdrew his arm from around the woman beside him. She turned slowly to see who had spoken and Marin's breath caught in his throat. She was the spitting image of Lindy, only slightly younger, and she had a bright red streak in her blonde hair that ran from her scalp to her shoulder. He stared at the red hair, trying to figure out what had happened to her, before settling his gaze on Gareth again.

Lindy ran to her sister and hugged her with a soft scream of delight. "Sara, oh my God, what are you doing here?" Looking her up and down, she acted as if they hadn't seen each other in years rather than weeks.

Sara's gaze flicked over to Marin, who stood watching from down the hallway. Squeezing her sister's hands, a broad smile lit her face while she rolled her eyes heavenward. "You naughty girl, why didn't you tell me about Mr. Delicious over there? Where did you find him?"

"It's a long story, Sis, and trust me, you wouldn't believe it if you heard it." She turned and beckoned Marin forward, jealously grabbing his arm when he stopped beside her. "Sara, this is my friend Marin. I see you've already met my other friend," she said, inclining her head toward Gareth.

"You know each other?" Sara couldn't have sounded more surprised.

"Yeah. I brought the guys to town for a fun-filled afternoon of shopping and dusty artifacts."

Gareth stood with his mouth open while he looked back and forth between the two women. He'd recognized her similarity to Lindy but couldn't place who she was because he didn't know any human women other than Lindy. Now he realized that it was the picture on her bedside table that he recalled, the photo of the four sisters. "You're Lindy's sister?" he asked her, his voice rising with excitement.

Sara nodded and placed her hand on Gareth's arm, flirting brazenly. She adored red-haired men, and even though Gareth's hair wasn't technically red but a few shades lighter, it was close enough. And he was cute, to boot.

"What are you doing here?" Lindy asked again. She'd thought her sister was away at college since the new school year had recently begun.

"Senior research project," Sara said disgustedly, her eyes wandering up and down Gareth's slim physique. Her fingers clenched his arm tighter, eliciting a soft whimper from him. *Strange guy*, she thought. *But very cute.*

"Hey, what do you say about all of us going out for some ice cream?" Lindy suggested, trying to think of something safe they could all do together. She wanted to catch up on her little sister's recent news and still show the guys a good time. Most of all, she didn't want to leave Gareth alone with her sister. The girl would have him in bed in two minutes.

"What's ice cream?" Gareth asked.

Sara's eyes widened. "Are you kidding me? You don't know what ice cream is?"

Lindy scrambled for an excuse. "When he was a kid, Gareth's mom told him he was lactose intolerant. But you should really try it again, right Gar?"

"Uh, right," he mumbled, having absolutely no idea what she was talking about. He was still reeling from the feel of Sara's fingers wandering sensuously up the inside of his arm and he didn't care where they went as long as she went with him. If he couldn't have Lindy, her sister would do just fine. He couldn't believe his luck.

"Maybe we should go home," Marin said gruffly, eyeing the way the two young people were acting. They couldn't keep their hands off each other.

"No, I'm not ready to go home," Gareth said, staring

Marin in the eye determinedly. He didn't want to challenge the Guardian but he wasn't about to end his dream early because of Marin's overprotectiveness, either. "Let's get ice cream." Without waiting for a reply, he shoved his way past Marin, dragging Sara with him.

She rolled her eyes at her sister as they passed. "Gotta love a guy who knows what he wants," she said with a shrug.

Marin gazed down at Lindy, his arms crossed over his chest again. He didn't like this development one bit but there was nothing he could do about it at the moment. She looked back up at him with an amused expression on her face and he knew she agreed with Gareth.

"Okay," he sighed. "So what is ice cream?"

Sara dug her spoon into the mound of chocolate ice cream and held it up to Gareth's mouth. He stared at it for a moment, not certain what she wanted him to do. His eyes rolled toward Lindy for help.

"It's okay, Gar, just taste it."

Opening his mouth tentatively, he let her guide the spoon in and dump the dessert on his tongue. The cool sweetness melted in his mouth, sending shivers through him at its delicious creamy flavor. Nothing bears ate in the wilderness tasted this good.

Marin saw Lindy's wistful expression as she watched her sister feed Gareth and knew instantly what she was thinking. She was remembering the way she'd fed him that night, reliving the first time her fingertips had brushed his lips. He'd been so humiliated, and yet so swept away by his own desire in spite of it.

She looked across the table at him and smiled, realizing that he knew her thoughts. It was a comforting feeling, knowing how much alike they were sometimes. Glancing down at his untouched ice cream, she wanted nothing more than to offer him a taste of it, to perform the simple loving act of feeding him, but she knew he would hate it. She respected his feelings too much to do that. Instead, she took a spoonful from her own dish and slid it slowly in her mouth, noticing how Marin's eyes followed every move she made.

Marin didn't realize he was holding his breath, until his lungs began to ache. Then breathing in sharply, he followed her lead and took a bite from his bowl. The food was strangely cold and smooth on his tongue, but pleasantly delicious. He looked at Lindy and smiled, unable to stop himself from wondering how delicious she would taste.

"So where are you guys from?" Sara asked Gareth, feeding him another spoonful.

"Around here," Marin replied for him. He wasn't about to take the chance of Gareth screwing up and saying something he shouldn't.

"How'd you meet my sister?"

Gareth opened his mouth but this time Lindy answered before he could speak. "I, uh, went to high school with Marin. He was a couple years ahead of me. And Gareth is a friend of his."

Sara scooped a dollop of whipped cream on her spoon and shoved it in Gareth's mouth before turning to Marin. "I bet you were on the football team or something, right? Quarterback?"

He looked at Lindy helplessly, totally lost at Sara's question and uncomfortable being out of his element. She smiled back reassuringly.

"Yeah, he was quite the jock. Still is, as a matter of fact," she said.

Sara nodded and returned her attention to Gareth, leaving Marin to breathe easier. He hated playing games like this, especially when one mistake could cost the clan so much, but he knew there was no way out of this predicament. It was exactly what he had been afraid of. Gareth couldn't do a single thing without getting into some kind of trouble. At least this was damage he could control. Or so he hoped.

It was mid afternoon when they arrived back at Lindy's cabin. She unlocked the back door, escorted the men in and dumped her purse on the kitchen table. Gareth leaned back against the sink with his hands in his pockets and stared at her.

"What?" she asked.

"I was just thinking about everything you've done for me. I mean, first saving me after I was shot, and now saving me from a slow death by boredom." He laughed softly and walked over to pull her into his arms, ignoring Marin's heated gaze. "Thank you, Lindy, for all of it. Thank you for trusting me enough to stand up for me on this."

Marin growled softly at Gareth's jab.

Lindy kissed Gareth on the cheek and stepped back to look at him. His honey eyes were bright with excitement. It was obvious how much the day had meant to him. There were few pleasures in the life of Bearwalkers, especially with a zealous Guardian like Marin, so it was good to see him happy.

"You're welcome, Gar. Maybe we can do it again sometime."

He nodded furiously while he withdrew a slip of paper from his pocket. "Your sister said I should phone her. She gave me this number." He stared at it with a bewildered look on his face. "What's a phone again?"

Lindy shook her head and chuckled. He was so innocent that she sometimes felt more like his mother than his friend, not that she minded. She rather enjoyed looking after her *boys*, as she was coming to think of them. "Tell you what, since you don't have a phone, the next time you're here we'll call her together and then you can talk to her."

"Good. I'd like that."

Marin cleared his throat to get their attention. "It's time for us to go. Give Lindy your clothes, Gareth."

She whirled around to look at him, shocked by his words. "You're going?"

Despite the sad look in her eyes, he knew he had to. The clan had been alone for far too long, and he needed to get back to them. His needs, and hers, would have to wait. "I'm sorry." He slipped his clothes off and handed them to her, relieved to be free of them again.

"I was hoping you'd stay a while," she said, taking the clothes and laying them on the table. They were still so warm from his body heat that she didn't want to let go of them. "I thought maybe we could talk. I can fix us something to eat..."

"I'd like to, but I'm concerned about the clan. I've been away too long."

She bit her lip for a moment, feeling irritated that his first consideration was always the clan. "When are you going to worry about *you*, Marin? When are you going to take care of your needs?"

Her words puzzled him. The clan had never thought to concern themselves with his needs or care about what he wanted. No one ever asked what he cared about. He had no idea how to respond to her question, so he merely did what he knew how to do best.

"Good bye, Lindy," he said, walking out the door.

Gareth patted her arm to cheer her up and followed Marin out.

Chapter Four

Arlin saw them approaching from the corner of his eye and dropped the berries right out of his mouth. He snorted to get Shara's attention, motioning with his head for him to check out what was coming on the path out of the meadow. Shara gazed in that direction and his eyes grew huge at the sight of Lena and Lilea walking in human skin alongside a man. They were all chatting and laughing as though they were old friends. He looked back at Arlin and chuffed in alarm.

They ran back to the clearing where the rest of the clan were browsing.

"A stranger is coming," Shara growled to the others. "Someone like us."

They stopped eating and looked at him with stunned expressions on their faces. It was unusual for another bear to wander into their territory and even rarer when the bear turned out to be a Bearwalker. The clan knew that others of their kind existed, but they didn't know where they lived or how many there were. It was only by happenstance that they had the opportunity to meet one at all. And now, for one to walk right into their home was practically a miracle.

Everyone rushed forward to greet the visitor. They'd never seen such a big fellow, or one with such strange coloring. His black hair shimmered in the sunlight with a reddish glow that accentuated the red-tinted eyelashes above his deep, dark eyes. His face was square and thick, rather broad in a brutish way, but still handsome. He walked with an air of confidence and power that matched his physical stature.

Lilea walked so close beside him that their sides touched. He was over a foot taller than her, making it difficult for her to keep up with his long strides, but she didn't seem to mind.

Every so often she gazed over at him, letting her eyes drink in the sight of his powerful, deeply tanned body. Despite the muscles rippling on every part of him, he moved smoothly with the easy grace of a feline rather than a bear. She couldn't tear her eyes away from him. Even Marin didn't command her attention the way this bear-man did.

The she-bears led Lucien to the boulder marking the clan's gathering place and offered him a seat. He climbed up on top of the flat boulder, crossed his legs in front of him and waited, seeming completely at ease, while the clan assembled on the grass around him.

Lilea shot a worried glance at Lena. "He's in Marin's spot," she whispered nervously.

Her friend brushed it off with a laugh. "Yes, but Marin's not here, is he? Why not let our guest have the seat of honor—what can it hurt?"

Lena had a point. It might be hours before Marin and Gareth returned, and by then everyone would be asleep in their dens.

Lucien took a long look around him to appraise the clan. It was fairly evenly split between females and males. There were several cubs running annoyingly around in the grass nearby, but his attention was drawn to the adult males gathered around him. His gaze swept over two strong young adults, Shara and Keeran, who both appeared to be around twenty. They were powerfully built but probably not very experienced in defense. He doubted that either of them had ever challenged an older bear for dominance.

Sitting beyond the younger men were two older adults. One was an overweight bruin called Arlin, while the other was a thin, strange looking man called Balen. Both of them appeared to be middle-aged and out of shape. Definitely non-threatening. The only other man in the group was an ancient fellow with grizzled gray-brown hair. His strength was failing with his great age and he seemed to be on his last legs. When he moved, his body shook with wild tremors that looked painful to watch.

Lucien growled softly to himself. None of these males appeared to be capable of acting as Guardian except the younger ones, and they seemed too inexperienced to have assumed such an important role. *Maybe this is my lucky day,* he thought, letting his gaze drift back over to the females. Maybe *they have no Guardian.* There were seven females, all ages and sizes, some beautiful, some plain. If he wanted, he could have his choice of any of them. Maybe *all of them.* He laughed to himself. Yes, he decided, this was definitely going to be his lucky day.

Marin loped into the meadow just ahead of Gareth and stopped cold. In the distance, he could see the clan sitting around the boulder in the clearing. They had all shifted into human skin and were staring up at a man who sat on the boulder, looking as comfortable as if it was his usual resting place. Marin growled at the sight of the man perched on *his* rock, speaking to *his* clan. He lunged forward, raising his torso from the ground as he ran, and shifted smoothly into man skin.

"Who are you?" he roared, striding between Arlin and Lena to stand beside the rock and glare at the stranger.

The man looked up and gazed at Marin with a cool, impassive expression on his face before slipping off the boulder to stand beside him.

Marin's face froze as the man straightened up to his full height. He was huge. Marin had never seen anyone bigger than himself and could hardly believe the size of the stranger. The man's icy stare lingered on him for a moment before his lips curled up in a forced smile.

"I am Lucien of the Bear Clan."

"What Bear Clan?" Marin snarled. "We're the only clan in this forest."

Lucien dropped his gaze from Marin to Lena, who stared up at him with fascination. He gave her a seductive wink before returning his gaze to Marin. "I take it you're the Guardian of this delightful clan?"

Delightful clan? Who is this guy? His eyes narrowed with suspicion. "I am. Now answer my question."

Lucien sighed slowly, making a show of his patience in tolerating Marin's inquisition. "My clan lived in a forest near the horizon. I doubt that you've ever been that far."

Marin burned at the man's inference, even though he was correct that Marin had never been outside the immediate area of forest home. But he would be damned if he'd let him know that. Cocking his head to one side, he stared harder into the man's dark eyes. "You said 'lived'. Where are they now?"

Lucien looked past Marin to gaze at the darkening sky. A single ray of sunlight remained above the horizon, illuminating the gray twilight with a soft golden haze. "They're dead."

A rush of murmurs rippled through the clan at the news. His whole family was gone?

"What happened to them?" Marin asked.

"They were killed by humans. The vermin invaded our forest intending to harvest the trees and found it more convenient to slaughter my clan than to deal with them."

"How awful," Lilea gasped before a harsh glance from Marin warned her not to speak again. She looked down at the ground and grew quiet, respecting his order.

"So why are you alive if your clan is dead?"

Lucien looked at Marin with a sad, strange look on his face that Marin found disturbing. "I was the strongest. They tried to kill me but they couldn't."

"If you were the strongest, why didn't you protect your kin?"

"I tried." The sad look changed to a blank one oddly devoid of any emotion.

Marin felt a chill ripple down his spine. For someone who had lost his entire family, Lucien was surprisingly calm, and that just didn't sit right with him. If he himself had lost his whole clan, he'd still be hunting down the killers. "You tried and yet you couldn't save one of them? Not a female? Not a single cub?"

"I wasn't their Guardian. It wasn't my responsibility, though I tried." His voice was flat, toneless, without a trace of sorrow.

Marin shook his head, unable to comprehend how a bear of his size and power could fail to save the life of even one of his kin. Either the man was a coward or he was hiding something. Either way, Marin didn't like him. "You were sitting in my spot."

Lucien glanced over his shoulder at the boulder behind him, then back at Marin, a lopsided smile on his face. "I'm sorry, I didn't see your name written on it."

A snicker came from somewhere behind Marin. He whirled in time to see Gareth wipe a smile from his face and look away. If he could've grabbed the young he-bear by the throat and strangled him at that moment, he would have. Instead he forced his anger down and turned back to face the stranger. "What are you doing here?"

Crossing his arms over his chest, Lucien mimicked Marin's aggressive stance. He was not only taller than the Guardian but broader and even more muscular. Just the sight of him was enough to intimidate anyone.

Anyone but Marin. He glared at the man with a growing hatred that he didn't know how to control. He couldn't even pinpoint when he first decided he hated the man or exactly why. He just knew that something about Lucien wasn't right. Or more exactly, something was very wrong. He could feel it in his gut. It was at times like this that he missed Thoren the most. He had always counted on the wise, old warrior for advice and support, and now that he was gone, there was no one he could turn to.

"Answer me," he said again, his patience wearing thin.

Lucien smiled and looked at the Bear People seated around him. Their eyes were locked on him, giving him their full attention. *Excellent.* Gazing back at Marin, he raised his hands and shrugged his massive shoulders helplessly. "I seek only the kindness of strangers to help me through this painful time. I ask only for the companionship of your kin until I move on. Is it too much to ask of you, Guardian?"

Marin tipped his head back and stared into the sky. Darkness had fallen and stars were flickering overhead, but he didn't see them. The only thing visible to him was the box Lucien had trapped him in. He marveled at the man's ingenuity. If he granted Lucien his request, he'd be inviting the stranger to dwell among them against his better judgement. And if he refused, the clan would question his hostile response to the man's understandable request. Either way, Lucien would get what he apparently wanted.

He looked over his shoulder to assess the clan's expressions. All eyes were now on him, awaiting his response. Doubt suddenly welled up inside him—was he being paranoid? After all, the visitor had done nothing to warrant anything other than a warm welcome. If he refused Lucien's request, he would have to explain himself to his kin. Damn. Why had he let Lindy talk him out of stepping down as Guardian?

Taking a slow, deep breath, Marin looked back at Lucien and knew that he really didn't have a choice. "Very well," he said, unable to hide the rumbling growl that slid from his throat along with his words. "You may stay. Temporarily. You will sleep in Thoren's den."

Everyone rose to their feet and rushed forward to gather around Lucien. The she-bears nudged Marin rudely aside as they struggled to take positions closest to the attractive newcomer. Marin stepped back out of the circle to allow them more leeway and watched his kin make fools of themselves in their quest to befriend the stranger. Why couldn't they feel what he felt, that something was very wrong?

"You may stay," he muttered again under his breath. "But you will answer to me."

Chapter Five

Every darn tomato was rotten. Lindy plucked another one off the wilted vine and held it up in the afternoon light. Just like the others, it was riddled with tiny black spots from last night's frost. She dropped it on the ground by her knees and watched it splatter like a burst water balloon. Then her eyes fell on a perfect red orb dangling from a thick stem nearby. Aha! So one did survive. She pulled it gently off the stem and raised it up to eye level.

Her gaze assessed the perfect fruit before darting away beyond the garden toward a movement at the edge of the forest. She could just make out a large black bear standing in the shadow of the trees, so well hidden that she almost missed it. Its head lowered to better focus its small dark eyes on her. Her heart skipped a beat. She wasn't sure whether to be afraid or excited.

"Marin?" she called hesitantly, keeping her voice soft in case it was only a wild bear.

The creature walked slowly out of the shadows to close the distance between them. Its huge feet moved silently over the leaf-littered ground, as stealthy as a wolf hunting prey. It was a massive animal, all power beneath the thick coat of jet fur.

Lindy froze in place, afraid to move or even take her eyes off it. Her heart began to thump in her chest, pulsing harder as the distance between them closed, until finally she drew in a sharp breath and scooted backward across the cold ground. It was too late to escape the animal, too late to do anything but say a quick prayer for her safety.

Sniffing the air, the bear continued forward and stopped a few feet away from her. It didn't make a sound but merely watched her with intense black eyes for a moment before dropping its gaze to the tomato still clenched in her hand. Then it chuffed softly and opened its mouth.

She stared at the bear for a moment, shocked that it seemed to be waiting for her to feed it. Its mouth hung wide open, revealing a thick lower jaw lined with powerful teeth. The eyes lifted from the tomato to focus on her face, then dropped down to the food again. Slowly she raised her arm and offered the fruit on her outstretched and shaking palm.

The bear lowered its head and placed its mouth tenderly around the red sphere. Its dark fur tickled her palm and at the feel of her skin, its eyes focused deeply on hers. Then arching its back, the bear growled softly and brought its arms to its mouth.

Marin gazed at her intently while he took the tomato into his hand. He looked down at it for a moment, and then held it up before him like a sacred offering. Moisture glistened in his penetrating eyes as the memory came flooding back. "It was the second of two kindnesses you showed me," he whispered, lowering the fruit to his lap. "First you warmed me, then you fed me. No one has ever cared for me that way. Only you."

Lindy looked into his eyes, wanting only to fall into his arms and gaze up into those dark depths, but she forced herself to remain still. Her body cried out for him, for the warmth of his skin against hers and the taste of his lips on hers. Rarely had she seen him so vulnerable and open the way he was right now, and the look on his face was seared into her heart.

"Sometimes the simplest acts demonstrate the greatest love," she said, holding her hand out to take his.

He dropped the tomato and pulled her into his lap, drawing his arms gently around her until she was caught in his embrace. The flowery scent of her hair drifted around him and mingled with his own woodsy scent. They held each other for a long time without speaking, knowing that their bodies would speak more eloquently to each other than words ever could.

Lindy slipped her arm out of his embrace and swept her fingers through the tangles of his thick black hair. She loved how soft it felt in her hand, how wild and handsome it looked framing his rugged face. She could gaze at that face all day, swim in those dark eyes, smother under those firm lips forever. Could he ever really know how deeply she loved him? How much she wanted him?

He leaned to the side and laid her gently on the ground, still nestled in his arms. Her blonde hair spilled over the grass like a golden disk beneath her head and shimmered in the sunlight. Until he'd met her, he had never seen a female with hair the color of the sun. It was one of the prettiest things he'd ever laid eyes on. His mouth curled up in a smile as he ran his fingers through the silky strands.

"Why do you desire me?" he asked, his eyes narrowing while he looked at her. It was something he'd wanted to ask for a long time but had never found the courage to do. Fighting, killing... they were easy compared to understanding human nature.

She pursed her lips and ran her fingers along the curve of his jaw while she thought about his question. She wasn't sure if she even knew the answer. Her finger slid down his neck and across the top of his muscular shoulder. "I didn't at first, you know," she said, her gaze following the track of her hand across his skin. "You scared me so much I just wanted to run away from you."

He nodded, grunting softly in acknowledgment. "I have that effect on everyone."

"You're supposed to. That's what makes you a good Guardian."

Sighing deeply, he raised her head up and kissed her on the cheek. "I suppose. But when did you stop being scared of me? When did the fear become affection?"

"Honestly?"

"Of course. I want everything you tell me to be the truth. Always."

She licked her lips and breathed deeply as the scene replayed in her mind. "It was the night we came to rescue you. The men had such a head start on us that we weren't even sure you'd still be alive when we found you. Then we heard you cry out, and we knew they were hurting you. It tore me apart to think of what they were doing to you, of how much pain you were in, but at least I knew you were alive. It was at that moment I realized I wasn't trying to rescue you for Gareth's sake, or the clan's, but for mine."

His eyes narrowed again as he cocked his head to look at her. "But why? Why did you want to save me when all I'd ever done was intimidate and threaten you?"

The corner of her mouth rose in a slight smile. That was easy to answer. "I guess deep down I suspected that you were as captivated by me as I was by you. Don't think I didn't notice when you strutted around in human skin when everyone else wore fur." Her eyes suddenly lit up to match her grin. "Or the way you looked at me when you saw me watching you at the waterfall. You *wanted* me to look at you."

"It was that obvious, huh?" His voice sounded almost sheepish.

"Don't worry," she laughed. "Believe me, the feeling was mutual. You made my heart pound then, Marin, and you still do."

Gently brushing the hair away from her shoulders, he gazed at her with a seriousness that seemed to well up from deep inside him. He took a deep, quivering breath. "Lindy, when you look at me, what do you see—a man or a bear?"

She thought for a long minute before answering. "I see both. To me, they're not separate things but two parts of the same soul. I guess it's sort of like me, being a woman and also a human, two different aspects of one being. I respect the part of you that's bear, but I love the part of you that's a man. I love knowing that you're part human, Marin, even if you're not so sure about it right now."

He rolled over and lay on his back next to her, one arm still tucked under her neck to cushion her, and the other draped across his forehead. "I don't know if I'll ever learn to accept it."

"You will. You must, because it's who you are. You need to give yourself time." She turned on her side to face him and laid her hand on his chest. It felt so good to feel his warm skin beneath hers. She brushed her fingertips along the curve of his pectoral muscle and swept them across his nipple. It grew hard at her touch, and he groaned softly.

"You once asked me what I was afraid of," he whispered.

"I remember. You wouldn't tell me then."

He nodded and shifted his arm to cover his eyes as though he didn't want her to see his face when he spoke. "Don't laugh when I tell you this," he begged, his voice quivering. "But I'm afraid to be with you. And afraid to be without you."

Lindy draped herself across his chest and kissed him lightly on the lips. "I would never laugh at you, Marin. I don't ever want you to be afraid of telling me things that are important to you. We should both feel comfortable talking about things that affect us." Her hand slid across his chest and around his side to hold him tight. "So please tell me why you're afraid to be with me."

He inhaled a deep, trembling breath that betrayed his nervousness. Never in his life had he needed to admit the inadequacy he knew he must now explain. Suddenly all he could think about was shifting into bear skin and escaping back into the forest, anything to get away from the pain and humiliation of what was coming. But he had never run away from anything before, and he'd be damned if he'd do it now. Dropping his arm to the ground, he rolled on his side to face her and looked her square in the eyes.

"What scares me most is the thought of sexual intimacy with you."

Her heart sank at his words. Even though she knew he loved her, a nagging doubt had always drifted in the back of her mind that he would never desire her as a woman. Maybe he couldn't, maybe he *wouldn't*, ever make love to her. "Oh," was all she could force herself to say.

The pain was evident on her face, and he mentally cursed himself for bungling this. "Lindy, listen to me. I mated with Terra more times than I can count, and with others before her. Believe me, I'm not inexperienced at such things. At least as a bear. But as a man..." His voice trailed off while he gathered his courage again.

Lindy stared at him, needing to watch his expression when he explained it to her. She knew he didn't want to say anything else that would hurt her, but she just wasn't sure if he would go so far as to lie to her to spare her feelings.

Marin licked his lips and took another deep breath before he continued. "Did you know that when I look at you, I want you so much that I have to force myself to back off?"

She looked at him but didn't answer.

"Every time you touch me, I feel like my heart will burst out of my chest. You have no idea how jealous I was every time I saw Gareth touch you. In my heart and in my mind, I had already claimed you for my own. I just hadn't... claimed you with my body. Because... I don't know how." He grew quiet to let her absorb what he'd said. "Do you understand?"

The look on her face said it all. "Uh... it's a little confusing, Marin. I'm just not sure what you're telling me."

Marin reached over and laid his palm tenderly on the side of her face, relishing the soft warmth of her skin. Telling her this was one of the hardest things he'd ever done. "Here's the truth, Lindy. I've never mated in man skin. It's not something that Bear People do, so I don't have the vaguest idea how it's done. I wouldn't even know where to start. And I'm so afraid of disappointing you..."

"Oh, Marin. No," she cried, rolling herself on top of him. She dug her arms under his back to hold him tight while the tears slipped from her eyes. "Don't you think I understand that? I don't expect you to know about human sexuality any more than you expect me to understand bear mating." She stopped to wipe the wetness from her face and from his shoulder, where her tears had fallen. "I don't want our relationship to be stressful you for. You've already got enough of that in your life."

He laughed softly in complete agreement. "You're right about that."

Pulling herself more upright, she looked down at him while her fingers swept through his dark hair. His brow was furrowed with concern but his eyes were bright with desire. "I think you know how much I want you, how much I dream of being with you as a man. But when it happens, I want it to be on your terms, when you're ready. And when you feel the time is right, we'll work it out together. We'll help each other. Until then, I'll be satisfied just to be your sanctuary, your safe place to come when you need someone. And please, please know that you could never, *ever*, disappoint me."

Marin closed his eyes and pulled her against his chest again, feeling like a weight had been lifted from him. "Thank you, Lindy. Thank you for giving me time. And for understanding."

"We've got all the time in the world. I hope you know that I'd do anything for you, Marin. Anything."

He stroked her hair, running his fingers through the golden strands again and again. "I know."

She kissed his cheek and gazed at the intense look in his eyes, watching how the tiny worry lines around them eased. A moment later they returned, this time deeper. "I'm so glad you came to see me. Is everything all right at forest home?"

He hesitated for a moment, almost reluctant to bring it up and spoil the mood. "I'm not sure," he said at last. "A stranger has come among us."

"A stranger? A human?"

"No, one of our kind."

"What?" She couldn't believe it. So there really were other shapeshifters besides the clan. "Tell me about him. Her?" She said a quick prayer that it wasn't a *her*.

"He was there when Gareth and I returned from our trip to town with you. Lucien, that's his name. There's something odd about him. When he talks, things he says don't make sense to me."

"Like what?" She hugged him tighter at the feel of his heartbeat quickening with concern.

"He said that his entire clan was killed by humans who came to log the forest."

"Well, with as much logging as they do around here, that's certainly possible, isn't it?"

Marin pulled her closer to calm himself, feeling his gut churning with growing apprehension. "It's possible, but that's not what disturbs me. He told us that he couldn't save any of his clan. Even the cubs were killed."

"Oh God, that's awful. The guy sounds like a coward. If he gives you any grief, just force him out."

"That's just it, though. Lucien is... huge. Taller than me. And I suspect that he might even be stronger than me. I don't think anyone forces Lucien to do anything he doesn't want to do."

"Where did he come from? There must be other clans around here, then."

"He said he came from a forest near the horizon. We don't really associate with other clans, so I'm not sure which forest they lived in, nor do I know how he happened to find us. But he's certainly made himself at home with my kin."

She tried to keep the smile off her face at the jealousy in his voice. It wasn't funny, but the emotion he was revealing was so *human*. Not that it would comfort him to know she thought that. Clearing her throat, she forced her voice to sound serious. "What does he want from the clan?"

"A place to stay. Companionship." He turned his head to gaze at her. "It's the companionship part that has me concerned."

"Why?"

"Like I said, he's strong. I don't want him hurting any of our she-bears."

"Hurting them how?"

A smile lit his face while he shook his head at her. "You ask a lot of questions."

Lindy pursed her lips in exasperation. "I want to learn all I can about Bearwalkers, Marin. How can I help you if I don't even understand your people? I don't want to make any mistakes. Surely you can appreciate that."

His eyebrows arched at her logic. "Point well taken. Okay, I'm concerned that Lucien may try to mate with our females."

Now her eyebrows raised. "I always thought that bears mated in the spring."

"We do. But the part of our spirit that allows us to assume human form also allows us to experience sexual excitement at any time of the year. And believe me, the girls are plenty excited with Lucien around."

She stroked his arm with her fingers, tracing the muscles that bulged from his olive skin. He was so strong, she couldn't imagine there being anyone stronger. "What are you going to do?"

A long sigh slipped from his throat as he cupped his fingers over hers. "Right now, just watch him. I don't trust him, but he hasn't done anything that would justify running him off."

"Is there anything I can do to help?"

"Not unless you can change into bear skin and help me keep an eye on him."

Lindy sat up and smiled at him, wanting so much to be

by his side when he guarded the clan. Sometimes she felt so useless. But as always, he was right, there wasn't much she could do to help except just be supportive. Another thought suddenly came to her mind. "While you're here, there's something I've been wanting to ask you."

"What is it?"

"I want to mark a path to forest home so that I can find my way to you if I need to. I hate having to depend on you or Gareth to lead me there every time, and I thought that if I made a small paint mark on the tree trunks, then I'd be able to come to you by myself. No one will know about it except you and me. May I, if it's all right with you?"

Marin sat up and stared at the edge of the forest, trying to imagine how she felt entering the wilderness that she had so little familiarity with. In the past he would never have considered leaving a trail that might endanger them, but Lindy had raised a valid concern. What if she needed to contact him and couldn't? Even worse, what if she tried to find her way alone and was lost or injured? She could die before he even knew she was missing. He looked back at her and nodded. "I think that's a good idea. Do you have the paint?"

"Yes."

He stood up, pulling her upright along with him. "I have to return to the clan now, so why don't you come with me and we'll mark the trail together."

Lindy placed her hands on his shoulders and pulled him to her for a kiss. She didn't want him to leave, but then she knew she never would. She'd just have to get used to the fact that the clan was his life and his first priority. She smiled sweetly at him and kissed him again, hoping that some day she would have the same importance.

Chapter Six

Lucien eyed Lilia like a morsel ripe for devouring. She was tiny and fragile, even by bear standards, and oh so tempting. Even better, she had a taste for big bears like himself. He made a mental note to thank Arlin for sharing that tidbit of information with him. Looking at her now, he pictured the way she must have pursued Marin, pouting her dark little lips at him in the hope of mating with him, and then being so rudely rebuked. The Guardian must be crazy refusing a pretty thing like her. *Well, don't worry, sow, that ain't gonna happen with me*, he laughed.

She was lying in the meadow about ten yards away from him. Though her black fur blended in with the shade underneath the old hickory tree, he could still see that her eyes were focused on him. She lay with her head resting on her outstretched paws, watching every move he made. He wondered how long it had been since she'd seen any action. Damn Marin. If he hadn't ordered him to sleep in the dead bear's den, Lilea would have seen plenty of his action.

He watched her for a while longer before his thoughts were distracted by a movement nearby, and he turned to see who it was that plopped down next to him. It was the young cinnamon-colored bear.

"What's your name again?"

"Gareth."

Lucien cast a slow, cool glance over the bear, sizing him up. He was pretty scrawny but Lucien had seen him return to the clan in the company of the Guardian the other day.

What that meant, exactly, he wasn't sure. Marin didn't look like the young bear's sire, but they apparently had been away together all that afternoon. *Curious.*

"Sorry about your clan," Gareth said, looking Lucien over. He still couldn't get over how big a bear he was.

"Yeah, that's the way it goes," Lucien replied casually, as though the thought of it didn't even phase him.

Gareth just shook his head. Poor guy, the hurt must still be so fresh that he was numb. It was probably better just to drop the subject. He followed Lucien's gaze and saw that he was staring at Lilea in the shadows. "Pretty, isn't she?"

Lucien nodded with a grunt but another thought had already replaced her in his mind. He looked over at Gareth. "I saw you return with Marin the other day. Is he training you to replace him?"

"Oh, no. There's no way anyone could replace Marin. No, we had just visited a human friend."

Now that's interesting, Lucien thought. "A human friend, huh? Do you have many of those?"

"No, just the one."

"And Marin trusts this man?"

Gareth cleared his throat softly. "Woman. It's a her. And yes, he trusts her."

Oooh, things are definitely getting more interesting. "I see."

"But she's actually my friend. She saved my life."

"Is that so? Have you mated with her, then?"

Gareth cocked his head to look at him. "Of course not."

Lucien grinned and nodded to himself. "So how long has Marin been your Guardian?"

Gareth gave him a strange look. Didn't he know that Guardians were born into the position? The only way for an ordinary bear to assume that important role was if a Guardian died or was defeated in a challenge. "Marin has been our Guardian all his adult life."

"Is he a good one?"

"The best."

"He seems strict, overbearing. Highly unreasonable."

Gareth had to think about that. "Sometimes, but we know that it's because he cares about us."

Lucien uttered a loud, barking laugh full of scorn. "A good Guardian is protective without keeping his clan in a cage, and all of you," he said, nodding over his shoulder toward the clan, "are well caged."

"That's not true," Gareth replied defensively, offended by the visitor's rudeness.

Lucien continued to stare at him, trying to make him uncomfortable. "You don't think so? When was the last time you raided a human campsite?"

"Raided a campsite?"

Rolling his eyes, Lucien snorted out a laugh. "Don't tell me you're never done that?"

Gareth didn't want to lie, but he hated to admit the embarrassing truth, too. He stammered for a moment trying to come up with a reasonable excuse, but couldn't find one. Finally he exhaled softly and confessed. "I've never done it."

"Why on earth not? Every bear raids campsites."

"Marin won't let us."

A soft, slow breath of air came from Lucien's throat as he shot a look at Gareth that was pure pity. "I don't suppose you've *ever* mated in man skin, then, either."

The look on Gareth's face told it all. His eyes grew huge and round while his jaw dropped open. Was Lucien serious?

The bear swatted him sympathetically on the shoulder. "You are in one small cage, my friend. Maybe it's time to break out from behind those bars and start living life the way it was meant to be." He chuckled sarcastically. "Oh, that's right. Marin won't let you. But I bet he lets himself."

"I... I don't think Marin does those things either," he mumbled.

Lucien rolled on his back and lay in the cool grass laughing. "Sure, whatever you say." He swiped one huge paw across his nose and snorted.

"Do most Bear People do things like that... raid campsites and mate in man skin?" Though he'd heard of such things, they had long been forbidden in his clan.

The big bear rolled on his side and stared at Gareth's face while his voice grew serious. "I'm sorry, son, I didn't mean to start something here. I just assumed that if your clan was like mine, you'd be doing all the fun things that put a little excitement into life. Damn... sex and raiding... that was just a typical day among my kin."

By now Gareth was fuming. Why had Marin kept this from him and his clanmates? What else had he kept from them? And might he be enjoying things that he denied them? A burning sensation began to gnaw in his gut at the thought of what might have happened when he sent Marin to Lindy's home. The vision of it roared into his mind—Lindy pulling Marin into her arms, pressing her lips against his in a passionate kiss. She had refused *him* when he'd tried to kiss her during Marin's rescue, but she didn't hesitate when Marin stood before her.

His anger seethed as he pictured Marin slipping the clothes from her luscious body. It was all clear in his mind, as if it was happening right before his eyes. Marin pushing the jeans down her long, slim legs, then pulling her shirt over her head until she stood naked before him. He could almost hear the growl of passion coming from Marin's throat while the Guardian took her body.

Oh, wasn't Marin clever? Gareth thought back to a conversation the he-bears once had when they were trying to figure out how humans mated. Marin had played along so convincingly, making everyone believe that he knew nothing about it. Gareth chuffed angrily, wondering exactly how many human females he had taken over the years. It wouldn't surprise him if that was the reason hunters had killed Marin's mate. Maybe Marin had taken the hunter's mate first.

The more he thought about it, the more plausible it seemed. Did Marin really expect them to believe that he had spent the last seven years in celibacy? Who did he think he was fooling? He didn't need to mate with the she-bears when he could take his pick among human women.

What happened in the café the other day was a perfect example. The waitress had practically torn Marin's clothes off with her eyes. Even Lindy's sister had made some comment about how delicious he looked. In just that short amount of time, it had become clear that human women wanted to be with him in a sexual way.

Gareth closed his eyes and forced the painful images away. All his life he had admired and respected Marin. He'd trusted him. The thought of Marin playing *him* like a fool made him sick to his stomach and he wondered if anyone else suspected that the Guardian had been fooling them, too.

Well, Marin's days of deceit were over. As far as he was concerned, so were his days as Guardian. No one was going to treat the clan like that and get away with it. No one would treat him like a fool.

He'd make damn sure of that.

"Hello, Gorgeous."

Lilea looked up and shivered. Lucien stood above her, his dark eyes traveling across her body in slow, admiring sweeps. The way the sun shone behind him made the red in his fur glow as if he was on fire.

He was stunning. Every movement he made demonstrated his power and strength. The muscles in his shoulders and haunches rippled beneath his skin when he walked and propelled him forward with smooth, easy strides. Despite his bulk, he moved quietly through the forest, as soundless as the needles falling from the pines in the autumn breeze. Everyone turned to look when Lucien walked by.

"Hello," she murmured. *Well, it's about time.* He'd been watching her all afternoon but hadn't made a move. She'd wondered if he was toying with her or just too shy to approach her immediately, though she had the feeling that the last thing Lucien would ever be was shy.

The big boar lowered himself down beside her and spread out on the grass with his paws almost touching her. She was so small that it took two of her paws to equal one of his. He was amazed that she could be a mature sow, but from the way she'd wagged her rear end at him, he knew it to be true. It made him hot just thinking about it.

"Thank you for making me feel so welcome here," he said. His voice was deep, almost rumbling when his black eyes gazed at her from within the ebony fur of his broad face.

Lilea wanted to melt beneath his stare. There was something in his expression that was vaguely unsettling but she didn't know what it was. Maybe it was his recent loss that had darkened his emotions, or his loneliness. Whatever it was, she wanted to help him fix it. "You're very welcome, Lucien. Anything to help you through this terrible time."

Now that's an offer I like, the bruin smirked to himself. Lapping his tongue in the air, he sniffed to absorb the intoxicating scent of her. *Just a little longer,* he reminded himself. "I wish there was some way to repay you for your kindness."

"That's not necessary."

Believe me, it is. Lucien rolled his eyes to gaze at her sadly. "You have no idea how alone I've felt since I lost my clan. Do you know how miserable it is to wander alone, with no companion, no friend, no one to talk to? It's terrible."

She reached over to touch his paw with her own. Even in that momentary touch, she could feel his awesome strength. "I've never been alone like that. My clan has always been here with me."

"You're so lucky. I'd give anything to feel someone's soft paws holding me again. I haven't had a good night's sleep since it all happened."

"Nightmares bothering you?"

He sighed and rolled heavily onto his side, appearing exhausted. "No, I'm just not used to sleeping alone."

Lilea's dark eyes grew huge. "You don't sleep alone?" She thought every bear slept alone in his or her den. "I don't understand."

A puzzled expression clouded his face when he answered. "You know, no one's keeping me company at night. I really hate that. It's so cold." His shaggy body rippled with a shiver.

The sow turned away to gaze at the forest, deep in thought. Lucien was a strange bear, but very intriguing. Was it commonplace for his kin to share their dens with each other? It was a behavior she'd never heard of, yet he spoke of it as though it was an everyday occurrence. What an odd thing to do. But then, who in their right mind wouldn't want to spend a night with Lucien?

Her eyes wandered across the meadow and settled on her friend Lena, who grazed on wild berries. She made a promise to ask her if she'd ever heard of this. But when she looked back at Lucien, she saw his eyes glued to Lena, watching every move she made. Without warning, a slow soft growl slid from her throat. Why was he watching *her*? Lena was big and clumsy, not to mention having her cub Notch tagging along at her side constantly. Still, the way he was looking at her didn't betray any hint of disinterest because of it. In fact, he looked very interested.

"You know," she said quickly, "there's no reason why you should sleep by yourself, Lucien. My den is large enough for two."

He swung his huge head back to look at her and smiled. "Why, what a thoughtful offer, Lilea. But I really couldn't impose. Especially when I get the impression that it's not a custom among your clan. Pity though."

She snorted loudly. "Just because we've never done something doesn't mean we can't start. Personally, I think it sounds like a lovely tradition, and I'd very much enjoy your company tonight. If you want to, of course."

His smile grew even bigger. Lucien lifted his huge body up and walked over to nudge her side gently with his own. "How could I refuse such a delightful lady?" Then his expression grew solemn. "But I forget. Your Guardian won't allow it, I'm sure."

"Marin doesn't have to know. Besides, it's none of his business. I can entertain whomever I want, whenever I want. He doesn't own me."

Lucien nodded appreciatively. "Indeed. You're a grown, intelligent sow who needs no bruin's permission. Especially Marin's. He's a virtual tyrant from what I've seen of him. The Guardian of my clan actually encouraged us to be more open with each other, more free to pursue the physical pleasures of maturity. I can't understand why Marin feels differently. Did I hear that he hasn't mated for... what... seven years?"

She nodded. "Hard to believe, isn't it? What strength he has."

Lucien laughed contemptuously. "I'm surprised that you actually believe his lies, Lilea."

She swung her head sharply toward him. "What do you mean by that?"

"Surely you don't believe that a bear of his strength and vitality has been alone for so long? Why would he deny himself the greatest pleasure in life, especially with his prestigious position as Guardian? It's unthinkable."

"But I know for a fact that he hasn't mated with any of us," she declared. "Believe me, I've tried to interest him, and he just walks away."

Lucien shot her a steely glance that was dead serious. "But who does he walk away *to*?"

Lilea blinked rapidly, her face blank. She didn't understand what he meant. There was no one else, no other clans in this forest. No other females, at least ones with fur...

Then it hit her. Humans. Human females. Like Lindy,

the woman whose life she had spared with her vote. No, it couldn't be. Marin couldn't be satisfying his body with human women! The thought of it made her nauseous.

She looked at Lucien with panic on her face. "Humans? How can you be sure? You don't even know Marin."

Tilting his head back as if her question was ridiculous, Lucien sighed slowly. "I'm male, I know what it's like to be without female companionship for a short length of time. And I can guarantee you that there is no way, absolutely no way, that a handsome, prime-of-life boar like Marin has gone seven years without sex. Nope, no way. He's definitely been humping someone. Or more likely, several someones."

Lilea closed her eyes. Waves of anguish rippled through her body at the thought of Marin denying her advances in favor of a human. It was sickening. How could she have been so blind not to see it? Not to even wonder about it? How stupidly naïve could she be?

Lucien reached over and covered her delicate paw with his own. She was shaking badly. "I know, dear, it's hard to believe that some bears can be so cruel, isn't it?" he whispered, nuzzling her small black ear. "You think you know someone and then you find out it's all been a game. Damn him. Damn Marin for hurting you."

She tipped her body sideways to rest against him, glad to have his warm strength for support. Maybe she wasn't good enough, human enough, for Marin's taste, but she was certainly good enough for Lucien. Sharing a den with him tonight was looking better and better all the time.

Chapter Seven

Marin worried about what was happening. Every day for the last three weeks, Lucien had made his way through the clan. One by one, he had sat down with them or strolled off into the forest with them and spent hours talking. It was an unnatural thing because bears were, by nature, solitary, and to let a stranger into their lives like this was, well, it was just wrong. He'd been amazed when they'd first accepted Lindy and now it was happening again with Lucien.

He sat on top of the boulder where he always sat to keep an eye on his kin and gazed down over the meadow. Lena lay on her side in the shade of the hickory tree, sprawled comfortably in the cool grass. Every time the wind blew, dried leaves drifted down from the crown of the massive tree, dotting her brown fur with golden speckles. Suddenly a huge black paw swept across her fur to swat the leaves away, causing her to burst out laughing.

Lucien rolled over until his taut belly nudged up against her back. His mouth opened in a broad grin while he ran his paw gently over her fur. Neither one of them seemed to be aware of Marin perched on the rock watching them, or if they were, they were simply ignoring him.

The longer Marin watched, the more the fur stood up on the nape of his neck. Something was changing. The atmosphere among his kin was completely different; they were cooler, more aloof. When he spoke to them, they responded less respectfully—if they responded at all. It was a change he didn't like one bit. And he knew that everything hinged on Lucien.

As if that weren't enough, he had caught the bruin sneaking out of Lilea's den the other morning. Lucien had shot him a look of pure contempt and continued on his way without the courtesy of an explanation. Shortly after, when Lilea emerged from her home, Marin had questioned her about the incident, worried that Lucien had hurt her. Instead of thanking him for his concern, she had snubbed him by turning and walking away. Stunned and hurt, Marin didn't force the issue but simply let her go on her way.

He couldn't do that anymore. Things were getting out of hand and he knew that the only way to rectify the situation was to talk to Lucien. It wasn't something he looked forward to. He had never confronted a bear bigger than himself, though he felt confident that if it came down to a challenge, he could defeat Lucien. He knew that at a minimum, he would get hurt, and after the beating he'd endured during his kidnapping, pain was something he'd just as soon avoid.

Knowing he could stall no longer, Marin jumped down off the rock and crossed the drying meadow grasses until he stood beneath the hickory. Lena and Lucien stopped their conversation and glared up at him.

"What is it, Marin?" Lena chuffed, obviously perturbed by his interruption.

"I need to speak with Lucien."

The red-tinged bruin rolled to his feet with an annoyed look on his face. "I'm listening."

Marin shook his head. "Alone."

Lucien's mouth opened in a broad grin. "Whatever you need to say, you can say in front of my dear friend here."

Marin growled deeply at Lucien's rudeness. Was there anything he didn't argue about? "This is not for her ears."

"Why Guardian, are you trying to hide something from your own kin? Surely she's worthy of hearing anything that I'm worthy of hearing." His grin grew broader, almost becoming a sneer.

"Yes, by all means. Speak to *both* of us, Marin," Lena prompted, following Lucien's lead.

Sighing angrily, Marin took a step closer until he could thrust his muzzle into his adversary's face. He felt the heat, the anger, rising in Lucien. "Your stay has been terminated. Leave."

Lena gasped. How could Marin do this? Lucien was the first visitor of their own kind in years. Why was he forcing him out when Lucien had brought such excitement to their boring clan? "No, you can't do that," she cried.

"I can. And I have."

A disgusted look crossed Lucien's face as he turned to look at Lena. He hunched his huge shoulders up in a helpless shrug. "What did I do? Have I done something wrong?"

"No," Lena said.

"Yes," Marin contradicted.

"I'd appreciate an explanation, Guardian," Lucien said. "If I'm being forced to leave, I'd at least like to know why."

"Fine," Marin replied, more than happy to let him have it.

Lena moved beside Marin and shoved him hard with her side, eliciting a fierce growl from him. "Just hold on. You can explain it—to all of us." Without waiting for him to respond, she loped away to alert the others and bring them back.

Within minutes, everyone shoved into a tight circle around Marin and Lucien. They didn't want to believe Lena when she'd told them that Lucien was being forced to leave. Why? For what reason? He'd done nothing wrong.

Shara forced his way through the crowd to stand beside the Guardian. His lips were tightly drawn together in anger before he spoke. "What is this nonsense about Lucien leaving us?"

Every head turned to hear Marin's answer.

"Our guest has taken advantage of our hospitality by

breaking every rule of the clan," he growled. He didn't mean to sound so angry, but they had him on the defensive and he hated it.

"What has he done?" Gareth asked, pushing his way forward to stare at Marin.

Marin was reluctant to embarrass anyone, but at this point he had no choice. "I saw him leave Lilea's den the other morning."

"So?" Lena snorted. "Lucien left *mine* this very morning."

"And mine the other day," another she-bear added from behind her. Instead of sounding embarrassed, her tone of voice was practically boastful.

Marin couldn't believe what he was hearing. Had they lost their minds? "In this clan, we have never shared our dens. We *do not* share our dens."

"And why not?" Lilea challenged. "Is it wrong to share our bodies and have some fun?"

"Fun? Mating is to be held in the highest regard. We aren't rabbits, breeding and popping out litters mindlessly."

Laughter rippled through the crowd. Marin was so old-fashioned, so straight-laced it was pathetic.

Shara wasn't laughing. His young face was heavy with anger when he spoke. "And why haven't we been allowed to raid campsites? Or dumpsters? Why have we been denied all the fun things that other clans enjoy? It's not fair, and I resent it."

Marin's jaw dropped. Shara had never, ever, mentioned doing such things. They were dangerous and foolish, a senseless risk to a bear's health. Why was he bringing this up now? Then he knew. Of course, it was Lucien. The bruin was planting thoughts in their minds to stir up discontent. What better way than to make them miss things they never had?

But Marin knew his reasons were valid. The things he had forbidden had been outlawed long ago. It was nothing new, nothing shocking. There was not one among them who had ever raided a campsite except Tabon, the oldest bruin, who had made that mistake in his youth and paid for it with a gunshot to his leg. Marin swung his gaze to the old bear hoping for support; but his head was down, and he refused to look up.

Lilea shoved Shara aside and stood beside Marin. Her eyes sparkled with moisture when she looked up at him. "How could you?" she said, her voice so soft and quivery that it was hard to hear her.

Marin snarled when he answered. "How could I *what?*"

She shook her head, furious at his blatant pretense of ignorance. "You know what," she hissed. "It's no wonder you never mated with any of us after Terra died. Why should you, when you found human females more to your liking? You hypocritical traitor."

Angry hisses rose up all around him at her words and every eye glared heatedly at him. There was no doubt about it. Marin had fooled them all.

"You're crazy!" he roared, swinging his head around to look at the clan. There was not a hint of compassion or understanding on any of their faces. His heart began to pound at the realization that they weren't just angry with him. They were *furious.* Suddenly it all became clear. Lucien had turned them against him.

"Don't you see what he's doing?" he cried, whirling to face each of his kin in turn. "He's telling you lies. Turning you against me. Don't believe him!"

Gareth shook his head sadly. "We trusted you, Marin. And you took advantage of us."

Marin panted heavily, feeling like he was trapped in a painful snare from which he couldn't free himself. His heart thumped so hard it hurt. "Listen to yourselves. We've known each other all our lives. I've guarded you... protected you. I've saved the life of each and every one of you. How can you listen to Lucien and trust anything he tells you when you don't even know him?"

Gareth turned to his kin. "Ask Marin what we did the other day when we left together."

Every eye shifted from Gareth back to Marin.

"Well?" Shara said impatiently.

Marin stood defiantly silent.

"We went to the humans' town," Gareth said. "I even met a human female there."

Gasps rose up from the clan. This was the first they'd heard of it. No one *ever* went into the humans' town, because Marin had forbidden it.

"You asked me to take you there," Marin growled. "It was *your* idea. I didn't want to go, remember?"

Gareth grunted. "The only reason you let me go was because Lindy went with us. You'd do anything to be with her. Wouldn't you?" He shoved his slender face toward Marin's threateningly. "How many times have you mated with her, Guardian? How many other humans have you enjoyed while denying us the same privilege?"

Marin couldn't answer; he was so stunned. The anger inside him had turned to ice. All he felt was numb. This couldn't be happening.

Lucien stepped forward, easing his way slowly through the crowd. He moved with a confident swagger that matched the smirk on his face. When he finally stopped, he stood face to face with Marin and shook his huge shaggy head.

"I'm afraid," he laughed, "that it's really time for *you* to go."

Lindy jumped and startled awake at the sound of a knock on her door. Gunther lurched to his feet and zipped through the cabin to the back door, stopping to bark at the window. She pulled a robe over her pajamas and walked through the kitchen, taking a quick glance at the clock so she could curse whoever had come visiting at such an ungodly hour. Whoever it was, she was ready to kick some butt.

She flipped on the back porch light and looked out the window into the darkness. A naked man stood there, his dark hair tumbled down to obscure his face. She threw the door open.

"Marin?"

It took a minute before he lifted his head to look at her. The light flooded down over him, illuminating his face. Blood trickled from a cut at the corner of his mouth and an ugly purple bruise swelled around one eye, forcing it halfway shut.

"My God, what happened?" she cried. In the harsh light, she could see that he was trembling.

He looked at her with an expression of utter despair on his battered face. "The clan has forced me out," he whispered, his voice creaking with anguish. "I have nowhere to go."

Chapter Eight

Marin didn't look up when Lindy sat down beside him on the sofa and raised the clean wet cloth to his face. His thoughts were miles away, his memory frozen on the faces of those who had hurt him.

"Are you okay?" she asked, dabbing gently at the cut on the corner of his mouth. Whoever had punched him had hit him hard enough to bruise his cheek the same sickening bluish-purple color as his left eye.

"Sure," he grunted harshly. "The only thing that could make my day even better is if you rip my heart out, too. So why not? Take a stab at it, Lind. Everyone else did."

She slapped the bloody cloth down on the end table and grabbed Marin's face in her hands, knowing it was the only way he was going to look at her. "Don't attack me, Marin. I'm the one who's here for you, remember?" She was torn between grabbing him by the shoulders and shaking him or just walking away. She settled for another option. Pulling his head toward her, she kissed him hard on the lips.

His eyes shot toward hers. He groaned, amazed that she could make him feel so good when he hurt so badly. But then, that was the way she always made him feel. That was why he had come here. He sighed and lowered his eyelids. "I'm sorry. I shouldn't take my anger out on you."

She released the hold on his head and slid her hands down across his broad shoulders. His skin felt so good beneath her fingers that she had to force herself to honor her promise not to jump all over him. "You're right. You shouldn't." She got up from the sofa and returned a minute later with a cold compress. "Why don't you stretch out here and relax while I tend to these wounds. Tell me what happened."

He turned on the sofa and stretched his long legs across the cushions while he rested his head on the armrest. Lindy sat down beside him and pressed the compress over his swollen eye, causing him to hiss at the sudden stab of icy pain shooting through his head.

"Hush now, it'll help with the swelling," she said, holding the cloth with one hand while she swept the fingers of her other hand through the mass of thick black hair falling around his face. Under the fluorescent glow from the kitchen light, it shimmered with a bluish cast that was stunning. It matched his gorgeous dark eyes perfectly. Her heart jolted at the sight of dried blood matted among the black tangles, spurring her to search for another wound. Just as she feared, two small holes pierced the side of his neck. "Did someone bite you?" she asked, forcing her voice to be calm when inside she wanted to scream.

"Shara bit me while Gareth was pummeling on me."

"*Gareth* hit you?" She didn't want to believe her friend could do such a thing. "But you're stronger than either of those boys, Marin. How were they able to jump you?"

His head tipped back harder against the armrest while the scene played in his mind. "Lucien attacked me head-on and knocked me on my back. Once I was down, he and Arlin held me to the ground while Gareth and Shara beat me. I'm strong, but not strong enough to fight off four mature bears at once."

Lindy lifted the compress to check the swelling. His face seemed less puffy, but his eye was bloodshot and the lid was now almost completely closed. A shiver swept through her at the sight of him, and at the memory of him looking this way the night he was kidnapped and beaten by the humans. Somehow, this time seemed even worse because it came from the paws of his own clan. "I just don't understand why on earth they did this to you. They love you. Jeez, Arlin reveres you."

A skeptical growl slid from his throat as his good eye focused on the blonde hair that fell in a cascade around her shoulders and glimmered in the subtle light. Reaching up, Marin ran his fingers across the golden strands before letting his hand slide down the front of her shoulder. Beneath her terrycloth robe, her pajamas were silky and shimmery, and he wanted nothing more than to slip his hand beneath the fabric and touch her warm skin. Her soft blue eyes burned into his while she waited to see what he would do. There was no doubt in his mind what he wanted to do, but he was just too drained to do it. He dropped his hand back to the couch and closed his eyes.

Swallowing down her disappointment, Lindy laid the cloth gently back over his eye and gazed at his naked body. She hadn't noticed it before, but his arms and legs were bloodied with red parallel scratches where they had held him down with their sharp claws. Anger burned inside her as she wiped the blood carefully away. How could this have happened to the man who had spent his life protecting them?

As if reading her thoughts, Marin drew in a ragged breath and shuddered. "It was Lucien. Somehow he turned them against me. It's my own damn fault this happened."

She shook her head, wondering why he would say such a thing. "How can it be your fault they attacked you? I don't get that at all."

"Because I saw it coming and I didn't do anything about it. I can't believe I was so stupid. I saw him taking them aside one by one, befriending them. No doubt he pumped them for information about me. I watched while he broke every law of our clan, and still I did nothing. I figured he was one of *us*. I never thought that he would betray one of his own kind like that."

Lindy stroked his arm tenderly, her heart breaking for him. "It sounds to me like you were just giving him the benefit of the doubt. You were trying to be nice."

He grunted angrily and whipped the compress off his face to stare at her. "And look what it got me. Disowned by my own kin."

"Why did he do it?"

"I'm not sure. He's been mating with all the she-bears, but I'm not convinced that's his real motive. Maybe he wanted to take over a clan and become its Guardian. I just don't know." A shiver rippled down his body, raising a carpet of goosebumps on his flesh.

"You need to rest, Marin. When you're exhausted and sore, the best thing for you is a good night's sleep. Lean forward, and I'll help you up." She slipped her arm behind his broad back to help him sit up.

Marin rose unsteadily to his feet, still overcome by the pain of what had happened. With Lindy beside him, he took three steps toward the guest bedroom and stopped. His eyes lingered on the door of the familiar room.

"What is it?" she asked.

Inhaling sharply, he swung his head to look into her eyes. He had always cherished his privacy, but the last thing he wanted now was to be alone. She gazed at him so sweetly, her eyes so full of affection. He felt the heat rising in his body despite the pain, and all he could think about was being in her arms. "Can I sleep in your bed tonight?" he whispered.

His request caught her off guard, so she didn't answer for a moment. She forced down the lump in her throat, a bit confused by what he wanted. "You want to sleep in my bed— with *me?*"

Shaking his head slightly, Marin smiled at her self-doubt. "No, Lindy. With Gunther."

I'm such a dork, she told herself, and laughed nervously. "Sorry, I just wasn't expecting you to ask that. Of course you can sleep with me," she said, barely able to contain her excitement. Deep down, she knew he was too tired and sore for anything to happen between them, but the thought of being beside him all night still made her heart race. She'd dreamed of this a hundred times since the first and only night they'd slept in the same bed together, the night he'd shifted into bear skin during his sleep.

They turned around and walked slowly down the dark hallway to her bedroom. The bedcovers were thrown back across the mattress from her abrupt awakening. Marin eyed the colorful fabrics while she helped him onto the bed. He sank down into its softness gratefully, thanking fate that Gareth had ended up here the day he was shot. Now that he had no clan, Marin couldn't imagine what he would've done if he hadn't been able to come to Lindy.

The mattress dipped as she crawled in beside him and pulled the covers up over both of them. Then reaching up on the wall above the headboard, she flipped the switch that cast them into darkness. She turned on her side and slid her arm gently across his chest.

"Does it hurt if I put my arm here, Marin?"

Heat washed through him at the feel of her hand on his skin and he laid his own hand over her arm to hold it in place. "It never hurts when you touch me," he said, trying to keep the emotion from choking his voice. His senses were overwhelmed by the scents drifting around him: the flowery perfume of her hair, the sweet lotion she always put on her body, and most of all, the exotic sensual perfume of her femininity. Despite his fatigue and the pain of his bruises, he felt his groin tighten with desire. He shivered and forced her arm tightly against him to prevent her from moving and discovering his aroused state. Sometimes he just couldn't figure out how he could want her so much and still be so afraid.

He swept his fingers up and down her lower arm, feeling the delicate curve where it dipped in at the elbow. Her skin was velvety to his touch, her body so delicate. He realized he did know why he was afraid. He didn't want to hurt her. Bear People were stronger, tougher than humans. They were prepared for the rough mating suited to their animal nature. They could meld their bodies without worrying about someone breaking a neck or suffering internal injuries, but he knew that the same couldn't be said for human bodies.

For a few moments, he resigned himself to the idea that he and Lindy would never mate. She was too fragile for his strength. But slowly the thought drifted into his mind that maybe he was different from the other he-bears. After all, he was part human. Maybe if there was any benefit to that embarrassing part of him, it was that he would be able to control the roughness with which he mated. If he could just tame his body, there might be hope that he could be gentle enough for her.

"Marin?"

Her voice pulled him out of his thoughts, and he turned to look at her. Even in the darkness he could tell her eyes were locked on him, searching his face. But was she looking at the hideous bruises or trying to see what lay beneath in the thoughts rushing through his mind? "Yes?" He felt her fingers open and brush softly across his ribs.

"What are you going to do?"

Exhaling slowly, he stared into the darkness. He'd been wondering the same thing, but he still didn't have an answer. "I don't know," he replied honestly, feeling unsure about everything in his life right now. "I'm not sure what to do. I want to win my clan back, but I don't know how to do it since Lucien has turned them all against me. If it was a simple matter of challenging him physically, I wouldn't hesitate. But with their minds closed to me now, the clan wouldn't accept me even if I defeated him."

"What about if you got rid of him? Or if he mysteriously disappeared?"

Marin chuckled quietly, surprised by her question. It was so unlike her. "Are you talking about murder?"

She ran her fingers up his ribs and across his chest, noticing how hard his nipple had become. Her own breasts tightened at the feel of it. She took a deep breath and forced herself to control her urge to roll on top of him and smother him with kisses. "I think," she said, "that we should do whatever it takes to get rid of that asshole and straighten out the clan again."

His interest piqued at her words. "We?"

"Yeah. You and me. Guardian and Protector together. Isn't that the way it's supposed to work?"

He laughed again, charmed by her optimistic naivete. She made it sound so simple, so easy and clean. Just walk in, kill Lucien, and win back the clan. No problem. But he knew it wouldn't be that quick and painless. They would be waiting for him, watching for him to come back because they knew he would never give up without a fight.

Despair overwhelmed him at the hopelessness of it. There was no way he could get his clan back now. It was too late. And as much as he appreciated Lindy's offer to help, there was really nothing she could do, either. Except... she could be his sanctuary, the one safe place for him now. Now that he had no family, no home. An anguished cry choked in his throat before he could stop himself.

Lindy raised up on the mattress to look at him. He rarely expressed his emotions but there was no doubt about it now. He was in agony. "What is it, my darling Marin?" she whispered, brushing her mouth across his cheek. His skin was warm and sweaty, burning against her cool lips.

He raised his hand to her head and grasped her hair, holding her firmly against him, not wanting to lose the physical connection with her. He had nothing in the world now but her. His voice was so hoarse he could hardly choke the words out. "I have no one now, Lindy. I have no home, nowhere to go..."

She swept her lips down his cheek and onto his mouth while she held him. "Don't you know that you *are* home when you're here with me? I love having you here, and you're welcome to stay as long as you want..." Her voice trailed off as sadness welled up. "But as much as I want you to stay with me, I think I know you well enough to understand that you really wouldn't be happy living here. I've seen the way you look in the wilderness, the way you breathe in the fresh air. Your spirit is with the forest, Marin, just as your heart is with your clan. And even though your being here makes me so happy, it's more important to me that you be truly happy. If that means helping you go back to your kin, then that's what I'll do. But until then, as long as we're together, you are home."

Marin opened his mouth but couldn't speak. He was stunned that she really did understand his wild nature, and even more stunned that she wasn't trying to change it. She obviously accepted him as he was, a creature that was both man and animal. Even knowing that his true form was a bear, she was okay with that. It was complete acceptance.

All the despair, all the doubt he'd felt about her vanished. His heart soared with the freedom her words gave him. She loved him, but she didn't want to own him. She offered her home to him but didn't insist that he live there. And most important, she wanted him as a man but was content accepting him as a bear.

Ignoring his painful bruises, Marin rolled over and lay gently on top of her. He couldn't stop himself. He didn't want to stop. All he could think about was melting into the body of the woman he loved, of filling her with the most private part of him. Even through the silky pajamas, he could feel her breasts pressed against his chest. Her heat drove him wild. He slid his hand through her golden hair, separating the long strands with his fingers before sweeping them down the curve of her slender neck.

"Would you take this off for me?" he asked, slipping one finger beneath the collar of her pajama top.

Her breath caught in her throat at the shock of his request. It was the most assertive he'd ever been with her and she hadn't expected it in his present condition. But there was no way she was going to turn him down. "Why don't *you* take it off me?" she suggested, hoping her grin wasn't too brazen.

Marin smiled at the thought of it. He rolled off and knelt beside her, looking down at the row of buttons fastening her shirt closed. His fingers trembled as he fumbled with the small round disks, and he hoped she didn't notice how nervous he was. A maddening length of time seemed to pass before the last button was freed and he swept the sides of the shirt back to expose her breasts.

He was sure that his heart had momentarily stopped beating at the sight of her. Her breasts were full and round, perfect womanly mounds just the right size for cupping in his hands. His eyes traveled over her generous curves and settled on the pink nipple crowning each breast. The chests of she-bears were nothing like this. They were small and muscular, rather than soft and voluptuous like Lindy was.

She smiled at the sight of his eyes locked on her body. She could tell he was enchanted by what he saw, just as she was enchanted when she looked at him. But at the same time, he seemed frozen and unsure what to do, almost lost. "Touch me, Marin."

His gaze flicked to her face for a second, seeking reassurance that she had actually said that. The last thing he wanted to do was upset her by doing something wrong.

"It's okay. I want you to touch me," she assured him.

He raised one finger and let it hover hesitantly above her chest while he wondered where to start, then he slowly lowered his knuckle and ran it gently across her right nipple. A soft breath of delight escaped his mouth at the feel of the swollen skin, the way it looked sliding beneath his finger. Opening his hand wide, he took her breast in it and cupped it carefully as if it were the most precious and fragile thing in the world.

The look on his face was instant bliss. Immediately his other hand rose up and he laid it on her other breast. "Tell me if I hurt you," he said with a concerned edge to his voice. He ran his hands across her chest, gently squeezing while his thumbs flicked softly over her taut nipples.

"It feels wonderful. I promise you're not hurting me,

so relax," she said, her voice breathy. Every time his fingers touched her breasts, her core tightened with desire. She had never wanted any man as much as she wanted Marin, but she forced herself to be patient. Rushing could ruin everything. "Would you like to know something else I enjoy?" she asked with a smile.

He nodded without answering but his good eye was wide with interest.

She raised her hand off the bed and pointed to her nipple. "Kiss me here."

Marin's jaw dropped open before his lips curled up in a grin. Bending over her, he slowly lowered his head and placed his lips on her. The taste of her flesh against his mouth was more delicious than he could have dreamed. Growing braver, he parted his lips and took her firm peak into his mouth to tease it with his tongue.

Shivers of delight shot through her body. Unable to hold back a groan of pleasure, Lindy arched her back and drove her breast harder against his lips. Her sudden movement worried him and he tried to pull away, but she held his head and kept it gently in place against her. "Don't stop," she begged him. "Please."

Feeling more confident, he swept his lips across her chest and took her other nipple into his mouth. He was forced to lean over her and realized that his erection was rubbing against her hip. Searing hot spasms of pleasure wracked through him with the friction of his body on hers.

Being this close to him when he was hard and ready was almost more than she could bear. Unable to restrain herself any longer, she slipped her hand between their bodies and took him in her fingers, cupping her palm around every inch of him. His body was hot and throbbing to her touch.

Marin groaned at the feel of her hand on him and he laid his cheek gently down on her chest to savor every stroke she gave him. He'd had no idea that humans touched each other like this, or that they treated each other's bodies with such care. No one had ever touched him this way, because it wasn't something Bear People did when they mated.

He was still reeling from the warmth of her fingers sliding over him when she did something else that stunned him. She wiggled beneath him and pushed her pajama bottoms down, and then he felt her hand grip his and guide it to the cleft between her thighs. She was damp and warm there, and he knew instinctively that this was where she would receive him. Gently guiding his fingers, she showed him how to stimulate her core while she continued to caress him.

Lindy couldn't believe how good it felt to finally have him touch her like this, and she prayed silently that he wouldn't get frightened and back off at the last minute. She needed him so badly, yet she owed it to him to make sure he was ready emotionally. Fighting back the moans that were coming with her spasms of pleasure, she threaded her fingers in his hair and raised his head gently up to look at her.

"Marin," she said between deep breaths. "I'm ready for you. Do you want to take me now?" *Please, God, please. Let him say yes.*

His dark eyes steeled onto hers. The desire was so clear in her eyes that it almost made him cry out. He wanted her so desperately and his groin throbbed so fiercely with desire that he couldn't stand much more. This is what he had dreamed of for months, but he was so scared, so afraid that if he hurt her he would lose her.

"Is it really what you want, Lindy, knowing what I am?" If she'd changed her mind, she needed the chance to get away from him before it was too late. Every fiber of his being hoped that it wasn't necessary. He didn't know what he'd do if she told him to stop.

Moisture wet her eyes when she looked at him, but it was the smile on her face that gave him his answer and made his heart race. "I want you, Marin. All of you."

He swallowed down the lump in his throat and lowered

his head down to her chest in relief. *She wants me. Man or bear, she wants me.* "Then what do I do?" he asked, suddenly unsure of himself again.

Still holding him gently, she guided him between her legs and arched herself up to meet him. Tiny beads of sweat formed on his chest as he slowly entered her, but he couldn't have stopped if he'd wanted to. He gasped as her heat surrounded him, and he drove himself deeper into her, his confidence growing. She moved in time with him while she watched his face. He was trembling, but she knew it was from pleasure rather than worry or pain. Deep slow growls slid from his throat as waves of passion rolled through him for the first time. She held him tight, matching him stroke for stroke, until she felt him release himself inside of her. Marin threw his head back and roared at the ecstasy washing through his body. Even with Terra, mating had never been like this.

Still trembling with emotion, Marin sank down on top of her and held her tight without withdrawing from her body. Lindy clutched him against her, savoring each moment he remained inside her. It felt so good, she didn't ever want him to move from her. He was still for a long time before he reluctantly pulled out and collapsed alongside her.

Neither of them could talk. It was enough just to lie together with their hands clasped and their fingers entwined. Outside, the darkness deepened as the night passed, but in this room, love burned brightly in two souls that had set each other on fire.

Chapter Nine

"Well, now, isn't this comfortable, girls?"

Lucien leaned back against the tree trunk with his long legs stretched out on the grass in front of him. He had Lena nestled in the crook of his left arm and Lilea in his right. All three of them lounged in man skin, looking for all the world like human nudists.

Lilea tipped her head back to look at the man. In the bright afternoon sunlight filtering through the branches of the hickory, the red tint in his dark hair glimmered seductively. The light made his tanned skin a deep, dark gold that matched the drying leaves in the branches above him. "You're right," she murmured, her dreamy eyes focused on him. "Everything feels so much better in man skin. I had no idea it could be this way."

"That's because you lived under a dictator for so long, my dear. I don't know how you did it, to be honest," he laughed. His voice was deep and rolling with an underlying edge to it that was somewhat grating. He gazed down at the petite woman who lay against him, eyeing her naked body hungrily. Though he'd taken her several times in bear skin, he had yet to sample her with his human body. The mere thought of it stirred the desire in him.

She sighed softly, remembering how strict the Guardian had been. "Wouldn't Marin have a fit now?" she muttered, an angry sneer rising on her delicate mouth. "I hope he's happy with whatever human bitch he crawled away to."

Lucien nodded appreciatively as he pulled her closer

against him. She was so petite that she practically melted into the side of his massive body. "The old fool didn't know what delights he was missing among his own clan."

"It's strange, though," Lena said, turning sideways in his embrace to rest her hand against the side of his thick neck. "Marin was never away from us for very long. An hour maybe, after we'd leave the waterfall. The first time I can remember him leaving for any longer amount of time recently was the day he took Gareth into the humans' town. So when did he find time to meet up with his human lovers?"

"Think about it," Lucien replied. "When is a Guardian really off duty? There's only one consistent timeframe that he had entirely to himself."

"When we're asleep in our dens at night." From the tone of her voice, it was clear that Lilea wondered why she hadn't thought about that before. "It would have been easy for him to sneak away and still be back before we woke up. How stupid could we be?"

"Now, now, don't be so hard on yourself, my luscious. Marin thrived on deceit. It wasn't just you he fooled, but everyone. You all trusted him implicitly, and he used your trust to his own advantage." Lucien clicked his tongue. "Such an evil bear."

Lena shook her head, sending her long brown hair tumbling around her shoulders. The thought of what Marin had done was still troubling. She had tended to him after Terra's death, had seen how it ripped him apart. The Guardian had sunk so deep inside himself in his grief that it seemed odd that he would find comfort in human arms after what they'd done to his mate. Still, Lucien's explanations about him made sense, especially when Marin had ended up in Lindy's company. She pushed the disturbing thoughts out of her mind and focused her attention on the gorgeous man at her side.

Lucien was the biggest, strongest bear man she'd ever met. She had thought Marin impressive, but she wondered if he could've held his own against Lucien in the fight— if it had been a fair fight. A shudder ran through her at the memory of what they'd done to their Guardian. She saw in her mind how Arlin and Lucien's claws ripped into Marin's flesh while they pinned him to the ground so the younger he-bears could beat him into submission. Despite her anger at Marin, her stomach turned at how unfair the fight had been. The agonized look on poor Marin's face when they drove him away was forever burned into her memory. An uneasy feeling settled over her as she pulled her hand off Lucien's neck and dropped it to the ground beside her. Despite what Lucien said, things just didn't seem right.

Lucien felt her body tense up against him, and he stared down at her, trying to figure out what was running through her head. Unlike the other sow in his embrace, Lena had a sharp mind and an innate curiosity that made her dangerous. When a she-bear started to believe she had a mind of her own, it was time to teach her a lesson. And he was always ready to give a sow one of his lessons.

"What is it, my dear?" he asked with a soft, caring tone. "Are you uncomfortable here in my arms?"

She forced a smile to her face before she answered. "No, not at all. I was just thinking about Marin. He once saved my cub's life, you know."

"Awww, isn't that sweet?" Lucien mocked. "Marin's a real hero, isn't he? Well, you put your hero out of your thoughts right now because he's as good as dead to you." He stared down at both women and sneered. "His name will not be spoken again. Ever."

Irritation began to smolder in Lena when she looked up at him. Who did he think he was, giving such an order? "I can't just forget someone who was part of my life for so long. Marin is not dead to me, nor will he ever be."

Lucien shoved Lilea away from him and whirled to pin Lena to the ground beneath him. His dark eyes pulsed with fury at her nerve. "You will not question my orders, bitch. What I tell you to think, you will think. Is that clear?"

Lena's brown eyes grew huge and round as she trembled between his outstretched arms. She'd never seen such rage on his face or heard such fury in his voice; even the way he had turned on her so quickly was terrifying. No he-bear had ever treated her this way before, because Marin would have killed him if he had.

"Just lay there and cower like the stupid sow you are, then," he laughed. Adrenaline coursed through his body in strong pulses that felt almost as good as sex. Almost. Lucien looked over his shoulder, ignoring the panicked look on Lilea's face, and called to Arlin, who grazed nearby.

"Arlin, get your furry, fat ass over here right now."

The heavy-set bear sauntered over and paused a few feet away. He didn't take it kindly when someone made a derogatory comment about his weight, especially someone who threw his own weight around so arrogantly. "What is it, Lucien?" A moment after he'd said the words, he noticed Lena pinned beneath him. Her face was twisted with fear. "Are you okay?" he asked, bending low to look at her.

Lucien swept his arm out and knocked him back. "She's not the one I'm worried about," he hissed, still looking over his shoulder at Arlin. "It's *that* one." He nodded to his other side where Lilea stood frozen in place. "I want you to stand tall and then take her, Arlin. Keep her... entertained."

Arlin shook his head in confusion while he shifted. "Take her where? Where can we go in man skin?"

Lucien's eyes blazed with disgust that he'd apparently fallen in with a clan of morons. "You imbecile. I want you to *take* her—mate with her. Take her to your den and have fun with her. Then keep her there for a while."

Lilea screamed a screeching wail that was part cry and part growl. She backed away, shaking her head furiously. "No. I don't want to mate with Arlin. You can't make me."

A deep, rolling growl slid from Lucien. "Oh baby, that was the wrong thing to say to a big ole' boy like me." Before she could even react, he took one leap and was on her. She cried out while he yanked her by the hair and threw her roughly at the other man. If Arlin hadn't been watching carefully, the force of the throw would have knocked them both down.

He reached out and grabbed her just in time, then pulled her into his arms. He couldn't tear his eyes off her face, her beautiful face that was grimacing in pain and panic. "I... uh, I don't think she wants to," he mumbled, groping for a way out of the situation. "Besides, I've never mated in man skin."

With two huge steps, Lucien was in Arlin's face, his breath hot on Arlin's cheek. "I don't give a damn what she wants. I want some time alone with my little friend here, so you will take Lilea to your den and do as you're told." He moved even closer, forcing Arlin to take a step back. "You're not neutered, are you? Am I correct that you *have* mated at least once before?" He laughed sarcastically, loving the way Arlin flinched before him.

Arlin looked down at the ground, too afraid to reply. This was a side of Lucien he'd never seen before, and it scared the hell out of him. His mind flashed back to the day they'd attacked Marin and forced him out, and he could still recall how fiercely Lucien had treated the Guardian. It was as though he enjoyed inflicting pain on him. What kind of person had they invited into their clan?

Lucien drew his arm back and punched Arlin hard in his upper arm. The man yelped and staggered back, shocked by the blow, but he couldn't say anything. He didn't even want to look at the bastard for fear that his temper would blow, and Lucien would lash out again.

Lucien just stood there with his hands on his hips and laughed. "Okay, scaredy-bear, here's what you do. Put the bitch on her back and hold her down with your belly while you stick it in her. Not too tough. Thank you can handle that?"

Arlin couldn't answer. Nodding meekly, he grabbed Lilea by the arm and pulled her away, only too glad to be out of Lucien's reach. When they were out of earshot, he looked down at her. She struggled in his grasp, and he was overwhelmed by guilt. "It's okay, Lil. I won't hurt you," he swore to her. Then holding her tightly to prevent her escape, he dragged her inside his den.

Lucien swung around to focus on his main concern, the sow with the big mouth. Lena had stumbled to her feet and was inching away when he came after her. Since she was too dangerous to allow to think on her own, a little persuasion might do the trick. With a quick maneuver, he was on her again and pinned her back against the tree.

"Shara, Gareth, can you hear me?" he yelled across the meadow.

Their large shaggy heads rose up above the drying grasses and gazed his way.

"Stand tall and come over here. I need you."

Within moments, the young men walked over to Lucien and stared wide-eyed while he held Lena roughly against the tree. It was such a strange thing for him to do that they were dumbfounded.

"Gareth," Lucien growled. "What is the fourth rule of the Bear Clan?"

The young he-bear thought for a moment, trying to recall the teachings of the Elders. The rules were a code of behavior that had been passed down from generation to generation, and he, like all cubs, had been taught the rules along with other necessary things like reading and speaking the human language. But it had been a long time since anyone had asked him a question like this.

"I think it's... 'the Guardian shall have final authority in the governance of the clan to maintain harmony and civil accord'."

"Smart boy, Red. Maybe someday you'll actually amount to something," Lucien laughed. He punched the young he-bear playfully on the arm before turning to address Shara. "I have a job for you two, and if you prove your worth to me, I'll see that you're rewarded well for it. See, here's the problem. Our lady friend is a little confused. She seems to think that clan order is a democracy, when in fact it is not. The rules clearly state that the Guardian makes and enforces the law, and since you no longer have a Guardian, I've decided to show my gratitude for your kind hospitality by assuming the task for you."

Shara's eyes widened with shock. "You're our Guardian now? But I thought I..."

Lucien clutched dramatically at his gut, looking wounded by the words. "Surely you don't think that a bear as young and inexperienced as yourself is suitable for such a demanding position? No offense, cub, but the clan would laugh you right out of the forest if you tried to order them around. But I'll tell you what. Be my backup, help me enforce my rules and orders and I'll train you so you're fit to take over some day. Once you've learned how to deal with troublemakers, you'll be prepared for the job. And speaking of troublemakers..." He shot an angry glance at the woman trembling before him.

Shara and Gareth looked at each other without speaking. Not once in all the time that Lucien had been with them had he voiced any desire to take over the clan. In fact, it was just the opposite. He kept reassuring them that he only wanted a place to stay and some gentle companionship until he moved on. They realized that he'd never actually stated when *that* would be.

"What do you want us to do?" Shara asked. Though Lucien made him nervous, he was still impressed by the authority and force with which he handled things. Shara admired power; he respected it. He'd often dreamed that one day he would assume the role of Guardian and then his kin would bend to his rules and desires. That should be the way of the world, he reasoned. The strongest should rule. But of course it wasn't possible as long as Marin was around.

Lucien strutted back and forth in front of Lena, enjoying the sight of fear in her eyes. It made him feel so masculine and virile to make her wonder what he might do to her. He stood still for a moment and gazed down at her panic-stricken face while his lips curled up in a smirk.

"Miss Lena here doesn't want to obey an order I gave her. It was such a simple order, too, nothing her tiny little brain can't understand. But she seems to think that she knows best regarding this particular concern, and she's wrong. So I've decided that correction is necessary to make her rethink her views. I just need you boys to hold her here until I return in a few minutes. I have no doubt about *your* ability to understand and comply." His eyebrows arched while he looked from Gareth to Shara and back again, then he watched while they each took one of her arms and held it tightly. He smiled smugly and walked away.

Lena panted heavily as she watched Lucien walk down the hill edging the meadow. Once he was out of sight, she moved to pull her arms out of the men's grasp but she couldn't. They held on tight. "Let me go," she growled, fighting against the strong grip they had on her. She looked from Gareth's face to Shara's and her terror grew. Neither man showed any hint of compassion. "Guys, please help me," she groaned. "Lucien is crazy. He's lost his mind. Let me go before he gets back."

Shara's mouth lifted in a smile. Her skin felt so soft and tender beneath his fingers, so fragile, so easy to control. There was something stimulating in the way she looked at him and begged for his help, and even more stimulating in his power to refuse it. There were very few times in his life when he'd felt that power—the day he killed humans to rescue Marin and Gareth, and the day he'd fought Marin and driven the Guardian away. It was a taste sweeter than honey, and he knew he'd never go without it again. "Sorry babe, gotta do as the big bear says," he replied with a shrug of his shoulders.

"We're kin, Shara. We're supposed to help each other," she hissed, feeling her panic growing. His fingers were digging harder into her flesh and the tighter he gripped her, the more he smiled. *He's enjoying this. He likes hurting me.* She swung her head to look at the other man. "Gareth, talk to him. Make him let go of me."

Gareth couldn't look her in the eyes. Lena had been his friend all their lives, but Lucien had promised him a reward for simply holding her here. And if he knew Lucien, he was sure the Bear Man would pay up big when the time came. If anyone could deliver Lindy or Sara to him, Lucien could. "Shut up, Lena," he scowled.

Lena bit her lip to keep from crying out. How could they do this to her? They were kin, her own clan mates, yet they treated her like someone they didn't care about. Her heart thumped furiously at the thought of what Lucien was planning for her. Then she saw him cross the top of the hill toward them and her heart stopped beating altogether.

He had Notch in his grip. Her cub dangled upside-down by his back legs, bellowing and growling with every ounce of ferocity in his tiny body. He struggled helplessly and bounced painfully with each step the man took. Lucien crossed the meadow and stopped beside her with an amused look on his face.

"Let my baby go," she screamed, struggling franticly in the men's tight grip. Lena kicked out at Lucien with her foot, only to have Shara stop the blow and return one of his own. He slapped her hard on the face, causing a vivid red welt to rise on her cheek.

"Mama!" Notch cried, wiggling even harder to escape his captor. Suddenly he felt himself being flipped right-side-up and pinned against the man's bare chest.

Lucien squeezed him so tightly the cub could barely breathe. "Shut your yap, little one, or I'll shut it for you permanently," he growled. Notch whimpered and became still in his arms. "Now, how can I make you understand the importance of your complete cooperation?" he said, addressing Lena again. "What can I do to get your undivided attention?" His gaze dropped to the tiny black furball in his arms. "Oh gee, how about this?"

"No," Lena cried again. "Leave Notch alone. He's done nothing to you."

Lucien laughed and shook his head back and forth at her futile plea. "When Lucien teaches a lesson, that lesson is never forgotten." Then grinning broadly, he lowered his head and took one of the cub's small black ears in his mouth. His eyes never left Lena's face while he yanked his head sharply and tore the ear off.

Lena and Notch screamed simultaneously as blood poured from the hideous wound in a crimson torrent.

Gareth recoiled in horror at the same moment and released his hold on the woman. It was all that Lena needed. She jerked away from Shara and ripped Notch from Lucien's grasp. She had to get away, had to save her infant from the evil that had come to their clan. Before Lucien could even react, she had shifted to bear skin and fled into the forest, clenching her screaming cub's scruff tightly in her mouth.

"You son of a bitch," Gareth yelled, taking a swing at Lucien. "He's just a baby."

Shara stepped forward and caught his arm before it hit its mark. Twisting it roughly behind Gareth's back, he forced the man to the ground in submission.

Lucien walked slowly around the prostrate man and clucked his tongue in reproach. Then he lashed out and kicked Gareth fiercely in the ribs until a sickening *crack* came from inside his body. "Keep an eye on him" he ordered Shara, who he was delighted to see was proving his worth. "Keep a tight rein on him, unless he wants to learn a lesson of his *own*, of course." He walked away with a snort of contempt.

Gareth moaned and clutched his side while he rolled on the ground in agony. White hot spasms of pain shot through his chest and back with each breath. He looked up to see Shara smirk and walk away, leaving him to suffer alone.

"Shit," he groaned, panting with each excruciating breath. For a moment his memory flashed back to a day just like this when it had been Marin on the ground taking a beating. Only then, Gareth had been the one inflicting the pain. And unlike him, Marin had been bear enough to suffer in silence and not cry out like a coward.

Gareth squeezed his eyes shut to hold in the tears as guilt crashed down over him in a smothering blanket. Suddenly everything became clear. Every terrible thing he'd done, each hurt he'd inflicted on the Guardian who had cared for him so well, had come full circle and returned to him by way of Lucien. Lucien had suckered them all.

"I'm sorry, Marin, so sorry," he cried, his sobs nearing hysteria. "What have we done?"

Chapter Ten

Marin opened his eyes and gazed across his pillow at Lindy. She breathed deeply in sound sleep, unaware that he was awake and unable to take his eyes off her. His gaze fell to the soft mounds of her breasts as they rose and fell beneath the sheet with each breath she took. Her arm was still draped over his waist from when she had briefly awakened during the night and hugged him tightly.

Was this how it felt to be human and in love? Every night for the last week, they had lain together in this very bed, laughing and talking like lovers who had known each other forever. Then they grew quiet and drew closer in each other's arms to make love. It was the most exquisite thing he had ever experienced, full of such passion and tenderness. Even now it took his breath away, and each new day with her helped him understand more how his great-grandsire had felt about the human woman with whom he had mated.

In some ways, it made him feel guilty. He had loved Terra, cared for her and protected her the way a mate should. But when they mated, it was rough and feral like the animals they were. The act was performed quickly and instinctively to satisfy the primal urges that surged through their ursine bodies. And when it was done, they resumed their daily activities as if nothing extraordinary had happened.

But it was different being with Lindy. His human body was much more sensitive and attuned to the nuances of sex.

When she touched him, every neuron in his body seemed to pulse with life. At the touch of her skin, his senses exploded with feeling and sensation. And when he entered her, it was as if their bodies became one organism that he never wanted to separate himself from. He needed to caress her, nurture her, the way he never could with Terra.

He pushed the blonde hair away from her face to see her better. She was so beautiful when she slept. Every morning, her cheeks flushed a soft pink when she grew warm beneath the blanket, and then she would turn on her back and draw her hand above her head to rest on the pillow. When she grew still again, he would reach out and touch her soft palm with his fingertips while he kissed her lips tenderly to avoid waking her.

He leaned over and swept his mouth across her cheek now, wondering if she could feel his touch in her sleep the way he could feel her in his. It didn't matter whether he was awake or asleep or what he was doing. She was in his thoughts and dreams constantly, luring him to desire love and sex.

When she didn't stir, he lay down and turned on his back to stare at the ceiling. Ever since Dean had revealed the terrible truth about his human ancestry, Marin had tried to force it from his mind, refusing to deal with it. All his life he had hated humans and everything they stood for. And then fate had deemed that he be one of them.

At first it was almost unbearable. Every time he took a drink from the stream, he'd stare down at his reflection and try not to search for the part of him that was human. He didn't look any different, but he felt it. There was something in him that had changed when he'd learned he wasn't a full-blooded Bearwalker. He felt as though his clan pitied him, the way they looked at him sometimes. The last thing he wanted was anyone's sympathy.

But now, things were better than he could have imagined. Being with Lindy opened his eyes to the part of himself that he had shunned. He could be gentle and affectionate and not be judged as weak. He could speak softly and passionately without being viewed as submissive.

There was no longer the fear of being a man. In fact, he was astonished at just how much he enjoyed it. Maybe being human wasn't the curse he had thought it was.

To his amazement, he was even feeling more at ease with the human world. Her home was warm and comfortable, much more so than the clan's earthen dens. Water and food were always on hand without needing to forage for hours. He had sampled more exotic and delicious foods in his short time with her than he had in his whole life. If he wasn't careful, he warned himself, he might end up looking like chubby Arlin.

He thought back to the day that Lindy had taken Gareth and him to town and dragged him through all the stores. He hadn't been impressed with human gadgets then, but now he found himself amused by them. More than once, Lindy had caught him playing with the microwave, nuking hotdogs until they exploded. He was even beginning to enjoy music, which he had never heard until she introduced him to it.

But his favorite human thing was the bed. Whoever invented it should have been well rewarded, he decided. In his wildest dreams, he couldn't imagine a more perfect place for two people to share their nights and their bodies. He loved the way the mattress creaked beneath them, offering its own musical accompaniment to their lovemaking. The soft feel of the sheets, the way her feminine scent lingered on her pillow, it all made his senses reel. Each morning, he woke up already anticipating the end of the day when they would lie in bed and hold each other once again.

He smiled to himself, happier than he'd been for a very long time.

"Morning," her soft voice said from beside him.

Marin turned his head to look at her, surprised that she was awake. "Hi."

She placed her hand tenderly on his shoulder to roll

him toward her. "Why are you smiling? Did you have a good dream?"

He snuggled his arm around her waist and pulled her close. "Sometimes I wonder if this isn't all a dream. It's too wonderful to be real."

She looked at him for a moment, noticing that something in him had changed. It wasn't anything physical, no outward sign, but rather a serenity and calmness of his spirit. He wasn't fighting her, or himself, anymore. She leaned over and kissed him firmly on the lips, eager to feel his warm, hard body against her, and gazed into his luminous dark eyes. "But it is real. What we feel is real."

At the warmth of her body on his, his groin tightened and a throbbing rush of desire coursed through him. He had never wanted anyone this way before, and no matter how much he was with her, it wasn't enough. Growling low in his throat, Marin pushed his head back against the pillow and raised his chest, hoping that she would understand what he wanted.

Lindy smiled as she slid her hands over his powerful chest. There wasn't any part of his body that she loved to touch more than that. His curves were so sleek and firm. She could easily make him her mattress and sleep like a baby. Only now, sleep was the farthest thing from her mind. Her kisses fluttered down his chest, across his washboard abs and trailed down to the flare of his hip. She felt him hard and throbbing against her.

He tried to slip his hands around her waist to roll her underneath him, but she pushed them gently away. A disappointed look marred his handsome face for a moment, before she straddled him and guided him inside her. Marin gasped when he realized what she was doing and his eyes widened with delight when she began to rock herself rhythmically against him, sending wave after wave of pleasure through his body. He didn't know this was even possible, that she could make love to him. He closed his eyes and groaned while he focused on the feel of her riding him, controlling his body. It was unlike anything he had ever experienced.

When she brought him over the edge, he almost regretted it. Having her on top of him was so incredible that he wanted it to go on forever. She slid off him and sank down beside him with her head on his chest. His heart thumped wildly beneath her ear, bringing a smile to her lips. There was nothing she enjoyed more than pleasing him.

Marin clutched her head to his chest, refusing to let her go while his fingers slid through the golden strands of her hair. Everything about her made him love her. Suddenly he realized that he was more content than he had ever been. There was no clan to worry about, no hunger pangs needing to be satisfied, no cold wind whipping in his den to chill him at night. And no loneliness. For the first time in seven years, he didn't feel alone.

He sighed contentedly and let the image of Lucien come into his mind. How he had cursed the bear man, hating him for taking his clan away. But Lucien had done him a favor by forcing him to confront the part of himself he feared. Now he knew that being part human wasn't bad at all. In fact, he thought he could easily get used to living here with Lindy. If she would let him.

Only one small thought remained to worry him, something that he knew was beyond his control. Like all bears in the Northwoods, his body shut down in the winter. When nature told him it was time, he curled up in his den and fell into a deep sleep until spring. That was the nature of a bear.

Marin forced down the lump that had formed in his throat at the thought of it. He couldn't help feeling that now, when he had accepted his human nature and adjusted to a human way of life, his bear nature would rip it away from him. He would lose Lindy for half the year.

He closed his eyes against the pain of it. *Please, Mother Earth,* he prayed silently. "*Let me stay with the woman I love. Please don't send me to sleep when the first snow falls.*"

Chapter Eleven

"Thanks for helping me with this," Lindy said, yanking another dried tomato stalk from the ground.

Marin laughed at how downright domestic he was becoming. He'd already learned how to vacuum the floor and make the bed, and now he was gardening. He gathered up the withered stems and threw them in a pile for burning. "It doesn't seem like work when we're together. I guess I'm turning out to be some human, and I mean that in a good way," he said.

Lindy stopped for a moment to watch him. His long, muscular body was clad in jeans and a gray sweatshirt. Even through the thick material, the curves of his muscles were evident. He handled the rake expertly, as though he'd done it a hundred times. Then he bent and picked up the debris and added it to the growing pile. Her eyes lingered on his taut rear end when he bent over.

Sensing her staring at him, Marin swung around to look at her without standing up. His thick black hair had grown long and hung down around his face, giving him a feral, wild man look that made her body burn with desire. He grinned, knowing what she was thinking.

"You need a haircut," she laughed. If she kept thinking about his butt, she'd never get any work done. "You look like a shaggy dog."

He stood up and crossed his arms over his chest while he glared at her, feigning offense. "Please don't insult me by comparing me to that mangy hound of yours. If I'm shaggy, at least call me the dignified creature I am. And I'd think twice about trying to give a bear a haircut, if I were you." His grin grew bigger, daring her.

"Well it's a good thing I like to live dangerously," she said, setting down her plant trimmers. She walked slowly around him, figuring out how to trim those jet locks. Even though she liked his hair long, when it started to hide his handsome face it was time to go. She ran her fingers through the thick mop, feeling the smooth strands slip sensuously against her palm, and decided that she could easily take off two inches and still leave his hair just above shoulder length.

"You keep touching my hair like that and I'll have to send you to bed," he threatened from beneath arched brows.

Lindy stopped in front of him and gazed up at that masculine face. It was amazing how this seriously scary bear had become a warm, funny man. She raised up and kissed him hard. "Is that my punishment, then?"

He nodded. "I may have to keep you there all day."

"Then I'll have to cut your hair more often," she laughed, pulling away from him to return to work. "Seriously, I would like to trim a little of the length off."

There was no answer.

"Marin?" She turned around to see why he hadn't answered.

He stood with his back to her, his gaze focused on the forest abutting the rear of the yard.

"What are you looking at?" she asked, coming to stand beside him. As far as she could tell, the woods were quiet and deserted.

"Shhh," he whispered, motioning for her to remain still. He moved toward the woods and stopped. "It's all right," he called loudly toward the trees.

Lindy still didn't see anything. There was no movement, no sound anywhere. Her pulse began to race. *Dear God, please don't tell me the clan has come after him here.*

He moved slowly forward again; his eyes locked on a spot straight ahead of him. Every muscle was tensed and alert, ready to respond to whatever waited ahead. His bear instincts took command of his human body as he stalked silently across the yard like a predator.

Lindy had seen him do this many times in bear skin while he guarded the clan, but this was a first. He was a man moving like a bear, sniffing the air, listening with ears more receptive than her own. She was spellbound by how interwoven the two parts of his spirit were.

Finally reaching the edge of the forest, Marin disappeared among the trees. Lindy held her breath, wanting more than anything to run to him and be by his side when he faced whatever was out there. He had told her to stay put, because as always, he was not thinking of his own safety, but hers. She couldn't stand it. She just couldn't wait here and let him face danger alone. She took two steps and froze.

Marin walked out of the forest with a large brown bear by his side. Something small and black dangled from the bear's mouth. Marin was talking to the animal but his words were too soft for her to hear what he was saying. Lindy walked cautiously toward them.

At the sight of her movement, the bear hesitated, seeming unsure and ready to bolt. Marin quickly reached down and touched its shoulder in a comforting gesture while he urged it forward. Gathering courage, the bear followed him closer to Lindy.

"It's Lena," Marin told her when they neared. "Notch has been hurt and needs your help." He turned to face the bear while he spoke to her. "Lena, it would be helpful if you would stand tall so you can tell us both what happened."

Her brown eyes were wide with fright but she did what Marin asked. In an instant, a brown-haired woman stood before them, cradling her black cub in her arms. His tiny body was limp. A tear rolled down Lena's cheek at the sight of her injured baby.

"What happened, Lena?" Lindy asked, moving closer

to look at Notch. She stopped about a foot away, knowing better than to get too close or try to touch either of them.

Lena could hardly force the words out of her sob-wracked throat. Her brown hair was matted with tangles and briars as though she hadn't groomed in days. "It was Lucien. He wanted to... to teach me a lesson. He... he bit my son's ear off." She burst into tears again.

"Oh my God," Lindy groaned, echoing the fierce growl that came from Marin's throat. "How could someone do that to a baby?"

Marin wrapped his arm around Lena's shoulder and guided her toward the house. She eyed the building warily, slowing her steps the closer she got to it. She'd heard so many stories about this place, this house of healing. The human woman had healed Gareth, and then Marin. She was terrified of being here but she had no choice. Her cub needed some of that magical human healing.

Lindy held the back door open while Marin led Lena in. He pulled out a chair at the kitchen table and helped her sit down. Then taking Notch carefully from her arms, he laid the cub on the table beneath the kitchen light while Lindy hovered next to him so they could examine the injury.

The ear was ripped off near its base, leaving a jagged tatter of flesh protruding from his small head. Scabs formed a thick, crusty line from one side of the stub to the other. Judging from the stains on his fur, he had lost a fair amount of blood, but apparently the bleeding had soon stopped.

"When did this happen?" Lindy asked. Her heart broke at the sight of Lena's pained face when she looked at her son.

"Three days ago. I've been hiding in the forest since then, because I thought Lucien would come after us and kill Notch." An agonized shudder rippled down her spine.

"I'm just going to open his mouth," Lindy said. Her hand trembled as she separated the tiny jaws and peeked inside. His gums were pale and dry. "When was the last time he drank anything?"

"He didn't take any water from the stream yesterday or today." She stopped to choke back another sob. "Yesterday he was alert and could walk. Today... well, look at him." Lena reached out and stroked his dark fur tenderly, willing him to live. "Please, Notch, get well for Mama."

Lindy left the room and returned a minute later with a baby bottle in her hand. She filled it with cool water and screwed the top on. "I'm going to hold Notch and try to get him to drink some water. He's dehydrated." Her eyes shot to the cub's nervous mother, who watched every move she made. "If it's okay with you, Lena?" She hesitated, the bottle still in her hand.

The look on Lena's face was utter confusion. How could Notch drink when he was barely able to hold his head up? Her watery brown eyes swept across the table toward Marin, silently asking his advice. He nodded *yes* without speaking. Lena looked back at Lindy and nodded, fighting back her mistrust of the human. "Yes."

Lifting Notch from the table, Lindy cradled him carefully in her arms like a human infant. She slipped the rubber nipple in his mouth and said a silent prayer that he would accept it. A few drops trickled slowly down his parched throat and then he whined softly. A minute later his tiny lips sealed around the nipple and began sucking on it ravenously. Lindy rolled her eyes toward Marin and smiled, delighted to hear the loud sucking noise coming from the cub.

"How did you know to do that?" Lena asked, her mood considerably brightened.

"This is how we feed human infants," Lindy said. "I've bottle fed my sister's two children. The last time she came here to visit, she left a bottle behind and thank goodness I didn't throw it out." She leaned over to let Lena take her baby back and continue the nursing.

Marin's eyes followed Lindy curiously, amazed by her way with the cub. She seemed so self-assured, so confident and comfortable the way she handled Notch, as though she was a natural healer. Or a natural mother. He realized then he'd never asked her if she'd borne any children, or if she ever desired to. There was no doubt in his mind that she would be a fine mother, and he couldn't help but wonder how she would feel birthing a child that was a shapeshifter. *Stop*, he warned himself. *This is dangerous ground to tread.*

A broad smile lit Lena's face while she fed Notch. After several minutes, she set the bottle down and held him to her breast. He latched on and fed hungrily while his small ebony paws kneaded her skin contentedly. A single tear slid down her cheek when she looked up at Lindy. "Thank you," she mouthed.

Lindy sat down across from her and smiled. "I've got some antibiotic cream we can rub on the wound, too. It'll help prevent infection. But if Notch keeps eating like this, he should be better in no time."

Marin sat down between the two women and gazed at Lena's face. Her eyes were drawn as though she hadn't slept in a long time. "What's going on at home?" he asked with a heaviness in his voice that betrayed his anxiety.

When Lena met his gaze, she was sure the guilt inside her showed on her face. She shook her head sadly, not wanting to admit the terrible truth. "It's bad, Marin. Lucien has declared himself Guardian and taken over the clan. Shara and Keeran are acting as his assistants, but they're just being bullies like him." She lowered her head and shuddered at the memory of how they had handled her so roughly. "He ordered Arlin to..." She stopped and swallowed hard. "He told Arlin to mate with Lilea, though she begged him not to. Lucien tells us what to think, what to do." She sniffled softly, unable to contain the sobs that wracked her body again. "We were so wrong about him."

Marin wasn't at all surprised by her admission. His instinct had always served him well during his years as Guardian, and his instinct had fired a loud warning the day Lucien first walked into their forest. The arrogant son of a bitch was pure evil. "I'm curious, Lena, what he told the clan about me."

She exhaled loudly, embarrassed to have to repeat Lucien's words. Her gaze settled on Notch, because she couldn't look Marin in the eyes. "He told us that for the last seven years, you've spent your nights in the company of human women. He said that one of your human lovers was responsible for what happened to his clan because you told her about the existence of our kind, and she told the loggers who then came to exterminate his kin. He said that's why you never mated with any of us—because you had your... humans." Her eyes flicked up long enough to cast an accusing glance at Lindy.

Marin lowered his head into his hands and groaned, devastated by her words. It took him a few moments to shake off the shock and pull himself together. When he raised his head to look at her again, his dark eyes glistened with moisture. "And you believed him?" There was a trembling in his voice that was painful to hear. "You've known me all your life, and you believed *him*?"

Tears streamed down her face at the sight of his emotional anguish. "I'm so sorry, Marin. He made it sound so... so plausible. When Lucien talks to you, it's like he crawls right inside your mind and makes you believe. He makes you believe anything." Her voice trailed off, leaving the three of them sitting in uncomfortable silence.

Finally Lena cleared her throat and stared at Marin until he was forced to return her gaze. "I need to know the truth, Marin. All those years you kept to yourself and revealed so little to us about your private life. I'm going to ask you straight out, and I ask that you respect me enough to answer me honestly." She took a deep, quivering breath before she continued. "Is it true? Have you taken human lovers?"

Marin stared at her blankly, torn between answering and telling her to go to hell. It was none of her business, none of the clan's business what he did or didn't do. All they ever cared about was what he could do for them. Yet he knew that if he didn't answer, it would look like he was hiding something. He ran his hands through his hair and locked his jaw while he debated.

Lena waited patiently, watching him. It was clear that he was debating in his own mind and it gave her a bad feeling. Maybe Lucien had been right, after all.

Finally he took in a deep breath and chewed on his lip. "I've always spoken the truth, Lena, and I'll speak it now. For seven years after Terra died, I was with *no one*, bear or human. I've never experienced such loneliness, but I just didn't have the heart or the desire to be with anyone because there could never be someone who meant as much to me as her. Until now." His gaze swept to his right and settled on Lindy while he took her hand in his own. "I won't lie to you. I have mated with Lindy, but it happened *after* I was cast out of the clan."

Lena looked at Lindy. "Is it the truth, Protector?"

She nodded solemnly. "Yes, it is."

Lena bowed her head. "Then I owe you an apology, Marin. I'm sorry for believing Lucien when he accused you wrongly. I'm sorry for not standing up for you when they fought you. You've been a fine Guardian, and you didn't deserve what happened to you." A disgusted growl rolled under her breath. "And now we're stuck with him."

Lindy looked at Marin expectantly, sure that he would respond, but he just sat there and stared at the wall. *This is strange. Doesn't he want to get the clan back?* She wasn't sure whether she should say something or mind her own business.

After a few moments, Marin spoke, but his voice was heavy with resignation. "I wish I could help, but it's too late. Like I told Lindy, even if I challenged Lucien, the clan still wouldn't accept me. Not if they still believe him and his lies."

"They're beginning to see how he really is, how evil and sick he can be," she said, desperately wishing he would change his mind. "He's still got some of them twisted around his finger, but others are beginning to see through his lies."

Lindy cleared her throat hesitantly and looked at Marin, wanting to interrupt. He nodded courteously. "I'm wondering about Gareth. Is he... is he still supporting Lucien?"

Lena shook her head. "He was one of the men who held me down while Lucien tortured my son. But when he saw what that bastard did to Notch, he took a swing at Lucien. The last I saw, Gareth was taking quite a beating of his own. I doubt that he's much of a Lucien supporter now." The corners of her mouth upturned in a satisfied smile at the justice of it.

Lindy's heart sank at the news. It was still hard to believe how quickly Gareth had turned against Marin. Even though she knew they were rivals as far as she was concerned, she also knew how much he respected and cared for his Guardian. Lucien must have done some pretty fancy talking to sway not only him, but the entire clan so quickly. It hurt to think of him being beaten by Lucien—not that he didn't deserve it for what he'd done to Lena. She wondered... if his mind had been so easily swayed by Lucien, maybe he could be as easily persuaded to change his mind again.

"I have an idea," she said, drawing Marin and Lena's attention. "Gareth trusts me. Maybe I can talk to him and convince him that he was wrong about you, Marin."

He thought about that for a minute but his expression was gloomy. "I think he would just assume that I sent you to talk to him. He may love you, but that doesn't mean he'll believe you."

"But from what Lena said, maybe he's more convinced now about Lucien's real intentions. Besides, once you get the snot beat out of you, you tend to be a little less friendly with someone."

Marin struggled to withhold his grin. *What does she know about getting the snot kicked out of her?* But knowing how courageous and persistent she could be, he made a mental note to ask her about her past when they had time alone.

Lena stared at Marin for a moment. Even after hearing the terrible news about the clan, he had a look in his eyes that she had rarely seen. When he looked at Lindy, his face practically glowed with contentment. She'd never seen anything like it. Every so often, his fingers opened to take her hand and squeeze it tightly, as if her mere touch gave him some kind of serenity and acceptance. He appeared perfectly at ease staying here with her and living the way humans did. But then, he was part human, so why did that surprise her?

"Marin, I need some advice," she said at last, beginning to feel uncomfortable with the touchy-feely going on in front of her. It was just so unlike Marin to be touching someone like that, it was so... human.

"Whatever I can do to help," he said, pulling his hand into his lap. He didn't like the disapproving look she was giving him. It was the same warning look he had always given his clan when they misbehaved.

"I don't know what to do," she frowned. "Where can I go to keep Notch safe? I just can't go back to forest home as long as that bastard is there."

Marin cast a questioning glance at Lindy.

She understood immediately what he wanted. "Lena, you can stay here with us. You and Notch will be safe, and it'll give me a chance to keep applying the antibiotic to his wound. You're welcome to stay as long as you want."

Lena hesitated, torn between jumping at the offer and refusing it. She had serious reservations about moving into a place where a human actually lived, but at least it helped that Marin was here. She knew he'd never let anything happen to her. On the other hand, if she refused Lindy's generous offer, where else could she go? No matter how uncomfortable she was, her first priority was seeing to Notch's safety and there was nowhere safer than wherever the Guardian and Protector were. "I appreciate your offer,

Lindy. I'd like to stay."

Lindy nodded and rose from her chair. "Why don't you let me show you around?"

Marin quickly stood up and caught her gaze. "It might be better if I do it," he offered, sensing how tense Lena was about her decision. He stared at Lindy, hoping she wouldn't question him.

"Oh, okay," she said, taking the hint. "There's something I need to do, anyway."

Marin led Lena toward the guestroom where she and Notch would stay. When they were gone, Lindy grabbed the phone and punched in a number.

Sara answered on the third ring. "Yeah?"

"Jeez you sound grumpy. A little PMS going on there?"

A tired sigh whooshed through the phone. "Sorry, Sis. I sooo need a break. I'm really stressed right now with homework up the wahzoo, so just ignore the mood. What's up?"

Lindy sat down on the kitchen chair and ran her hand absently across the top of the table. "Who is your roommate dating now?"

"You called me to talk about my roommate?"

Lindy chuckled. "Yeah. Would you just answer the question please?"

"Same guy. Josh."

A small smile crossed her face. Perfect. "He's the one who wants to be a wildlife biologist, right?"

"Yup, that's him. Although why someone would want to make a living studying animal pooh is beyond me."

"There's a lot to be said for caring about wildlife." *If she only knew the half of it.* "Can you get Nikki to have Josh do me a favor?"

Sara's laugh echoed over the phone, sounding just like her sister's. "Sure, as long as it doesn't cost anything. Josh is so cheap he could bleed a vampire dry."

"Well, this won't cost him a cent. I just need him to

do some investigating."

Her curiosity piqued, Sara's voice rose questioningly. "About what?"

"A group of bears were supposedly killed by loggers somewhere around here recently. I never heard anything about it on the news, so I don't know if it's true or not."

"How many bears?"

"I'm not sure. Lots, I think. Do you suppose that Josh could find out something like that?"

"I think so. He really gets into stuff like that. The other day he was telling me how he helped do a population study on foxes for one of his classes. If he can't find out about the bears, no doubt he knows someone who can."

Lindy nodded to herself, encouraged by her sister's optimism. "Will you let me know as soon as you find out?"

"Sure, no problem. By the way, have you seen Gareth lately?"

"Uh, not recently."

"Did he ever mention me after we met that day?" A wistful tone came over her voice.

Oh shit. A relationship between Gareth and her sister was not something she wanted to encourage, but she'd do anything before she'd hurt her baby sister. "Yeah, he did mention that he thought you were pretty cute."

"I gave him my number, but he hasn't called. I don't think he likes me." She sounded dejected.

"Gareth lives out in the boonies. I'm not sure he even *has* a phone, sweetie."

"So, what is he, like a caveman or something?"

Lindy laughed again. "Yeah, something like that." She looked up as Marin walked in the kitchen and sat down beside her. "Hey, I gotta go. Call me as soon as you get that info, okay? And don't let school get you too stressed out. Love you."

Marin waited until she'd hung up the phone before he spoke. "They're asleep. Lena was exhausted."

"I can't believe Lucien would do something that heinous." She shook her head at the horror of it as she visualized what he'd done. She gazed steadily at Marin. "He should be stopped."

He returned her look with a cool stare of his own while his jaw cocked sideways in thought. Could he just ignore his kin after a lifetime of caring about them, even after what they'd done to him? He was more angry at them than he'd ever been in his life, but he didn't want them to suffer at the hands of a lunatic. Finally he rolled his eyes toward the ceiling and stared at it blankly. "I don't know how. And I don't know if it should be me."

Her eyebrows arched at him. "What does that mean?"

The dark depths of his eyes flashed ominously. "I don't know if I can, Lindy. I don't think I can do this anymore. They don't want me. So let them do without me."

The expression on his face told more than his words did. They'd simply hurt him too deeply for him to care anymore. Now that he was adjusting to human life and human comforts, the fight seemed to have just left him.

Lindy stood up and took his hand in her own, cupping his strong fingers comfortingly. "Let's go to bed," she said softly. "I don't want to talk about this right now." The thought had just entered her mind that she'd gotten her wish— the clan didn't come first anymore. She should have been elated, but she wasn't. She led him toward the bedroom for the long night ahead, knowing that her dreams would probably be nightmares.

Chapter Twelve

Lucien pulled Keeran and Shara to a halt beside him and motioned for them to be quiet. His eyes focused on a spot just ahead of them beyond a copse of tall pines where two distinct human voices mingled. He couldn't see the humans but he could smell them, and their food. He'd had enough of bear food to last a lifetime and couldn't wait to sink his canines into something raw and bloody.

The human couple stood beside the fire with their arms locked around each other and gazed at the pink sunset settling over the lake. They'd camped in the national forest several times before but had never had such a beautiful vantage point as they had now from this campsite. They were on a small rocky promontory that jutted out into the lake. It was private and perfect for their last camping trip of the season.

Kim turned and rubbed her cold hands briskly over the crackling flames while she cast her gaze to the man beside her. Terry was tall and slim with dark brown hair that glowed with golden highlights in the firelight. Sensing her gaze, his piercing green eyes met hers, sending a shiver of desire rippling through her. God how she loved the man.

He bent down beside the fire. "The steaks should be ready soon," he grinned, sniffing the meaty aroma rising from a pan sizzling in the flames. He could almost taste the meat, feel the crunch of the slightly blackened and seasoned beef. This meal was the perfect end to a rigorous day of hiking in the autumn-scented woods and the perfect start to their new life together.

The woman knelt beside him to check two foil-wrapped potatoes baking in the glowing coals. Her fork slid into the steaming bundles easily. "These are done," she said over the growl of her stomach. It was funny, she thought, how fresh air heightened the senses and increased the appetite. Now she just had to figure out what she was hungrier for—the steak or her sexy new husband.

She rose and walked toward the tent to bring back the aluminum dishes they used when they camped. She withdrew two plates, silverware and coffee mugs from their green knapsack and froze. "Terry."

Her voice was so soft he wasn't sure she'd even spoken. "Yeah?" he said without looking up. The steaks were beginning to burn, and he'd be damned if he'd ruin their supper.

"TERRY." This time her voice rose with alarm.

He turned and glanced over his shoulder at her, his expression instantly freezing in panic. "Hold still, Kim." Grabbing the long wooden stick he'd been using as a poker in the fire, he stood up and slowly moved to her side. "Stay here," he warned.

She grabbed his arm, clutching him tightly to her. "Be careful, honey."

Terry nodded and moved cautiously toward the bear. It was a huge animal, bigger than any he'd seen, and he'd seen plenty of them over the years. You couldn't grow up in the Northwoods without seeing them. The creature stood motionless and stared back at him with dark squinting eyes that seemed to be intelligently appraising him. It gave him the creeps. He raised the stick over his shoulder and grabbed an aluminum pan from the knapsack beside the tent.

"Get out, bear!" he yelled, crashing the stick hard against the pan while he dashed forward. The animal was only yards away from him, and he covered the ground quickly, expecting the bear to turn and bolt into the forest. It didn't.

Kim's hand rose to her mouth. "Terry, get back here," she whispered. She'd never seen a bear act like this before. They *always* ran away in fear.

He stopped where he was and stared at the bear, feeling shaken by its weird behavior. In the fading sunlight, he noticed that the animal's fur had an unusual reddish tinge that seemed to glow. It was unlike anything he'd ever seen, and he couldn't tear his eyes off it.

A pan clattered to the ground behind him. The couple turned simultaneously, their attention pulled back to the fire where the sound originated. Another bear stood just beyond the reach of the flames and swiped its paw at the hot steaks that had tumbled to the ground.

Kim's breath caught in her throat. She raised her arm and pointed toward the lake shore where yet another bear had appeared among the bushes and was moving silently toward them as stealthy as if it were stalking prey.

"Jesus," Terry said, stepping slowly backward until he stood by his wife's side. He'd camped for years and had never seen anything like this. Three mature bears in a single campsite was unheard of.

They watched with growing fear as the three bears shuffled toward them, moving gradually closer in a tightening circle. Kim clutched his arm so tightly it hurt.

"What are they doing?" she whispered, her eyes darting from one bear to the next.

"If I didn't know better, I'd say they were hunting us."

Kim shook her head furiously, her long auburn braids swinging behind her. "Bears don't hunt humans."

"I know." Terry didn't sound confident when he said the words. He pulled her backwards and stepped inside the safety of the tent. They huddled together on the floor, Terry still grasping the pan and the stick in his trembling hands. Through the zippered opening, they could see the bears nosing through the camp, overturning the canvas packs in their search for food.

Shara eyed the frightened couple and snorted contemptuously. Cowards. He almost wished for the man to come after him with the stick and show him what a strong, courageous human he was. But of course he wasn't. He was hiding in the tent like a frightened cub, too afraid to do anything but cower beside his female.

Lucien stalked to the fire and sniffed at the meat cooling on the ground. The smell was irresistible and without hesitation, he snatched the entire steak in his mouth and swallowed it down. It tasted of fire and ashes, but he didn't mind. Anything was better than the ants and berries the clan had been feeding him. Downing the second steak, he swung his head to his companions and addressed them in bear-speak.

"You've served me well, boys. Now take your reward."

Shara and Keeran looked at each other and chuffed with excitement. Lucien had kept his word, just as he'd promised, and brought them on their first camp raid. They were free to do whatever they wished. Shara wheeled around to return to the knapsack beside the tent, eager to dump it out and explore what lay within it.

Keeran had other plans. He gazed behind him to a thick rope tied to a nearby tree. Following the path of the rope with his eyes, he saw that it connected to a huge dark sack suspended from a limb of the tree about fifteen feet in the air. The unmistakable odor of food drifted downward from the sack, carried by the soft evening breeze, and he knew immediately what he had to do. Taking a running leap, he landed beside the rope and slashed it with his powerful claws, severing the rope quickly and cleanly. The sack crashed to the ground with a *thud* and split open, spilling its bounty of human food.

Lucien smiled with satisfaction while the bruins entertained themselves. Now that his stomach was full, it was time to satisfy the other hunger that constantly gnawed inside him. He'd denied himself long enough, but no more. Swiveling his huge shaggy head, his eyes focused on the canvas tent on the other side of the fire and the humans that hid within it. Their fear was growing stronger, he could smell it, and it made his hunger grow even more powerful. He quickly crossed the campsite and charged into the tent.

Shara and Keeran froze at the sound of screams. They recognized the haunting sounds of death, knew them from the dying screams of the men they'd killed during Marin's rescue. But these screams were different, they were helpless and undeserving. Together they whirled toward the source of the terrible wails and stared at the opening of the tent.

After a moment, the fabric parted and Lucien strolled out. Calmly arching up into man skin, he reached down and yanked one of the tent stakes from the ground, ignoring the blood that streamed off his chin, then leisurely crouched down to sift through the human things that Shara had dumped from the knapsack. He picked up a flashlight, rope and a knife and joined them with the stake in his hand. Only then did he notice the other bears staring at him. "Whazzup?" he asked, grinning.

The younger bears looked at each other, barely able to believe what had happened. Finally Keeran worked up the nerve to ask. "Lucien, did you... kill those people?"

Lucien nodded and replied in a cold voice. "Yup."

"But why?"

When he looked up, a puzzled expression filled his broad face. "Why not?"

Shara shook his head back and forth, still mystified by Lucien's bizarre behavior. "They weren't threatening us. And one of them was a female."

"So?" Lucien snorted, amused by the younger bear's logic. "A human's a human and the best kind of human is a dead one. Get it?"

The bears stood silently before him, left speechless by the man who'd taken over their clan and promised to teach them everything Marin hadn't. As much as Marin hated humans, he would never have killed them without provocation or just cause. He wouldn't murder for the sake of murder.

Lucien stood up and took a step nearer the bears, his fingers opening and closing around the handle of the knife. "Is there a problem, boys? Any complaints about the way I do business? Because if there are, we need to settle it right here and now."

Shara and Keeran inched backward, realizing the foolishness of challenging the man.

"Good," Lucien said, returning his attention to the things scattered on the ground. "Now gather up as much stuff as you can and let's head back home.. We've got us some partying to do."

Chapter Thirteen

"I need to go to town and do some errands," Lindy said, rising on her toes to kiss Marin. "I'll be back this afternoon. You'll be okay here with Lena?"

He pulled her close to give her a hug, reluctant to let her go. He hated even short separations. "We'll be fine."

"Don't forget to use the antibiotic ointment on Notch at noon, okay?"

"I'll remember." He watched her put on her jacket and walk out the back door with a quick wave. She slid into the driver's seat, started the car and pulled out onto the long gravel driveway, disappearing a moment later down the blacktop road that passed by her house. When she was out of sight, he sank back down on the sofa to finish reading the morning paper.

Lindy drove less than a block down the road before she parked the car on the shoulder and walked into the woods. All night, she'd tossed and turned with thoughts of the clan running through her mind. Something had to be done about Lucien, and quickly. He'd already hurt Notch and Gareth, and who knew how many others that she was unaware of. There was no doubt in her mind that if he wasn't brought under control soon, other clan members would be hurt. She wasn't sure how to stop him; but if Marin wasn't willing to do it, she knew she must.

She backtracked through the trees and picked up the trail leading into the forest from her back yard. Every thirty feet, a tiny orange paint circle blazed from the trunk of a pine tree to show her the way to forest home. The trail she and Marin had marked worked perfectly. She walked quietly, her footfalls padded by newly fallen needles that lay brown and dry beneath her shoes. Dark clouds drifted overhead, obscuring the sun and making the forest appear even darker than it was. Autumn was passing quickly, and she had the uneasy feeling that whatever had to be done to rectify the situation at forest home needed to be done before the first snow fell.

Pulling her fleece jacket closer around her against the cold wind, she plodded along the trail, her thoughts lost in the fear of meeting Lucien. From the sound of it, he didn't think much of women, especially when they had minds and opinions of their own. And judging by what he'd done to Notch, he was cruel and sadistic with no apparent conscience. If he could torture a cub, he would surely have no qualms about hurting or killing a human woman.

She checked her watch. Two hours had passed before she finally spotted the meadow of forest home just ahead. It wouldn't be surprising if Lucien had posted a guard nearby, anticipating that Marin would try to reclaim Guardianship of the clan. She pushed herself flat against the trunk of a huge white pine and peeked around it, scanning the woods for any sign of a sentry. Seeing nothing, she crept slowly closer, being careful to keep herself hidden as she moved from tree to tree. The closer she got to the meadow, the harder her heart pounded in her chest. *Please don't let me run into Shara or Keeran*, she whispered to herself, remembering Lena's words about how the young men were acting in league with Lucien.

She edged cautiously forward to the border of the meadow and stopped. A small black bear grazed on the drying grasses about twenty yards away, seemingly unaware of her presence. Lindy squinted against the glare of the sun as it peeked out between clouds, knowing that if she was caught, she was probably as good as dead. Raising her hand to her forehead, she carefully scanned the open area but saw no one else.

The bear trampled softly over the grass, her small paws moving soundlessly. She appeared to be an adult, but she was so small she could only be Lilea. None of the other sows were that tiny.

Lindy swallowed hard and took a step into the open. It was a calculated risk but one she had to take. If Lucien had forced Arlin to take Lilea against her will, chances were that she was no fan of his now. Maybe she could be persuaded to help. Lindy took another step closer to the bear and crouched low to the ground. "Lilea?"

The bear swung her head around in the direction of the sound. It took only a moment for her small black eyes to zero in on the woman hiding in the tall grass. She didn't move, but stood frozen in place.

"Lilea, come closer so I can talk to you."

The bear quickly looked around, uncertain whether they were alone. She sniffed the air to check for any scent and finding none, took a hesitant step closer to Lindy.

"I need to talk to you, Lilea. Please, will you shift into man skin and help me?"

Lilea stared at her for several moments while she debated. Her thoughts were so confused she didn't know what to believe or who to trust anymore. The one thing she was certain of was that if Lucien caught her talking to a human, he would kill her. But she couldn't stop wondering why Lindy was here. Glancing over her shoulder once more, she shifted silently into man skin and crouched low to the ground beside the human. "You shouldn't be here," she hissed.

Lindy crawled forward to close the distance between them so she could whisper. She cast a careful glance over Lilea's petite body, noticing a series of ugly bruises on her arms. "Are you all right?" she asked.

Lilea looked away, unable to look her in the eyes. "Yes. What do you want?"

"I need to speak to Gareth. Can you bring him to

me?"

Lilea shook her head back and forth, her black hair swinging down to cover her face like a dark curtain.

"Please," Lindy begged. "It's important. Please, Lilea."

Finally she looked up and settled her uneasy gaze on Lindy. "I can't."

Lindy exhaled softly, trying to figure out how to convince her. "Why not? You can trust me."

"I know, Protector," Lilea whispered. "I do trust you. I just can't bring Gareth to you." She hesitated again, working up her nerve. "But I can take you to him."

Lindy's breath caught in her throat. She wasn't convinced of Lilea's sincerity about her trust and knew it could easily be a trap. Lilea owed her no loyalty. Still, there was nothing else she could do. She had to trust her. "Okay."

Checking the meadow around her again, Lilea rose and darted into the safety of the forest. Lindy barely had time to follow her before she disappeared among the trees and circled around the meadow. Lindy followed silently behind her, her heart pounding so loud she was sure Lilea could hear it. They worked their way down a steep slope and emerged in the woods at the bottom of the hill.

Lilea stopped and pointed to a dark area of forest directly ahead of her. "He's in there. I'll stand guard while you talk to him, but hurry. If Lucien discovers us, he'll kill us both."

Lindy nodded and moved quickly through the trees toward the dark area. As she neared, she realized that it was a cave carved out of the rocky side of the hill. She entered it cautiously, terrified of what awaited inside, and suddenly wished she'd thought to bring her gun. She blinked hard, giving her eyes a moment to adjust to the darkness.

A moan drifted up from the floor of the cave. He could see someone standing in the entrance, just a black shadow against the brightness of the daylight outside. The shadow came closer and bent down beside him, and he flinched, fearing more punishment. He closed his eyes to the sight of an arm moving down to strike him.

"Gareth?" she whispered, laying her hand gently on his trembling head.

He jerked up to look at her, hardly daring to believe that it was her. "Lindy?"

She crouched down lower beside him and swept her gaze over his body. He was curled in the fetal position on the cold dirt floor of the cave. A heavy chain encircled his neck and connected to a huge metal spike that had been driven into the ground only two feet away. The chain was so short he couldn't even rise to a sitting position. Bruises and dried blood covered his battered body and his breaths came fast and shallow between shivers. She lowered her face to his and kissed him tenderly on the cheek. "What has he done to you?" She couldn't contain the horror in her voice.

Gareth reached up and tried to pull her into his arms, but his broken ribs throbbed in protest. A single tear escaped from his eye and fell to the dirt beneath him. "You need to go before he finds you. He'll kill you."

Lindy turned and ran her hand along the length of cold, dirty chain to where it met the spike and gave it a yank. It didn't budge. "Can't you shift to bear skin and pull this out?"

His head shook slowly, painfully. "The chain around my neck is so tight that when I shift, it strangles me. I have to stay in man skin just to breathe."

"Dammit," she cursed, her voice trembling with rage at Gareth's treatment. "I'll get you out of here, Gar, I promise."

He looked out the cave entrance as a shudder rippled through him. "Is Marin with you?"

"No." She tugged at the spike again, using all the strength she had.

"Where is he?"

She sank back to the ground and dropped her hands

into her lap to answer him. "He didn't come. He won't come."

Gareth stared at her with his mouth open. Then his gaze fell to the ground, and he swallowed so hard it was audible. "But you came."

"I'm your Protector, whether you like it or not." As soon as she'd said it, she knew her comment stung him, but she couldn't help thinking about how his words had hurt her when he had approached her about going into town. He hadn't wanted her protection then.

He began to sob softly, his thin shoulders trembling in the darkness.

Why am I such a bitch sometimes? she scolded herself, hating what she'd said. She huddled beside him and hugged him tight. "I'm sorry, Gareth. That was mean."

He reached up and slipped one arm around her, needing the comfort of her warm touch. He was so cold, so scared. "I need your help, Lindy. I want you to protect me because no one else can."

She ran her fingers over his head to smooth his cinnamon-colored hair, noticing the scabs and bumps from the blows he'd taken to his skull. The bastard had done a hell of a number on him. "I'll come back for you, Gar, just hang on a little while longer. Is there anything you can tell me about Lucien? Any weaknesses that I can use against him?"

Gareth shook his head weakly and sobbed again. "He's got half the clan still supporting him, and Shara and Keeran are working with him to keep everyone else in submission. Lucien has beaten Arlin, Lilea and me for disobeying his orders, but at least they're not chained up like I am. I don't know what happened to Lena and Notch, either. They disappeared."

"They're at my house, and they're both okay. Why did he do this to you?"

"Because I took a swing at him. I think he's afraid that I'll try to find Marin and bring him back, too." Gareth grasped her hand and held it so tightly her fingers ached.

"Tell him I'm sorry," he begged, his voice quivering with cold and pain. "Tell him we were wrong, and he was right. Maybe he'll come back for us."

"I'll tell him. But no matter what he says, I'll still come back for you."

She rose to her knees to leave when he grabbed her arm and pulled her close to his face again. His frightened eyes stared hard into hers. "I just want you to know that I love you," he whispered. "Whatever happens to me, I'll always love you."

Lindy fought back her tears and hugged his shoulder carefully to avoid hurting him. "I know, sweetie. I love you, too." She pulled away before she lost it and broke down in front of him. Peeking out the cave entrance, she saw Lilea beckon her to come out.

The she-bear pointed to a deer trail leading into the woods. "I don't know how you found your way here, but if you take this trail until it circles back up the hill, you'll end up where I met you."

Lindy nodded and wiped the sweat off her face, unaware that she had become drenched from her nerves. "Thanks, Lil."

Lilea grabbed her arm as she passed. The expression on her face was dire. "Lucien hasn't given Gareth food or water for three days. I've been sneaking a little bit in, but I don't know if he'll make it much longer. You've got to help us, Protector."

"I will," she said, forcing herself to sound confident. She laid her hand over Lilea's and squeezed it reassuringly. "I'll find a way."

Marin's attention perked up at the sound of the car pulling into the yard. He handed Notch back to his mother and rose from the kitchen table to look out the window. Lindy was standing beside the car, her head tilted in thought. *That's odd*, he thought, opening the back door for her. He looked again, noticing that she carried no packages, and a suspicious growl slid from his throat.

Lindy walked up the steps and smiled at him, wondering why he was frowning. She walked by him, then turned around at the sound of him sniffing her. "What are you doing?" she asked, trying to sound nonchalant.

He grabbed her roughly by the shoulders and pulled her to stand directly in front of him, still sniffing at her neck. "I smell bear on you. More precisely, I smell Gareth on you." His eyes flashed in warning while his fingers dug into the tender flesh of her upper arms.

She knew she was in deep trouble. "Ease up, Marin. I can explain." She squirmed in his grasp, trying to loosen his grip on her, but he wouldn't let go.

"Are you out of your mind? Do you have any idea what danger you put yourself in by going there?" he screamed, unable to control his anger. "Lucien is violent and unpredictable—he would have torn you apart piece by piece without a second thought. Why on earth did you do something that stupid?"

"Because it's my job," she yelled back, breaking away from his grip. She stepped backwards away from him, away from his hurtful words.

"Your job? You think a little round piece of wood makes you capable of walking in there and rescuing my clan from Lucien? You must be able to work miracles, Protector." His words spewed out in a venomous stream.

"I saved *your* ass, didn't I?" she seethed, glaring at him with as much courage as she could muster. Suddenly she was facing the old Marin, the Guardian who had scared her half to death only a few months ago. "Or are you saying that it was just dumb luck that allows you to be standing here alive today?"

Marin blinked rapidly as though she had thrown cold water on him. Her face was red and sweating, full of hurt and anger, and she trembled. *What am I doing to her?* he asked himself. He took a step toward her and was stunned to see her take another step back. "Lindy, I'm... I'm sorry," he said, raising his hands helplessly.

She swung around and sank into the kitchen chair, ignoring the shocked look on Lena's face as the she-bear cradled Notch to her chest. Even though she knew she'd have a lot of explaining to do, she hadn't thought Marin would make it this hard on her.

He sat down beside her and laid his hand on her shoulder before pulling her body against him. He felt her resistance, the way she stiffened up at his touch, and he hated himself for acting the way he did. "Lindy," he said, forcing her head down on his shoulder. She tried to pull away but he didn't let her. "Please, don't fight me. I want to hold you." He ran his fingers through her hair and struggled to keep his voice from cracking with emotion. "You scared me, that's all. I don't want to lose you, and I know all too well what Lucien is capable of doing. And you don't need to remind me that you saved my life. Do you think I'll ever forget that?"

Lindy grew still in his arms until she felt his grip relax, then she yanked herself away and sat back in her chair to glare at him. "Someone has to help those people, Marin. Maybe I'm not the defensive genius you are, maybe all I have is my little round piece of wood; but my promise to protect them means something to me. And at least I'm willing to try and help them."

Marin leaned against the table and crossed his arms over each other while he gazed at her from the corner of his eye. She was absolutely right. At least she had done something while he himself had turned away from his clan like a self-righteous fool. Her courage never ceased to amaze him; and despite his efforts to stop it, the corner of his mouth lifted in a smile at her stubbornness. "Do you want to tell me what happened?"

Forcing herself to shelf her anger, she sighed and looked from Marin to Lena. "I found Lilea at the edge of the meadow. She's bruised but okay. She took me to see

Gareth..." She stopped and blinked her eyes, seeing again the way he huddled in pain in the darkness. "Lucien has him chained on a very short tether inside a cave. He's badly beaten and can't shift into bear skin because the chain around his neck is too tight. Lilea said he's gone without food and water for three days."

A loud, angry breath escaped Lena's throat while she clutched her cub possessively to her breast. "What can we do?"

Lindy shook her head, still helpless to offer a solution. "Gareth said that about half the clan still supports Lucien, and Keeran and Shara are still enforcing his orders. Arlin has turned against him, though."

Leaning back in his chair, Marin crossed his arms over his chest and scowled. "We don't have much time to free Gareth. At least now we know who we have on our side."

The phone rang on the hallway table, jangling everyone's nerves. Lindy rose and answered it.

"Hi Sara." She grew quiet while she listened to the voice on the other end. "He did? About fifteen miles from here?" She nodded now and then as her expression grew darker, until finally she said good-bye and set the phone back down. Her eyes focused on Marin when she sat back down at the table.

"What is it?" he asked.

She crossed her hands on the table before her and licked her lips, preparing herself to explain. "My sister has a friend who's studying wildlife biology in college. We asked him to check out Lucien's story about his clan being killed somewhere in this area and he was able to get some information."

Marin leaned forward on the edge of his seat, his body tensed. "What did he find out?"

Lindy chewed on her lower lip for a moment before answering. "Four months ago, eleven bear carcasses were found by DNR officers in the woods near High Lake, about fifteen miles from here."

A loud, angry growl rolled from Marin's throat at the news. He closed his eyes and laid his head back, too stunned to move. "So Lucien was telling the truth about humans slaughtering his clan."

"Not exactly," Lindy said, reaching to take his hand in hers. Marin opened his eyes and leaned forward to look at her as she continued. "Something killed those bears, but it wasn't humans."

He cocked his head, not understanding. "What do you mean?"

She squeezed his fingers, as much to comfort herself as him. "The DNR report said the bodies were slashed and mutilated. They weren't shot, Marin. Those bears were mauled to death."

Marin was silent for a long moment while he considered her words. Then he closed his eyes as understanding swept over him. "Sweet Mother Earth," he groaned, lowering his head. "The son of a bitch killed his own clan."

Chapter Fourteen

Lucien sauntered into the cave and stared down at his prisoner. The bear man was curled up in a tight ball on the ground, his naked skin turned dark by a cover of dirt and grime. Even through the dark smudges, Gareth's bruises shone through and jutted out of his body in huge swollen lumps. He squatted down beside the man and grabbed his hair. "Are you ready to obey my orders now?"

Gareth nodded weakly, too scared to answer. He didn't want to obey Lucien, but he did want to live, and he was willing to do whatever it took. At this point, he would do anything for a drink of water.

Lucien laughed and bent lower to slip his finger under the chain around Gareth's neck. The flesh beneath the links was raw and oozing from the abrasion, but he didn't mind the feel of it. In fact, he rather enjoyed it. Roughly, he jerked the man up, until Gareth's face was close to his own. Then the unexpected scent hit him. "What is this?" he roared, sticking his nose against Gareth's cheek.

Gareth looked at him meekly, unsure what he was talking about. Then his stomach turned as he realized what Lucien had detected. It was Lindy's scent on him. He quickly looked away, but it was too late.

Lucien thrust him roughly up until the chain was taut. The links around Gareth's neck strained under the force, tightening until he couldn't get a breath. "A human was here. Who was it?" he screamed.

Gareth clawed at the chain, struggling with what little

strength he had to pull it away from his neck enough to gulp in one breath. His neck throbbed as the rough metal tore his flesh and dug into the muscle beneath. In desperation, he kicked out one leg and caught Lucien in the knee, knocking him off balance. The chain flew out of his grip as he fell backward, freeing Gareth enough to gasp in quick breaths.

Lucien scrambled to his knees and pinned Gareth to the ground on his back. "Who was here?" he roared again, bringing the back of his hand down across Gareth's cheek. "Was it the human you saw that day, the one you and *Marin* went to visit?"

Gareth closed his eyes and clamped his mouth shut. He knew more blows were coming, but he didn't care. He couldn't give Lucien any information about Lindy. He'd die before he betrayed the woman he loved.

His silence only infuriated Lucien more. He grabbed Gareth's head and slammed it down against the hard earthen floor again and again, ignoring the man's cries of pain and the blood seeping from a cut on the back of his head. "Tell me!" he yelled until he saw Gareth's eyelids flicker toward unconsciousness. Sighing disgustedly, he yanked his hands away and raised them to his own head, holding on as if it would tumble from his body.

Lucien stood up and stormed out of the cave, leaving Gareth alone in his pain. He rolled onto his side as the world spun around him, and tried to focus his eyes. They wouldn't cooperate, showing him the world only as a gray blur. Every part of his body throbbed with pain and cold. He didn't know how long he had laid there when he heard someone come back into the cave.

A terrified whimper echoed from somewhere nearby. It was a soft, high sound, a female sound. Gareth strained to fix his eyes on the blur before him, hoping against hope that it wasn't who he thought.

Lucien cackled as he jabbed one foot into Gareth's side, torturing the already broken ribs. Gareth screamed and clutched his arm over the damage. “Now that I have your attention,” Lucien smirked, “let’s get this game over with.” He fell to his knees on the ground beside Gareth, bringing the woman in his grasp down with him.

“Who is it?” Gareth groaned, still unable to see clearly.

“It’s your pretty little friend Lil,” Lucien laughed. He ran his huge fingers through her hair until they were tangled in the dark mass, then jerked her head roughly back against his chest until she shrieked with pain. He loved the feel of her trembling against him, the look of terror marring her beautiful face.

“Let her go,” Gareth said, struggling to crawl onto his hands and knees. The pain took his breath away, and he sank back down with his stomach almost touching the ground.

“Tell me what I want to know, cub,” Lucien warned, tired of being patient. “Or pretty little Lil won’t be pretty much longer.”

Though her neck was clutched tightly in Lucien’s grip, she could turn her head enough to see that he had a sharp-edged rock in his hand. When he saw her looking at it, he lowered it menacingly beside her face to give her a better look at what was coming.

“He’s going to cut me, Gareth,” she screamed, struggling to break free of his armhold. He was so strong that he only needed one arm to secure her against him. The rock came nearer her face, and she saw that the edge was honed to a devastating sharpness. “No,” she screamed again, her voice high with panic.

Gareth rose once more and tried to move closer to Lilea but the chain held him back. A frustrated growl roared from his throat, but he couldn’t move close enough to help her.

“Okay, you’re not playing nice, cub, so here she goes.” He slashed the rock down, catching the top of her cheek.

Lilea wailed in pain. The sound ripped through Gareth, killing him at the thought of Lilea’s beautiful face being damaged. Even worse, he knew Lucien would not stop at her face when her throat was mere inches away. He sank down in a heap and sobbed, knowing what he had to do. He had to protect her, because he was the only one who could.

"Okay," he moaned, realizing he had no choice in the matter. "It was my friend who was here."

"That's better," Lucien said, lowering the rock to his side. "Why was she here?"

He scrambled to make up an explanation. "We meet once a month. When I didn't show up, she came looking for me."

"How did she find you in here?"

Gareth swallowed hard, forcing down the bitter tasting bile that was rising in his tight throat. "Sometimes we come in here to talk privately."

"Right," Lucien laughed, kicking his foot into Gareth's side again. "You know, you don't lie very well. Do you think I don't know about your human protector? You think my boys haven't told me all about how she and Marin got together like two freaks of nature? Yeah, that's where he's been, plotting with the stinking human bitch and sending her to spy for him."

Groaning weakly, his ribs throbbing in flooding waves that took his breath away, Gareth forced himself to his knees before his captor. The pain was so intense he could hardly speak. "Leave her alone, Lucien. Lindy is my friend. She saved my life. I'll do whatever you want, whatever you say, just please leave her alone."

"It's amazing what a little painful persuasion does," Lucien observed while he eyed Gareth curiously. "Makes one grovel like a little worm in the dirt. Well, little worm, it's too late to make a deal with big ole' Lucien. You had your chance to work with me and you screwed up, so the deal is done. But don't worry. I'll kill your Protector quickly." He stopped and grew quiet for a minute, deep in thought. "On the other hand, what fun is that?" He laughed heartily and kicked Gareth in the leg, rolling him onto his side. "Oh hell, I might as well take my time and let her suffer. Why spoil my fun?" Then grasping Lilea tightly against him, he stood up and dragged her out of the cave. "Nighty night," he called over his shoulder. "Sweet dreams."

When the cave was silent and Gareth knew he was alone, he rolled onto his stomach and cried. He tugged weakly at the chain holding him, knowing that it wouldn't budge, but he was too angry to lay motionless like a defeated dog. The night grew cold, and he shivered on the dirt floor, but the discomfort couldn't compare to the hurt he felt inside. "Lindy, I'm sorry, I didn't want to betray you. I should have let Lucien strangle me," he sobbed, his failing strength at last succumbing to his pain. "It would be best for everyone if I was gone." Then grasping the chain in his hand, he curled up in a tight ball against the cold and wished himself dead.

Chapter Fifteen

Lindy's eyes flew open and she turned to look at Marin. In the moonlit darkness of the bedroom, she saw that he, too, was awake and listening intently to whatever had awoken them. They lay in silence, listening to the wind rustle through the treetops and the waves lap against the lake shore. "What is it?" she whispered.

He slipped out of bed and walked to the window to look out at the yard. Nothing moved in the distance, but he had the unsettling feeling that something was out there. Raising the sash up slightly, he lowered his head and sniffed the cold autumn air coming in the window. He whirled back around to face her. "Get your gun!" he yelled franticly. "And keep the house lights off."

She jumped out of bed and ran to the family room to take her gun from the storage cabinet while Marin woke Lena. She grabbed Notch and stumbled from the bed, not saying a word as Marin led them down to the basement. The look on his face told her everything she needed to know.

"Just stay down here and protect Notch," he warned her. She nodded without speaking and watched him bolt back upstairs and close the door behind him.

Lindy had the loaded gun cradled in her arms when he entered the family room. Even in the darkness, he could see the terror etched on her face, and he pulled her into his arms to comfort her as best he could.

"They're coming, aren't they?"

"By any chance, did you touch Gareth?" he asked, trying not to sound accusatory.

"Yes."

Marin gulped down his fear and looked out the kitchen window. "Lucien must have smelled your scent on him, and no doubt Shara is leading him right to us."

"Oh God, I'm such an idiot," she groaned, burying her face against his bare chest. Because of her recklessness, they were all in danger of being killed.

Marin stroked her hair and nudged her ear with his lips. "It's okay, Lind. They would have come for me sooner or later. I knew Lucien wouldn't be satisfied letting me get away alive." He pulled away and stared into the darkness, thinking.

"How will they attack us?" she asked, feeling sweat beginning to bead on the back of her neck. Her heart raced so fast she almost felt faint, but she had to keep in control. Marin couldn't defend all of them by himself.

"Are the doors locked?"

"Yes, I always lock them."

He nodded, visualizing the attack in his mind. He wondered if it was the same plan he had devised when they had intended to rescue Gareth from her. "The windows. It'll be easier for them to crash through the glass than to break down the doors. We need more weapons."

She ran to the kitchen, yanked open one of the drawers and withdrew a large steel carving knife. "How about this?"

Marin took it and then looked into the drawer, choosing a cleaver and another knife to go along with the first one. "These will help." A frenzied growl came from the darkness, and he jolted his head up to look outside. "They're coming. Stand in the family room against the wall and shoot anything that comes through the window, is that clear? Don't hesitate because you won't get a second chance."

She tried to answer, but the words stuck in her throat, so she nodded yes and took her position near the wall. The gun shook wildly in her hands as she stared at the thin pane of glass separating them from the coming danger.

It wasn't a moment before the glass shattered in a thousand pieces around her, spraying her body with silvery shards that fell to the floor like tiny crystals. Lindy screamed and swung the gun up toward the huge black body hurtling through the open window toward her. She fired off one shot and slammed back against the wall as the bear tumbled toward her.

At the same moment, the kitchen window disintegrated and Marin ducked beneath a black mass of fur bounding over him in a shower of glass. The bear hadn't even landed when Marin charged him and thrust the thick silver blade into the tender skin of his belly, opening a ten-inch slit that spilled out a coil of steaming intestine. The bear bellowed in rage and rolled on the floor, sliding in a pool of its own blood. The dark, round eyes glared up at him while the pain shocked the animal into shifting. Balen gasped in a ragged, bubbling breath and snarled at Marin before closing his human eyes for the last time.

Lindy's shot caught the bear in the upper chest. The animal skidded over the floor and took a powerful leap right at her, barely even slowed by the bullet. She screamed and pulled the trigger again, this time catching the bear in the neck. It crashed to the floor on its belly, but still it wasn't enough. Ignoring the blood streaming from its wounds, the bear rose to its feet once more and staggered toward her. She aimed for the bear's head and pulled the trigger. Nothing happened.

Marin jerked backward as another bear crashed through the shattered kitchen window, but his attention was focused on Lindy. She was struggling with the gun, trying to fire another shot, but it wasn't working. The injured bear inched closer to her, spewing bloody spittle from its snarling jaws.

Ignoring the bear at his back, Marin ran into the family room and slammed the meat cleaver into the bleeding bear's face. It snorted out a foamy streak of blood from its slashed muzzle and sank to the floor.

"Duck!" Lindy screamed.

Marin dropped to the floor as the other bear hurled itself across the room at them. Lindy couldn't move, but stood frozen as the bruin crashed into Marin and knocked the cleaver from his hand. The weapon slid across the floor and lodged underneath the sofa.

Without a weapon, Marin realized his best chance was to fight in bear skin. He arched his back and shifted just as the bear rose to its feet and charged him with its jaws open and its gleaming canine teeth slashing the air. Marin rose up on his hind legs and threw his powerful front limbs around the bear, grabbing him in an ursine hug. His head twisted away, trying to dodge the sharp teeth snapping at his head, but one tooth caught him in the cheek and opened a gash that bled viciously. They struggled chest to chest, their roars filling the house with a deafening sound as they clawed and bit at each other.

Marin pushed the bear back and charged him hard, throwing him to the floor on his back. He sank his teeth into his opponent's neck, missing the jugular by inches. The bear screamed and bucked fiercely, throwing Marin off. Marin slipped in the blood pooling on the floor and couldn't get a foothold to rise up on all fours. It wasn't a second until the bear was on him, and he watched helplessly as it lunged at his throat with bared teeth.

Suddenly a huge white cloud shot out of nowhere and blasted the attacking bear in the head. It snorted at the cold blast and whirled to see what assaulted him. Lindy slammed the heavy metal fire extinguisher down on the bear's head with every ounce of strength she could muster. The crack of its splintering skull echoed across the room, and the animal fell dead to the floor.

Marin lay motionless on the floor, panting to catch his breath. His eyes were wide with disbelief. When he had recovered, he rolled over and arched up to man skin and came to stand beside Lindy. "You okay?" he asked, ignoring the blood seeping down his cheek.

She wobbled unsteadily against the wall and nodded yes while her gaze swept the room. She recognized Balen lying dead in the kitchen, but she couldn't tell who the other two bears were. The panic of what had happened took over and she threw herself into Marin's arms and cried.

There was nothing he could say to express his gratitude better than the hug he gave her. Again she had saved his life, this human woman who he had scorned and ridiculed for so long. She was as brave as any bear he knew, and his love deepened at the thought of how she protected him at the risk of her own life. She was not only the clan's Protector, but as true a Guardian as he or any of his predecessors had been. His heart swelled with pride for her.

When she could finally speak, she pointed to the two dead bears at their feet. "Who are they?" Her voice still trembled.

Marin looked down at them and shook his head with a grimace. "It's Keeran and Mara."

Lindy gasped and stared up at him. "Mara? She's a... *she.*"

"Even she-bears can put up a hell of a fight," Marin said, shaking his head. "I guess Lucien still had her totally under his control. The sad thing is, she has a yearling who's motherless now."

"Oh God, that's pitiful," Lindy whispered, thinking of the poor cub who was undoubtedly alone in forest home and waiting for his mother to return.

Marin climbed over her body and walked to the basement door. He opened it and called down. "Lena, it's safe to come up now."

Cradling Notch protectively in her arms, she left the safety of the cellar and stepped into the room. The color drained from her face at the sight of the devastation around her, at the blood and bodies everywhere. "Balen, Keeran... oh no..." Her words died in her throat as she stumbled across the room and knelt distraught beside Mara's body.

"Was she a good friend of yours?" Lindy asked, looking on from beside Marin.

Lena shook her head, unable to answer.

It was Marin who voiced her words. "Mara was her sister."

Shara loped back through the moonlit forest, his thoughts running in a terrified torrent. Lucien was waiting for him back at forest home, anxious to hear his report about the attack and expectant to hear that Marin was dead. But Marin wasn't dead. Somehow he had been able to fend off all three of his attackers and still survive. Shara had peered in the kitchen window and halted his own attack at the sight on his kin lying dead on Lindy's floor. Then he had turned like a coward and fled back into the darkness, too afraid to attack on his own.

A shudder rippled across his steaming fur, shaking him to his very bones. He didn't want to go back and face Lucien, but he had no choice. Surely he would understand. Shara swallowed hard and panted deeply in the cold night air, willing the chill to leave him. But he knew it wasn't the cold of the night that made him tremble. It was the thought of facing Lucien and admitting his failure. He growled softly to himself, wondering if he'd live to see the sun rise again.

Chapter Sixteen

Lindy closed the door and faced the bed to take a good look at Marin. He sat on the edge of the mattress propped up by his strong arms, his eyes fixed on her with a hungry stare. The corner of his mouth turned upward ever so slightly, betraying his thoughts.

She shook her head at his suggestive posture. Even wounded, the man was incorrigible when it came to sex. Her eyes fell to the long cut crossing diagonally over his left thigh, then to the smaller slashes marring his chest and shoulders. Above his smile, a large, shiny bruise was beginning to swell on his right cheek. "Why don't you take a nice warm shower, and then I'll patch you up?" she said.

He smiled broader, ignoring the ache in his cheek. "Why don't you clean me up in a nice warm bath?"

"I don't know how you can do it," she said, returning a smile.

Arching his eyebrows at her, Marin rose from the bed and took her hand to lead her to the bathroom. "Do what?"

"How you can fight time after time and put your body through such abuse."

He looked down at himself, surprised by her words. "This isn't abuse, Lind. This is what I do, what I am." He stopped abruptly, realizing what he'd just admitted. There was no way to deny it. He was a Guardian, and it didn't matter whether he protected her or the clan, it was what he was born to do. When he looked up again, a sheepish expression lit his face.

"So you're not turning your back on the clan after all?"

He swung his head back and forth. "How could I? They're my kin, regardless of how they treat me. They need my protection." He took a step before stopping again to gaze down at her sky blue eyes. "No, they need *our* protection."

Lindy smiled without answering, then knelt beside the tub to plug the drain and run the water. Marin watched from behind her, remembering the day she'd introduced him to this divine pleasure. It was only a moment until steam rose into the air once again, just as it had then when they had kissed for the first time. It had been a turning point for him, the moment when he'd finally admitted that he didn't want to live his life without her, and since then he hadn't looked back. Lindy was the best thing that had ever happened to him.

When the tub was full, she stepped aside and let him climb in. Marin closed his eyes and groaned at the warmth flooding through him as he sank into the steaming depths. Every ache in his muscles seemed to blissfully fade away, much as the anger he carried in his heart at his clan's treatment of him was melting away.

He jolted at the feel of something rough moving across his thigh and he opened his eyes.

"Did I hurt you?" She was sweeping a washcloth gently across the cut to clean it.

"No," he lied, eyeing the wound carefully. It was long but superficial, thanks to Mara's miscalculated slash, but it still hurt. He watched her move the cloth tenderly across his skin to clean even the smallest cuts, taking great care not to hurt him. He loved that about her, how careful she was with him, as though he was the fragile one instead of her.

Finishing his body, she raised the cloth to his face and held it carefully against his swollen cheek. His ebony eyes pierced hers with a stare that made her tremble. She remembered a time when he'd made her tremble with fear, but now it was only desire that made her body shiver and her heart ache with want for him.

"I..." she blurted, wanting desperately to tell him how she felt. *I love you, Marin.* But she couldn't. How could he be ready to hear such words or to handle such a human emotion when he was still learning to accept the human part of himself?

"What?" he asked, cocking his head curiously.

She stammered for a moment before recovering her composure. "I, uh, was just wondering what you're going to do about Lucien."

"Ah, Lucien," he replied, laying his head against the back of the tub. "I think our first priority is to get Gareth out of there before he's killed. Then we can worry about Lucien."

"Any suggestions how to go about it?"

"If Gareth is correct that half the clan still supports him, and we've killed Mara, Balen and Keeran, that still leaves Shara, Lucien and Balak to deal with."

"What about the she-bears who still support him?"

Pursing his lips, he thought for a moment while he sank deeper in the water. Moisture seeped up into his hair, tinting the black curls with a blue sheen that shimmered under the bathroom light. "Minus Lilea, that leaves five more, unless any have changed their allegiance."

Lindy dropped the washcloth in the water and slid her hand beneath Marin's hair. She loved the weight of it in her hands, the way it curled tighter around her fingers when it was wet, the way its darkness contrasted so stunningly with his olive skin. But then, there was nothing about this man that she didn't love.

Marin noticed the preoccupied look in her eyes and tipped his head up to catch her attention. "Are you all right?"

"Yeah," she smiled, bringing her fingers around the side of his head to rest on the curve of his chin.

Reassured, he laid back again and closed his eyes to concentrate. "We'll need a diversion to keep everyone away from the cave. We just need enough time to free Gareth and get him away before they come back."

"What kind of diversion?"

"There's only one thing guaranteed to keep Lucien's attention for any length of time."

Lindy dipped her hand into the water, then watched the droplets fall off and land one by one on Marin's chest. They trailed slowly down his curves, following the dip between his abs before blending smoothly into the surface of the water again. "And what's that?" she asked at last.

"Me."

Her head shot up to look at him. "No, you can't use yourself as bait."

Marin studied her face, wary of the panic that filled her expression. If anything could doom a risky plan, it was uncontrolled panic. She had to learn to control it. "Lindy, it's the only way."

"No," she argued, shaking her head furiously. "You already fought him once and lost. You can't do it again."

"It wasn't a fair fight. Last time he had three others helping him."

Her head still shook while she laid her hands on his shoulders. Why did he always have to be so stubborn? "What makes you think it will be a fair fight this time? Since when does Lucien give a damn about fairness?"

"It'll be different because this time I'll challenge him formally. The rules of the clan demand that a challenge be one on one with no help or interference from anyone. Besides, once he knows I survived this attack, that's what he'll be expecting, I'm sure. He'll assume that as long as I'm alive, I won't just walk away from the clan and do nothing to get them back."

"I still don't trust him. And what about me?" She gripped his shoulders tighter to control the trembling in her fingers. The thought of what he wanted to do almost made her sick to her stomach. "What can I do?"

"You'll have to be the one to free Gareth. With any luck, Lena will agree to help us and she can cover you while you cut the chain. If he's as hungry as Lilea says he is, he'll be weak and you'll probably both have to help him get back here."

Lindy slumped her head toward her chest, dreading what she knew had to be done. "And what happens to you, Marin? Whether you win or lose against Lucien, you'll still be surrounded by a clan of bears that have turned against you. How will you get out of there?"

Trying to act confident, he forced a smile to his face and rested his fingers on her flushed cheek. He wasn't sure if the heat radiating from her face was due to the warm steam rising above them or her nerves. "Don't worry. I'll figure out something."

She narrowed her eyes at his argument, finding it less than convincing. "We're not going until we have a solid plan to get you out of there. It's too risky to walk in with some half-assed scheme that might get you killed. I won't have it."

The corners of his mouth rose in an amused grin. She had been impertinent the day he'd put her on trial at forest home, and she was equally so now–much to his delight. He'd never known that humans could have such incredible fire to their spirits. "Is that so?" he laughed. "You won't have it?"

"No," she swore, ignoring his laugh to stare him in the eye.

Marin laughed again, then without warning pulled her into the tub with him. Water poured onto the floor as she landed in his lap with a splash.

"What are you doing?" she squealed, beginning to laugh with him.

He took her hand and guided it to his erection. "Tell me, Mrs. Anderson, will you have *this*?"

Chapter Seventeen

"I don't want any funny business going on in that tent tonight," Sara warned, flashing a smirk at her roommate. "Why should you two have fun if I can't?"

Nikki grabbed her boyfriend and kissed him hard, putting on an intentional show. "You know Josh and I wouldn't do anything like that," she giggled.

"Yeah right. Just every chance you get."

Josh backed away from the women and finished pounding the last tent stake into the ground with a roll of his eyes skyward. Why he had let the girls talk him into a campout, he couldn't fathom, but it was too late now. At least, he could look forward to a roll in the hay with Nikki under the stars tonight. That alone was worth the agony of listening to their nonstop chatter.

"Besides," Nikki continued, "it's not my fault that you didn't take Chad up. He offered to be your sleeping bag buddy and you refused him, remember?"

Sara stacked wood in the firepit, preparing it for the evening fire. "I know, I know. Chad's a nice guy, but he's just not my type."

"No, he's just not Gary."

"Gareth. Gar-ETH." A vision of the man drifted into her mind at the mention of his name. Even now, she remembered the feel of his arm around her back and the silly way he'd pretended not to know what ice cream was. She still wanted to run her fingers through his shaggy cinnamon-red hair and kiss that boyish face that was always in her thoughts.

"He never called you, did he?"

Slamming the wood down on the ground beside her, Sara gazed over her shoulder to stick her tongue out at her friend. "You just had to cheer me up, didn't you?"

"Sorry, but I don't know why you're so hot for him. You only met the guy once." She took the hamburger from the cooler at her feet and opened the package to form the raw meat into patties. "No guy makes *that* good of an impression on the first date."

"Hey now," Josh muttered, stopping his work on the second tent to shoot her an insulted look. "Surely you're not including me in that sexist generalization. I must have made a pretty damn good impression since you're still dating me."

A grin slipped across Nikki's face as her eyes traveled over his tall, athletic body before settling on the tight jeans covering his firm butt. "Yeah, it was definitely your intellect that caught my interest on our first date."

Josh snorted and turned back to the tent with a laugh. "Women."

"I don't know what it is about Gareth," Sara continued, adding another log to the growing stack in the pit. "There's something different about him, like he's a little boy in a man's body. I can't explain it really. I just get the feeling that he's special." Now that she was utterly dejected, she dropped her hands in her lap with a sigh.

"Well, you'd better get over him because the man is *not* interested," Nikki advised, piling the hamburgers in the frying pan. "No sense making yourself miserable over some jerk who doesn't give a rip."

Sara struck a match and held it to the tinder at the bottom of the firepit. When the spark flared, she blew softly on it until the wood burst into tiny flames. "I guess you're right," she said between blows to the fire. "I just really thought he cared." Her thoughts were suddenly distracted by a noise in the bushes to her right at the edge of the campsite. She turned her head to look in the direction of the sound but didn't see anything.

"Is that fire ready?" Josh asked. He had the salt and pepper in his hand and a hungry look on his face. "Maybe we could do a little less talking and a little more cooking?"

Nikki slapped him playfully on the rear end as she passed by and knelt down to set the frying pan over the fire. "What's this 'we' stuff? I don't see you over here cooking your dinner."

"And I didn't see you over here helping me set up *your* sleeping accomodations," he muttered, juggling the spices in his hands.

"Yeah, yeah, you made your point," she groaned. The smell of the sizzling burgers was already drifting around her, making her stomach growl. "These are going to taste great."

"So are you."

The three college students wheeled simultaneously in the direction of the unfamiliar voice. Three men stood beside their tent, seeming to have appeared out of nowhere.

"What the hell?" Josh said.

Nikki looked nervously at the two younger men who stood on either side of a huge, slightly older man. They were both tall, good looking and strikingly well built with wild, shaggy hair. Even better, they were stark naked. She swallowed hard.

Josh stared at the man standing in the middle. A good six foot six, he towered over all of them and had the intimidating body of a professional wrestler. His dark eyes burned within a frame of dark, red-tinted hair that appeared to glow like embers in the fading sunlight. Like his younger companions, he was completely naked. Josh drew in a slow breath to calm the butterflies churning in his gut. "What's going on?" he said, trying to deepen his voice.

The older man took a step forward and dragged his hand across the green canvas of the tent. With one quick jerk, he yanked the tent rope out of the ground, stake and all.

"Hey!" Sara yelled. "Leave that alone."

His mouth turning up in an amused grin, the man focused his attention on the woman who had spoken and took another step closer. He could always count on women to open their big mouths and invite trouble their way. "You're trespassing."

Nikki's brows knitted together in confusion. "Excuse me, but the last time I checked, this was still a national forest. How can we be trespassing on public property?"

The man shook his head slowly, at the same time sweeping his eyes across the other woman. She was as lovely as the first and equally mouthy. That suited him just fine. It made giving them their lesson that much more satisfying. "This is our campsite. You're trespassing."

"I don't see your name on it," Sara retorted.

Josh laid his hand on her shoulder and squeezed it firmly in warning. He had a real bad feeling about their visitors, not the least being their state of undress. "We'll leave," he said calmly, slipping his other hand over Nikki's. Holding on to both women, he took a step back and pulled them along with him.

"Too late," the big man said through a lopsided grin. He took another step closer with the younger men moving in tightly behind him.

Josh dropped his grip on the women and held both hands up imploringly before him. "Look, we don't want any trouble. Just let us pack up our stuff, and you can have the campsite. We don't care about it. We'll just go."

A slow, amused chuckle oozed from the big man's throat. The boy was trying to be brave and protective of the women, but Lucien could smell his fear. The kid trembled like a leaf in a strong wind. Lucien pursed his lips for a moment while he considered the offer. Then smacking his lips loudly, he shook his head. "No."

"What do you mean, 'no'?" Josh's eyes flared wide.

His heart pounded harder, and his pulse raced faster with every step closer the man took.

"No means no," Lucien said, as though he was speaking to a toddler. "You're not going anywhere." Then he cocked his head to the side and thought a moment. "Did I hear someone mention Gareth?"

Sara's eyes grew huge and round. "Do you know him?"

"As a matter of fact, I do. He's a good friend of mine. How do you know him?"

"My sister introduced us."

"Really?" Lucien's voice rose with interest. "Maybe I know your sister, then. What's her name?"

"Linda. Lindy Anderson."

Lucien's lips curled up in a sneering smile at the mention of the familiar name. Oh, life was indeed sweet. He turned to look at the men standing beside him. "Why don't we invite... what was your name, dear?"

"Sara."

"Why don't we invite Sara to come and visit Gareth? I know he'd be delighted to see her, don't you think?"

Shara and Balak nodded, understanding Lucien's meaning. "Yes, he'll be so happy to see you," Balak agreed. Shara moved forward and took Sara by her arms to drag her away.

"Hey," she said, trying to pull herself out of his grasp. He held her so tightly that her arms throbbed beneath his fingers, and she was overcome by the sickening feeling that going with him was definitely the wrong thing to do.

"Let her go," Josh warned. "She doesn't want to go with you."

"You're in no position to tell us what to do," Shara growled, shoving Josh roughly in the side with his elbow as he dragged Sara past. It pissed him off that humans always tried to have their own way, and he was not about to take any crap from this man.

Josh swung around and grabbed Shara by one arm to

yank him roughly back. He was scared to death but he knew he couldn't let Sara be taken without a fight. If anything happened to her, he'd never forgive himself.

Shara lost his balance and stumbled backward under the force of Josh's tug. He tumbled to the ground in a heap with the woman landing on top of him.

"Run!" Josh screamed to both women.

Sara was up on her feet and running into the forest before the naked men could respond, but Nikki didn't move. Her mouth hung open in terror, and she stood motionless while Balak stepped forward to pin her against him. His arms felt like steel bars around her, crushing hard into her lower chest, and the heat of his breath was thick on the back of her neck. She screamed and began to struggle, but it was like fighting a brick wall. Neither arm could move, and she had no leeway to even shift within his grasp. She kicked downward to stomp her shoe on his bare foot, but he merely bent backward and lifted her off the ground to raise her feet up. For a moment she dangled in the air, completely off the ground, and then she screamed again.

Lucien was already on Josh, pummeling him with his huge fists. A loud, humming roar came from the big man's throat as though he was propelled by a motor that was revving faster with each passing minute. Josh had never experienced anything like it, had never been so full of terror in his life, but his instinct to fight kicked in with a burst of adrenaline. He thrust his leg into a bent position to pound Lucien in the groin with his knee. The big man howled with pain and fell to his side on the ground.

Josh scrambled to his feet and sprinted across the campsite. Balak was heading into the woods with Nikki screaming and kicking in his grip like a wild banshee. Josh took a flying leap and landed on the man's back, forcing him to the ground on top of the woman. Nikki screamed again and huddled underneath the men, feeling as though every bone in her body was breaking from their combined weight.

Balak growled with rage and released his hold on her to whirl around and grab for the man instead. Josh backed away but moved too slow, allowing Balak to grab a handhold on the front of his shirt. The fabric split with a loud rip and fell away as Josh pulled free. Kicking his leg out hard, he buried the toe of his hiking shoe deep into the naked man's side until he felt the bones under the skin snap. Balak screamed in pain and clutched at his injured ribs.

Josh knew it was the only chance he'd get. He skirted around the groveling man and reached down to pull Nikki to her feet. Once she had gained her balance, he yanked her fiercely into motion and headed into the forest.

"Come on, come on," he screamed at her, barely able to control his panic. Over his shoulder, he could see the sun setting over the lake and the light fading minute by minute, and he knew they only had a short time before the forest was completely dark. They'd never find their way through the wilderness without a flashlight. They plunged into the woods and disappeared.

Chapter Eighteen

Johnny Thundermaker answered the knock at his door and couldn't believe who stood before him. "Well I'll be damned," he said, gaping for a moment before sweeping his arm to the side in a welcoming gesture. "I never thought I'd see you two here. Come on in."

Marin swept past him and entered the dimly lit room of the Thundermaker Trading Post. It took a few seconds for his eyes to adjust to the darkness and assess the appalling condition of the sparsely furnished room. What little furniture existed was dust-covered and decrepit. Cobwebs hung in tattered curtains from the ceiling and the one window that wasn't boarded up was shrouded in dust so thick that the glass appeared opaque. Marin shook his head while he waited for Lindy to follow him in.

"I didn't expect we'd meet up again," Johnny said, closing the door behind her. He walked across the room and motioned for them to sit in two ancient chairs perched in the center of the room. Running his hand nervously through the straight black hair that fell to the middle of his back, the young man dragged a sagging cushioned chair from the corner and sat down opposite them. "It's good to see you again. All is well with the Bear People, I hope."

Marin was quiet while he observed the man. Johnny's gaze was focused intently on him. He seemed surprised to see the Guardian dressed in human clothes, and it was a struggle to keep from staring. Marin cleared his throat and fought to keep the corner of his mouth from lifting in an amused smile before his mood turned somber. "That's why we're here. We have a problem at forest home, and we need your help."

Johnny's attention shifted from the Guardian's flannel shirt and settled uneasily on the dark eyes staring back at him from within the mat of thick black hair framing Marin's angular face. Small worry wrinkles lined the corner of those piercing eyes. "What's going on?"

Lindy leaned forward with her elbows resting on her knees. "Jack should be in on this, too. With his knowledge of Bearwalker history, he might be able to offer some useful insight."

Johnny nodded agreeably and stood up. "No problem, I'll get him." He turned, took a step and stopped to look over his shoulder at them. "You should know that he's lost his sight. He's completely blind now."

"I'm sorry to hear that," Lindy said. "What happened?"

The young man shrugged his shoulders helplessly. "He's ninety-two. Frankly, he's lucky to be alive." Then he turned and disappeared through a dark doorway.

Marin gazed at Lindy from the corner of his eye, his lips pursed with concern. Tension was clear on his face. "Even if he does know, can we trust his memory?"

She reached over and laid her hand on his arm to squeeze it reassuringly. "He's all we have, so we might as well ask and see what information he can give us. Maybe we'll get lucky. Besides, anything he tells us is more than we know now."

Marin's gaze swept past her to watch Jack enter the room. The old man shuffled slowly through the doorway, his thin arm entwined in the strong arm of his nephew. It took a few moments for him to cross the floor and sink wearily into the padded chair. When he was settled, he breathed deeply to catch his breath.

"Hi Jack," Lindy said. She was thankful he couldn't see the shocked expression she knew was on her face. The poor man looked like a walking skeleton. His one remaining eye had clouded over and was obviously sightless.

Jack's face shattered with wrinkles as his lips rose in a delighted smile. He reached his wobbling arms out in front of him, seeking to grasp their hands. Lindy took his left hand gently in hers and motioned for Marin to do the same. When their hands were clasped, Jack nodded approvingly. "I'm honored by your visit, Guardian, but I think it is not friendship that brings you here." Despite his weakened condition, his voice was steady and strong.

Marin couldn't help being impressed. Even with his advanced age and the sad deterioration of his body, the old Indian held himself with a dignity and determination Marin had rarely seen in humans. If Jack's character was typical of the Protectors from whom he'd descended, he could understand why the Guardians of the past had agreed to work with them. They were exceptional humans. He took a slow breath and focused his attention on the problem that had brought them here.

"Elder, you have knowledge of the old days, knowledge of the Bear People who have gone before. Something evil has come to forest home, and it's my hope that you'll be able to shed some light on what's happened to us."

His interest piqued, Jack squeezed the hands in his grasp before releasing them and lowering his tired arms into his lap. "I'll try. Tell me everything."

Marin sighed deeply, reluctant to relive the pain of it all again. "About a month ago, a Bearwalker came to us, saying that he was from a forest nearby. I asked him why he had come, and he said that his clan had been killed by humans. I became suspicious when he said he was the only survivor. You have to understand that Lucien is bigger than me, perhaps even stronger than me. I didn't understand how he could possibly have failed to save the life of even a few of his kin. Things became clearer with information that Lindy discovered." He grew quiet and waited for her to speak.

"I checked out Lucien's story and found out that it was true, at least partially. The DNR reported the deaths of eleven bears over near High Lake several months ago. The strange thing is, the animals weren't killed by humans. They were literally ripped apart, mauled to death. As if by an animal."

Johnny shifted uncomfortably where he stood beside Jack's chair. "What kind of animal kills bears? Especially eleven of them?"

Marin licked his lips. They had gone dry from the anger that roiled in his gut and was now burning in his throat. "There's no doubt in my mind that it was Lucien. He's the only thing big enough and mean enough to have done something like that. And now he's worked his way into my clan and twisted their minds to believe all the lies he's told them about me. He turned them against me and forced me out."

Jack's thin back straightened at the words. "How can that be? You're their Guardian."

"He had some kind of power over them. Lena said he crawls into your mind and makes his lies seem true. Then he uses threats and coercion, even physical violence, to enforce the changes his persuasion has brought about. He's declared himself Guardian and is using our young he-bears to enforce his will on the clan. I don't know how to stop him, or how to convince my kin to take me back."

The old man sat quietly for a long time while he considered Marin's words. His thoughts drifted back in time, sorting and sifting everything he'd been taught about the Bear People by his father, who had been their Protector. Slowly, bits and pieces of his father's stories coalesced in his mind. He nodded to himself as if acknowledging their importance.

"What is it?" Marin pressed. "Do you remember something?"

Jack remained quiet for a moment longer, wanting to be sure of his words when he spoke, needing to be confident of his memories before he told the Guardian of his suspicions. Finally he raised his head and stared directly at Marin, seeing him with his mind instead of his sightless eye. "I do."

Leaning forward in the rickety chair, Marin's breath caught in his throat at the old man's apparent apprehension. "Then tell me."

Jack swept his gnarled hand through the air in a horizontal path before him as if reaching into the past. "I was a boy, probably no more than six or seven, when my father sat beside the fire one night and spoke with his father. They thought I was asleep, but I heard their words. This was after the Bear People had broken off contact with humans." He stopped and coughed weakly into his hand, his frail body wracked by the disease that consumed him.

"Do you need some water, Uncle?" Johnny asked, placing his hand on the old man's shoulder.

Jack shook his head and frowned, and when he had caught his breath, he continued. "They were reminiscing about the old times when they had been welcomed by the clan. How proud they were to be a part of something so important."

"What does that have to do with my problem now?" Marin asked impatiently.

"There was something my grandfather said, something I had never heard spoken of before or since. He said that once he was involved in a mystery he had no idea how to handle. One of the members of the clan attacked and killed several of his own kin. He refused to obey the elders, refused to respect the laws of the clan, and refused to listen while they tried to reason with him. Grandfather said there was no reasoning with him, that he behaved as though his mind had snapped, the way he acted on his own with no concern for his kin."

"That's just how Lucien acts, completely oblivious to the laws of the clan. Totally intent on fulfilling his own impulses. He's out of control."

"Yes," Jack agreed. "He sounds much like this rogue Grandfather spoke of. The Devil Bear, they called him. The Bear With No Heart."

"What happened to him? What did the clan do to stop him?" Lindy asked. Her eyes widened with fear at the thought that Lucien might be unstoppable.

"He was killed, but I don't know how. My grandfather was forbidden to come back to them until the rogue was brought under control. He was told it was not a matter for a human to concern himself with."

Lindy's forehead wrinkled with confusion. "That's strange. I mean, isn't that what the Protector is for, to help deal with dangerous situations? Why wouldn't they want his help?"

Jack shook his head and exhaled tiredly. "Again, I don't know the answer to that. Grandfather just said that when he was allowed to return to the clan, the Devil Bear was gone and things appeared to have returned to normal. The rogue was never mentioned again."

Rising tensely to his feet, Marin walked around his chair and stopped behind Lindy, his hands resting gently on her shoulders. Jack's words were deeply troubling, and he couldn't imagine why his ancestors had refused the help of their human Protector. One thing he was sure of. When he figured out how to deal with Lucien, Lindy would be at his side.

"What happened to this bear to make him a rogue?" she asked, crossing her arm over her chest to lay her hand over Marin's. His skin felt cold and clammy, betraying the concern he was trying so hard to hide.

"Grandfather said..." Jack stopped abruptly, letting the words fade unspoken. He lowered his head for a moment, then shook it slowly from side to side. "He said he didn't know."

Marin stared hard at the old man, trying to read his face. He had the uneasy feeling that there was more to the story than Jack was telling. "Is there anything more you can tell us, Old One? Anything else that might help us?"

Jack raised one shaky hand to his face and stroked his chin thoughtfully. "I wish I had the answer for you, Marin, but I don't. But I can tell you this. You are descended from a strong line of Guardians. Their power flows through your veins, their courage beats in your heart. Trust yourself, your instinct, your knowledge. And trust your Protector. Together you'll figure out a way." He lowered his head to his chest, too exhausted to say anything more.

"He needs to rest," Johnny said. The urgency in his voice made his concern for his uncle very clear.

Lindy wrapped her hands around the old man's hands. "Thank you, Jack. Thank you so much for your help." Then she rose and wrapped her arms around Johnny. "I need to ask you for another favor," she said, hugging him softly. "Walk out with me, and I'll explain."

Jack started awake when the front door closed. It didn't matter how many hours he slept, he just couldn't stay awake for any length of time. "That you, Johnny?"

The young man laughed and sat in one of the chairs across from his uncle. "You fall asleep already?"

"Boy, you get nine decades in you and try staying awake," the old man grumbled.

Johnny laughed again, then quickly grew serious. "You were holding something back from them, weren't you?" When his uncle remained silent, he pressed again. "I think the Guardian suspected something."

"Some things are best left unspoken, Nephew," Jack warned with a sigh. "Nothing I can say to Marin can help him more than his own instincts. He'll find a way to solve this problem, but for now, I felt it best not to burden him with knowledge of his other problem."

Johnny's eyebrows arched curiously. "*Other* problem?"

"Mmm. I feel it here that Lindy is in danger." He tapped

a gnarled finger softly on his chest above his heart.

Johnny sat straight up in his chair, his heart pounding. "In danger? From the rogue?"

Jack shook his head slowly, his hand trembling on the arm of the chair. "No. From the one dear to her heart. The one she trusts above all others. Marin himself."

Chapter Nineteen

"Where are you taking me?" Sara wailed. Her wrist ached in the steel clench of Shara's hand and no matter how hard she fought against him, she couldn't escape his hold. "Dammit, let me go," she cried again.

Shara dragged her through the underbrush, a wicked grin lighting his face. The more the woman whined and begged, the better he liked it. Her cries reminded him of the spring day when he had helped rescue Marin and Gareth and slaughtered their human kidnappers, the day he'd first felt the addictive power of dominance over someone. The chill of those human screams had grabbed him and now each human cry for mercy or release stoked the need like wood feeding a fire. He looked over his shoulder at the trembling woman and flashed a satisfied smile.

"God, what's wrong with you? Don't you know that you can go to prison for kidnapping me?" Her voice was a shrill yell now, verging on hysteria, but the man just shrugged and looked away without answering. Her anger grew at his indifference. "They'll send you to prison until you're so old your dick rots, you jerk."

"They'll send me nowhere," he laughed. "No man will ever take my freedom."

"Oh, but it's okay to take mine?"

Shara stopped to turn and look at her. It was uncanny how much like her sister she was, even down to the big mouth that never shut up. But unlike Lindy, she had more guts than brains. He watched her gaze drop defiantly down across his chest and abdomen, then fall lower across his naked groin. She was powerless against him, and still she challenged him with her eyes. Oh yes, if Lucien allowed it, he would enjoy mating with her every bit as much as he would enjoy killing her. "Your freedom means nothing to me," he said at last.

"It should. You're not above the law, and what you do to me will come back and bite you in the ass someday."

The man's smile widened. "Interesting expression, but irrelevant. Your laws don't apply to my kind."

"Your kind? Of asshole?" Sara yanked her arm fiercely away from him, hoping that their talk had distracted him from his hold on her, but her wrist didn't budge from his grasp. "Look, I don't know what you want with me, but my friends are probably on their way to the police right now. Cops will be on your trail so fast..."

Shara smirked and gave her arm a vicious yank of his own that sent her body flying toward his. Before she could even react, he wrapped his arms around her and crushed her against him. The strength in his arms forced the air from her lungs, and she gasped in panic.

"Would you like to know what I want with you?"

Suddenly she knew what he wanted, because his erection was pressing against her thigh. Nausea rumbled in her belly and surged up into her throat, but fear choked any response from leaving her mouth.

"What? Nothing to say to me now, human?" Shara slipped one hand beneath her hair and sifted his fingers through the soft strands while his other hand kept her pinned tightly against him. "Do you think I'm afraid of human laws? There is only one law here, and it doesn't protect worthless humans."

Sara's eyes widened. "Stop talking to me like you're a freakin' alien. Maybe you haven't checked a mirror lately, but you look pretty damn human to me."

"But he's all animal, trust me."

Sara craned her neck to look behind her in the direction

the man's voice had come. Her heart sank at the sight of the huge man who'd appeared at their campsite and attacked Josh. "Ugh," she groaned.

Lucien took a step closer and eyed Shara's arms wrapped around her. "Nice to see you again too, Sara." His gaze rose to focus coldly on Shara. "What are you doing?"

Shara inhaled sharply and hesitated. Ever since Lucien had taken over the clan, he had demanded first claim on anything they'd taken from humans. 'Spoils of war,' he called them, as if the Bear People had declared war on the humans instead of simply avoiding them. But this was the first time Lucien had taken something *living*. Shara looked down at the frightened woman, then back up at the huge man towering over him. One corner of Lucien's mouth was drawn up in a faint sneer. Shara swallowed hard. "She was resisting. I was just motivating her."

Lucien's sneer dropped to a full-fledged scowl. "I don't have to remind you that I handle the discipline in this clan, do I? I count on you, Shara. Don't disappoint me."

Shara released Sara from his embrace and turned to drag her again. "I won't, Lucien. I didn't touch her."

"Hey, where are my friends?" Sara said to Lucien. She jumped at the brush of his arm against her shoulder.

"They won't be bothering us anymore."

"What have you done with them?" she cried, trying to keep the imagined horror from her mind. It didn't work. One look at these men told her they wouldn't give a second thought to murder.

Lucien shook his head and smirked "Don't worry your pretty little head about them. Let's just worry about you now. Shall we?"

"What is it you want? No one's going to pay a ransom for me, if that's what you're hoping."

He stared down at her and his smile grew. "Little girl, money is meaningless to me. The only thing that matters in this worthless world is power and control. And I have both."

Cold sweat trickled down the back of her neck. She had no idea where the men were taking her but one thing was certain. They were both crazy, and if she didn't get away soon, she knew with an agonizing certainty that something terrible would happen to her. Her mind raced to find a way to escape them, but she soon realized it was too late. Shara dragged her through a break in the trees toward a dark spot in the side of a hill that loomed before them. She strained to see it through the shadows. The mouth of the cave was barely visible in the gloomy darkness of the thick woods. Another young, naked man stood at the entrance of the cave, apparently keeping guard.

"I'm screwed," she muttered dejectedly to herself.

"Maybe later," Lucien laughed, grabbing her hand out of Shara's grasp.

The man guarding the entrance straightened up as the men approached. "Lucien," he acknowledged.

"Any problems?"

The guard shook his head. "It's been quiet."

"No sign of Marin?"

"No," he laughed confidently. "I guess he doesn't have the guts to fight anymore."

Lucien thrust his face toward the younger man's. "Don't be foolish enough to underestimate him. He'll show up, but it will be on his own terms—under conditions of his choosing. You can count on it. So don't make any mistakes."

The guard's face went red with embarrassment, his voice weak. "I won't."

Sara's attention perked at the big man's words. *Marin.* The name was vaguely familiar, but she couldn't place it. She didn't have time to think about it, when Lucien's hand pushed her ahead into the darkness of the cave. She tumbled to the ground with a shriek and came to rest on top of something soft. The thing beneath her groaned and quivered. She screamed again and crawled backward, her heart thundering in her chest. She'd only gotten a few feet when she bumped into Lucien's legs.

"Aren't you going to say hello to your friend?" he said.

"Wha... what?"

Lucien grabbed her by the neck and forced her closer to the bump lying on the cave floor. "Look familiar?"

"I... what?" Her eyes blurred as they strained to focus in the dim light.

"Take... a... look," Lucien snarled, thrusting her head down.

It took a moment before the prostrate form before her slowly came into view. Two arms clenched together over a bare chest. Tucked beneath them, legs were curled up, drawn tightly in toward the belly. She leaned closer, unable to tear her gaze from the man moaning on the ground. Even in the darkness, she could see the hideous cuts and bruises marring his body.

Lucien stepped around her and jammed his hands under the groaning man's armpits. Lifting him up as if he weighed nothing, he pushed Gareth nearer Sara so she could see his face.

She swooned for a moment and her eyes widened at the familiar face. "Gareth? Is that you?"

Lucien chuckled and dropped Gareth to the ground like an old rag.

She crept closer and swept his filthy hair out of his eyes, hardly able to believe it could be the same man she'd become enchanted by at the museum. "Is it really you, Gareth?"

He was so weak he had to strain to focus his eyes on her. But he knew from her voice that it was Sara, and his heart sank. He couldn't imagine where or how Lucien had found her, or why he'd brought her here. "S... Sara?" he whispered, lacking the strength to talk.

She inched forward to kneel over him. He smelled terrible, as if he'd been in this dank cave for some time, and his body was tinted with dark stains that she thought might be dried blood. "What happened to him?" she hissed to Lucien.

"He disobeyed me. I taught him a lesson."

"*You* did this to him?"

"Yup." The satisfaction in his voice was evident.

"My God," she moaned as she slipped her arms around Gareth's trembling shoulders and cradled him to her. His skin was so cold that the chill permeated her clothes and made her shudder. "It's okay now, Gareth," she whispered, though she knew she was lying. It was obvious that he was in bad shape, and she was in no position to help him. Still, if she could only comfort him...

Lucien snickered, his voice rolling like an echo in the cave. "So, human, how well do you know your friend Gareth?"

She gazed at the swollen face nestled in her lap. His breaths came slowly, painfully from his parched lips, but his half-closed eyes gazed up at her hopefully. She ran her fingertips gently along the line of his jaw and up the side of his boyish face, wanting him to be comforted by her touch. He whimpered softly. "Well enough to know he didn't deserve this." Her gaze rose to settle on Lucien as a hateful stare. "You're a sick bastard."

"Little girl, you haven't seen anything yet." Grabbing Gareth's ankles, he jerked the limp man across the filthy cave floor toward him and yanked him up by his throat. Gareth squeaked in pain but hung limp and helpless. Then reaching around to the rock wall behind him, Lucien grabbed a small silver key from a stony ledge and popped it in the padlock that held the chain around Gareth's neck. The chain dropped to the ground with a heavy thud.

Gareth gasped in a gurgling sigh and shuddered as a full breath of cool air flowed into him for the first time in days.

Sara rose up on her knees in hysterics. "He couldn't even breathe?" she screamed. "You fucker! You sadistic, evil, fucking bastard!"

Lucien just stared at her, amused by her tantrum. "That's not all he couldn't do," he said, interrupting her after a moment. "Watch this." He held Gareth by the back of the neck, half suspended in the air, waiting for what he knew was inevitable.

Gareth's body convulsed as he continued to gulp in huge breaths. The chain had been so tight around his neck that if he had shifted to bear skin he would have choked to death. Being forced to maintain his human body in his battered condition had drained every bit of energy from him and now that he was free, he couldn't hold back any longer. It didn't matter that Sara was watching him. He couldn't have stopped the shift if he'd wanted to.

His torso shook in violent shudders as thick strands of fur burst from every pore of his skin. His nose angled outward as his cheeks widened, and his ears rounded and drifted to the top of his head. He arched downward, his hands grasping for the ground, but claws scraped over the dirt instead of fingernails. He grunted loudly and collapsed on the ground, a quivering cinnamon-colored bear.

Sara's mouth formed an "O," but no voice came out. Her eyes glued to the whimpering creature huddled at her feet. She couldn't move, couldn't breathe, couldn't accept what her eyes had seen. But she had seen it. She'd watched him change from a man to a bear.

Gareth shuddered again and rolled his head to look up. His eyes searched the darkness, wanting to see her and comfort her. He knew she would be terrified of what she'd witnessed, just as he'd terrorized her sister the first time she'd seen him shift. Finally, he glimpsed a flash of white in the darkness, and his eyes settled heavily on her stunned face.

She knew the moment he looked at her. It was those beautiful honey-colored eyes, *his* eyes, that told her what she'd seen was true. The bear's eyes were Gareth's eyes. There was no mistaking it.

"Oh... Lindy..." she moaned, feeling her senses dull. The darkness closed in around her so quickly she didn't even know when she hit the ground.

Chapter Twenty

Shara stared hard at the figure moving quietly through the forest, his dark eyes following the man's quick movements as he made his way toward forest home. He knew well the familiar gait, the confident stride of the one he had always looked up to. "Lucien!" he called over his shoulder. "He's coming."

A slow, growling snarl came from the bear's mouth as he stretched up and shifted into man skin. "Well it's about damn time," he grumbled, stalking across the ground to stand beside his second in command. He shook his head. "Look at him, so cocky and sure of himself. Either he has a very short memory or he's just plain stupid."

Shara looked at Lucien, his eyes narrowed. *Who* was the cocky one? "If there's one thing that Marin *isn't*, it's stupid. I have no doubt that he's got some trick planned for us."

"No matter," he said with a wave of his hand. "I welcome his attempt to reclaim his clan. He won't win." Lucien spun around and charged down the path, more than ready to engage his adversary.

Marin stopped in his tracks as Lucien appeared before him. His breath caught in his throat at the size of the man, at the evil that seemed to eminate from him. Forcing himself to calmness, he took a deep breath and raised his head to stare Lucien in the eyes, seeing only an empty blackness within them. "I've come to force you from this clan."

"Of course you have," Lucien laughed, his voice deep

and resonating with sarcasm. He glanced at Marin's body, noting how the bruises and cuts they'd inflicted had healed. Marin looked strong, well fed. "I see your human bitch has taken care of you. I figured you would send her to fight for you, as well."

"You would be more familiar with that style of fighting than I," Marin snorted.

A sneer curled on Lucien's lips, bringing a wolfish appearance to his face. "I fight my own battles."

"In your mind, perhaps. It's obvious that you need the help of others when it comes to fighting a bear like me. Or have you forgotten how it took four of you to subdue me?"

"Are you issuing a challenge?"

Marin nodded, his dark hair falling in thick waves around his grim face. "You and I... alone. No interference from the others. The winner claims this clan."

"And the loser... dies," Lucien hissed, his sneer growing to a full-fledged grin.

Marin nodded. "Agreed."

Lucien looked around him to gaze at the clan members who had gathered to watch the spectacle. Every face was heavy with worry and dread. Their fear fueled the fire within him, driving his lust for blood and conquest. Swinging his head back toward Marin, he glared with madness flashing in his eyes. "Then let the war begin."

Lindy slipped down the steep, wooded slope, barely able to remain on her feet. She shook so badly the rifle trembled in her arms, but she cradled it to her as tightly as a baby. With the nearing of sunset, the woods grew dark, the shadows deepening as the golden light began to fade. It made walking treacherous and added to the tension already overwhelming her.

Landing at last on flat ground, she walked forward toward the dark opening in the side of the rocky hill and the cave that she knew pierced the earth. *Dear God, let Gareth be alive,* she prayed silently, knowing full well that they may have come too late. She summoned her courage and tightened her grip on the gun.

"Stop," a male voice ordered.

She lurched to a halt, sweat instantly beading on the back of her neck despite the rapidly falling temperature.

A large figure walked out of the shadow of the cave and stepped toward her. It was Balak, one of the younger he-bears of the clan, and one that Lena had said still supported Lucien.

He tipped his head up and glared at her from under hooded eyelids. "I thought I smelled human." His voice bore disgust. "Lucien said you would come."

Lindy tried to lick her parched lips but found that her mouth had gone completely dry. Balak was a big man, a powerful man, and he obviously had no love for her. She cleared her throat and took in a trembling breath. "Why did you betray Marin?"

Balak shook his head as he crossed his arms over his chest. "Stay out of this, woman. It's none of your business."

"I disagree, Balak. I'm the Protector of this clan. As I recall, I heard your voice say 'aye' when your kin voted to accept me in that role."

He snorted, his face full of contempt. "Marin deceived us. He tricked us into accepting you. We have *never* befriended humans. When he met you, he betrayed *us.*"

"You're wrong. Bear People and Protectors were friends once. They looked out for each other, cared for each other. Lucien is the one who's tricking you, Balak. He lied about everything, even about his own clan. His kin weren't killed by humans but by..."

"SHUT-UP!" Balak warned "You don't know anything about us. Lucien said..."

"Lucien's full of shit!" Lindy hissed back, stepping closer as her grip tightened on the gun.

Balak eyed the rifle warily and hunched his shoulders, tensing himself. "I know why you're here. You want Gareth. But that gun isn't going to help you get him."

Lindy shook her head, her expression softening for a moment. "I don't want to hurt you, Balak. I have nothing against you. But Gareth didn't deserve what Lucien did to him, and I'm going to get him out of here."

"He deserved everything he got," Balak spat, taking a step closer to Lindy.

"What has Lucien done to you?" she whispered, hardly able to believe that the quiet young he-bear had turned so cold-hearted. "Look what he's done to your clan. How many of you have died because of him? Do you want to be next?" But she never heard the answer as his powerful body slammed into hers. She hit the ground, smacking her head on the forest floor. The rifle flew from her hands and disappeared in the brush.

"The only one who is going to die is you, Protector," he seethed. His large hands clenched around her neck, tightening their hold on her tender throat. Thumbs squeezing, the cords in his neck throbbing with his power, Balak straddled her body and stared down at her terror stricken face.

Lindy struggled beneath him, but his weight was too much for her. No air remained in her lungs and stars flashed before her eyes as she pummeled franticly against his chest, but his grip on her neck never loosened. She gasped, begging for air.

Balak suddenly thrust his shoulders up and barked out a startled yelp. His hands released from Lindy's throat and rose to his own neck. Something warm and sticky coated his fingers. He looked down, saw the red dripping from his hand and running thick down the side of his body. Blood poured from the gash in his neck, spurting out of his jugular with each beat of his heart. Unable to make sense of it, he gazed slowly behind him and saw the bear. Her chocolate brown fur dripped with his blood, her gnashing jaws were bathed in it.

"L... Lena?" He struggled to get the word out. Blood clogged his throat; dark fog rapidly filled his vision as a cold weight settled over his body. His eyes still open to the sight of his attacker, Balak fell to his side as his last breath bubbled from his body with a final surge of blood.

Lena arched slowly into man skin and shuddered with revulsion. She couldn't take her eyes off the man's body, off the huge pool of red still flowing from the wound in his neck. The wound that she had inflicted. Giving a horrified cry, she slammed her trembling hands over her face. "I killed him."

Lindy struggled to her feet and staggered over to the sobbing woman. Despite the vicious throbbing in her throat, she knew she had to calm Lena and finish what they had come for before they were discovered. She slipped her arm around the woman's trembling shoulders. "It had to be done," she whispered, her voice raspy with pain. "He would have killed us both. Now let's get Gareth and get out of here. Where are the bolt cutters?"

Lena gnawed on her lower lip and nodded toward the bushes behind her. Lindy grabbed the heavy tool, retrieved her gun from the other bushes, and pulled Lena by the hand toward the cave. Together they stepped into the darkness.

"Gareth?" Lindy called softly. Fear knotted her stomach at the possibility that another guard might await them deeper in the cave. She squinted, forcing her eyes to scan the dark interior, but saw nothing. Glancing lower, she searched the damp floor for Gareth. "Dammit, where are you?"

A weak moan drifted from the floor to her left. Releasing Lena's hand, Lindy knelt down and crept forward, searching with her outstretched hand. Her fingers swept across something soft, something icy cold. "Gareth?"

He groaned again, a pitiful cry like an orphaned cub. It cut right to Lena's heart and she knelt down beside him and brushed her hands gently over his trembling furred shoulders.

"You're freezing," she said, her voice a shocked whisper. "We've come to take you to safety."

Gareth raised his head and looked from one woman to the other. "You came."

"What did he say?" Lindy asked.

"He's glad we came."

"I promised you, Gareth. We'll take you back to my cabin where you'll be safe. But we need to get going. If Lucien finds us here he'll kill all of us," Lindy said. She lugged the bolt cutters toward Gareth and searched for the chain that had held him to the cave floor.

"He took the chain off," Gareth said, his bear voice quivering and so weak it was barely audible. With a great grunt of effort, he rolled onto his stomach.

Lena translated again. "He said Lucien removed the chain."

"Well thank Heaven for small miracles," Lindy sighed. "Can you stand?"

Gareth shook his head no, then slumped over to the side, landing limply against Lena.

"Oh great, now how are we going to move him?"

"He'll have to shift to man skin so I can carry him. Gareth, listen to me. You must shift so that you'll fit on my back."

Groaning his understanding, Gareth wobbled unsteadily and allowed the women to help him to his feet. His body trembled with the exertion and pain, but he managed to complete the shift.

Lena pushed him against the wall of the cave. "Once I shift, you'll have to lift him onto my back."

"Are you sure you can do this?"

Lena shot her an irritated look. "Do we have a choice? It won't feel good on my back, but I don't see any other way to do it."

Seeing her point, Lindy nodded and sighed. "Ok. Go ahead."

Breathing deeply to prepare herself, Lena rounded her back and reached both hands to the ground. Within moments, her human skin yielded to chocolate fur, her fingernails lengthening into sharp, curved claws. Then lowering her heavy body to the ground, she rolled her brown eyes at Lindy to signal that she was ready.

Lindy stood and reached her arms down around Gareth, who had slipped down against the cold wall. Every rib seemed to protrude from his body. Swollen bumps of bruised flesh sank beneath her fingers as she clenched her hands together behind his back and yanked him up. He moaned with each movement, and though she did her best to be careful with him, it was a struggle to maneuver his dead weight onto Lena's back. Finally, after several minutes of struggle, his limp body fell forward and crashed down on her furry back.

"Ooomph," Lena groaned as Gareth's weight settled on her.

Lindy watched sympathetically as Lena forced herself to her feet. "You ok?" The bear nodded her head in the affirmative. "Let's go then. I'm ready to get the hell out of here."

Marin circled cautiously around Lucien, waiting for him to make the first attack. His paws thumped heavily on the leafy forest floor, almost stomping with anticipation. *Patience*, he warned himself. *Let him make the first mistake.*

The larger bruin grinned widely, exposing his large white canines. Even in the dimming light, they were impressive. "Come on, little bear," Lucien taunted.

Marin laughed. "I may be smaller than you, but my brain is bigger."

Snickers rose from the bears gathered in a circle around them. Those rooting for Marin chuffed loudly, letting him know that their support was now behind him. The rest, the ones with Lucien's lies still firmly tangled in their minds, snorted their support of Lucien.

"I know what happened to your clan, Lucien," Marin

snarled. "You killed them, tore them apart with your own claws."

"Really? And just where did you get this information?"

Marin circled around, waiting for an opportunity to attack, biding his time. "I have ways. Don't you know that evil always comes back to haunt you? You can't keep something like that hidden."

Lucien smirked and shook his head, sending a spray of saliva around himself. "I suppose not, when you have your human lovers spying on me. Not that it matters anymore."

"Why did you do it? Why kill your own kin?"

The grin faded from his face as Lucien's eyes flashed with anger. "They deserved it. All I wanted was a little control, a few changes in the way we did things. But they fought me, refused me every fucking thing I desired. I got tired of their resistance. It was time to find a more progressive clan, people who would be more *receptive* to my ideas."

"You mean people you could take advantage of."

"Your perception, not mine."

Marin stood still and glared at his opponent. "You're not taking my clan, Lucien. Not my kin. I won't let you destroy us the way you did your own people. I'll die before I'll let you waste any more lives."

The grin returned to Lucien's face. "That's my hope, Marin. There's nothing I'd like more than to see you die." Without warning, he charged and rammed Marin straight on. Their massive shaggy heads butted with a crack that made everyone cringe. Tiny rivulets of blood trickled from Marin's nose as he returned the charge and hit Lucien squarely in the side.

The force of the blow threw Lucien off balance. He stumbled, recovered and charged forward once again, aiming for Marin's face. At the last moment, he ducked and swept in underneath Marin's chest. Tossing his huge head with a massive thrust, Marin flew backward and crashed to the ground. The air rushed from his lungs as he lay momentarily stunned.

Lucien seized the opportunity and hurled his huge body on top of the prostrate bear. Jaws snapping, spittle spraying around him, Lucien was possessed. His dark, curved claws slashed into Marin's chest as thick tufts of ebony fur flew from the downed bear's body.

"Get up, Marin!" Arlin screamed. He had watched his Guardian fight more battles than he could count, but Marin had never faced an opponent like Lucien. More than anything, he wanted Marin to kill the son of a bitch and restore peace to what remained of their ravaged clan. As long as Lucien lived, the clan was doomed.

Despite the searing pain raging through his chest, Marin's mind raced to find a weakness in Lucien's attack. Finally seeing his chance, he lunged upward to grab Lucien's front leg in his mouth and jerked his head, tearing off a huge hunk of bloody flesh. Tendons and muscles popped with a loud *rip.* Lucien roared and staggered back, giving Marin time to roll out from under him and back away.

Lucien staggered backward two steps and stared down at his wounded limb. "You've scarred me," he growled, his anger rising to match the higher pitch of his startled voice.

"Come closer and I'll make it a matched set," Marin offered, wiping blood from his face with his paw.

Lucien charged again and pummeled Marin in his side, sending him crashing to the ground. Refusing to be pinned down, Marin deftly rolled over and struggled back onto his feet. His eyes were drawn to a ray of fading sunlight that suddenly penetrated the trees and fell upon Lucien, illuminating his fur. The tips of the coarse hairs glowed an eerie blood red, seeming to smolder against the black fur like embers. In the twilight it looked positively evil.

The clan members stepped back simultaneously, spooked by the unnatural glow of Lucien's fur.

"Freak," someone muttered.

Lucien spun around, his wounded arm dangling, and glared at those behind him. His lips drew back in a hideous snarl. "Shara," he growled to the young he-bear. "Help me finish this."

Shara blinked but remained motionless.

"SHARA!" Lucien roared. "Come here and join me in ending this half-breed bastard's misery."

The younger bear moved slowly forward, reluctant to get involved in their challenge.

One of the she-bears tried to pull him back. "It's forbidden for another to involve himself in a challenge," she reminded him.

"That was an order," Lucien screamed. "Kill him!"

Without another thought, Shara lumbered toward Marin, his mouth open to show his own canines. He took three steps and yanked backward abruptly as a bullet whizzed by his head.

As one, the bears turned to look for the source of the bullet. Just outside their circle, a young man stood with his rifle raised in readiness to shoot again. A long lock of ebony hair curled across his shoulder and down the front of his jacket.

"You all right, Marin?" he asked, never taking his dark eyes off the bears before him.

Marin arched painfully upright and shifted back into man skin. He looked down at the bright stripes of torn flesh covering his chest and took a quivering breath before answering. "I'll survive."

"Should I shoot him?" Johnny asked. His finger twitched in the trigger.

Marin looked at Shara, who stood motionless with his lower jaw dropped in shock. The young bear man had been in the crosshairs of a rifle once before and clearly remembered the gaping hole the bullet had torn in the chest of his beloved elder, Thoren. He looked terrified. Marin knew it would be so easy to let the human finish it here and now. At least there would be one less rebel he would have to deal with.

The clan stood stunned and motionless while they waited for Marin to respond.

He looked slowly from one face to another, reliving the agony of how they had betrayed him. His own kin, those he had grown up with, protected, loved. He didn't want to care about them anymore, or worry what they thought of him, but he couldn't help it. It was in his nature to lead them, to be strong for them. To bring honor among them.

Finally shaking his head, Marin looked back at Johnny. "No," he said softly. "This is for us to settle."

Johnny lowered the gun and watched silently as Marin raised his head to address his kin. "Do you not see how Lucien has played you for fools? He has no honor. He cares nothing for you–other than to take what he can from you. Though you drove me out of our family, I came back because I couldn't stand by and watch him kill you one by one. I was your Guardian once; and I will proudly be your Guardian again, if that is your wish. But you must decide if you will stand with me... or with Lucien."

Arlin broke the dead silence with a shrill cry.

"What?" Marin demanded.

He pointed to the blood-stained patch of ground behind Marin. "Look," he said. "Lucien is gone."

Chapter Twenty-One

Lindy wiped the cloth gently over the wounds slashed in Marin's chest. They were deep and wide, clear evidence of the power and ferocity of Lucien's temper. Marin winced as the cloth wiped away tiny pieces of dirt and fur that had found their way inside the tears in his flesh.

"I know this hurts, Marin, but you need stitches. They can fix you up at the ER and as long as you stay in man skin, no one will know what you are."

"I can't risk it, you know that," he snarled, angry less from the pain than the fact that Lucien had slipped away from him. "I'll heal. I always do."

She grew quiet, reeling from the venom in his voice.

Marin gazed at her face, at the sadness suddenly etched around her eyes, and knew that his words and tone of voice had wounded her. "I shouldn't direct my anger at you, Lindy, but it's difficult to control the rage I feel right now. He was right there, badly wounded, and I let him get away. It could have been finished by now if I had just paid more attention."

"You're not psychic. You didn't know that he'd slink away like the coward he is. I just thank God that we thought to have Johnny back you up. I hate to think what could've happened if he hadn't been there."

Marin raised his hand and held it gently over her hand as she held the cloth to his chest. His fingers squeezed hers gently as a smile came over his face. "I have you to thank for that. At the time I didn't think so, but your suggestion to have him accompany us to forest home was an excellent idea. Once again, you have saved my life."

"No," she shook her head, "Johnny saved your life. We owe him."

Across the room, Gunther perked up his ears and whined softly, then quickly jumped to his feet. He dashed to the kitchen window and skidded to a stop to look out at a car that had pulled up in the driveway.

Lindy set down the cloth and walked over beside him to peer out the window. In the dim glow of the porch light, she could barely make out the red bar light on the top of the vehicle. Her heart skipped a beat. "It's the Sheriff. Get into the guestroom now!" She swung around and motioned franticly for Marin to hurry. "And keep the others quiet." When he had disappeared into the other room, she pulled the dog aside and went to the door just as a knock echoed from the outside. She opened the door slowly.

"Linda Anderson?"

"Yes?"

The man pulled the brim of his dark blue cap up so he could see her better. "I'm Sheriff Caldwell. I'm here about your sister. May I come in?"

Lindy froze momentarily, trying to come up with an excuse to keep him out. With four Bearwalkers hidden in her guestroom, the last thing she needed was the police poking around. But she couldn't imagine which sister he wanted to speak to her about, or why. "Can we talk here?" she stammered. "I... I have a dog that's rather... unfriendly."

He peeked in the doorway, seeming not the least deterred by Gunther sitting on the kitchen floor beside his mistress. "Ma'am, it's a little cold out here, if you don't mind. Maybe you could put the dog in another room for a few minutes if you're concerned about him."

"Uh, ok. Sure." Lindy swallowed hard and stepped back, allowing the Sheriff to step inside the kitchen. She grabbed Gunther by the collar and guided him through the house to her bedroom. "Stay here, buddy," she whispered before returning to the kitchen. "You said you were here about my sister?" she asked as she entered the room.

The Sheriff removed his cap and turned to face her. "Do you have a sister by the name of Sara Tomison?"

Lindy nodded. "Yes, she's my younger sister."

"When was the last time you saw her?"

"Gosh, a month and a half, two months maybe. She's away at college."

The Sheriff bowed his head, wondering how to phrase his next words so they'd come out gently. When he looked up at her again, his expression was kind but serious. "We believe that your sister has been kidnapped."

Lindy stood frozen momentarily before slowly sinking down in the kitchen chair behind her. "I don't understand."

"Do you know a woman by the name of Nikki Carlson?"

"Nikki? My sister's roommate is named Nikki."

"Right. Miss Carlson and her boyfriend, a Josh Hardin, were picked up by some locals on Route 18. They were roughed up pretty badly, scared to death. They begged for a ride to my office. The folks brought them in and that's when they reported that Miss Tomison, your sister, had been kidnapped."

Lindy shook her head, floundering in shock and confusion. "But Route Eighteen runs the perimeter of the forest, *this* national forest right outside my door. What were they doing here?"

"They said they were on a camping trip, because they had a long weekend and wanted to get off campus for a few days. It was just the three of them, until they got to their campsite where three men attacked them."

"Attacked them? Why? Are they hurt?"

"Like I said, they were roughed up a bit, some scrapes and bruises, that kind of thing. Mr Hardin appears to have put up a good fight, but he'll be ok. Miss Carlson wasn't harmed. As for why they were attacked, we don't know.

What we do know is that one of the men took off with your sister and disappeared in the forest."

Lindy put her hands up to her head and tried to keep the tears from coming, but she couldn't. "My God, Sara," she cried. "What do we do?"

The Sheriff spoke confidently, trying to soothe her. "I've got a search party out right now. Your sister's room-mate gave us some good leads to pursue, so we should be on their trail soon. We'll do everything in our power to find her, Mrs. Anderson. But I need to ask you, are you aware of anyone that she felt threatened by? Anyone at school or elsewhere that she had a disagreement with? Was anyone upset with her for any reason?"

Lindy shook her head and brushed the loose strands of blonde hair from her eyes. "Not that I know of. Sara is so easy going that everyone likes her. I never heard her say that she'd had a fight with anyone or that she thought someone didn't like her. I just can't believe that something like this could happen."

Sheriff Caldwell chewed his lip for a moment, then gave her a gentle smile. "Well, I want you to give me a call at my office if you think of anything that might help us. But for now, just be assured that we're doing everything we can. We'll be in touch with you as information becomes available. Good night, Mrs. Anderson." He turned to leave.

"Sheriff, wait," she said. When he had turned back toward her, she gazed up into his eyes. "Did Nikki and Josh get a good look at the men? Were they able to describe them?"

"Yes. Two of the men were young, twenty-ish, good-looking, and the other was older. It was the older one that really spooked them. They said he was a huge man, and that he ordered the others around. And believe it or not, none of them were wearing clothes. Nudists of some kind, I suppose. I've been on this job for twenty-five years, and that's a new one for me."

Lindy couldn't speak, feeling like the life had been

sucked right out of her. Forcing herself to stand, she walked with him to the door. Her legs trembled so hard she wondered if they'd even support her. "Thank you, Sheriff," she mumbled as she closed the door behind him. When he was gone, she sank to the floor and cried.

Lena looked up from the edge of the bed, a glass of water poised in one hand and Notch tucked against her other side. Marin stood on the opposite side of the bed, and Gareth lay stretched out on the mattress between them. They looked up simultaneously when Lindy entered the room.

Marin gasped, shocked by the ghostly whiteness of Lindy's face. Her cheeks were mottled with tears. "What is it?" he asked, rushing to her side.

Lindy sank into his arms, oblivious to his pain as her shirt slipped across his bleeding wounds. "My sister, the one you met at the museum... she's missing. Kidnapped by three men right here in the forest. They took her. Three men took her."

Marin stroked her head gently, wanting desperately to ease her anguish. She shuddered against him, her skin cold to his touch. "I'm sure the Sheriff will find her. They handle things like this all the time, do they not?"

Stifling her sobs so that she could speak coherently, Lindy pushed herself back to look up at the handsome face that gave her such comfort. "You don't understand, Marin. The men that took her... they weren't wearing any clothes. One was a huge man... oh God, it had to be Lucien."

Gareth shuddered in the bed as the memory suddenly raged into his mind. *Sara!* He barely had the strength to speak but he had to let Lindy know. After she risked her own life to save him, he could do no less. "Lindy..."

She sniffled softly and turned to look down at him. It was still a shock to see the terrible condition he was in. "Gareth, you're awake." She sat down beside him and swept her hand gently across his forehead.

"Lindy, listen to me. I saw her. I saw Sara." He stopped to gasp in a breath as beads of sweat shimmered on his brow. The struggle to talk, to breathe, was an immense strain on his damaged body, but his will forced him on. "Lucien and Shara brought her to forest home. They brought her to the cave and made her watch when I shifted to bear form."

Lindy leaned lower to mop the sweat from his face. She studied his eyes, how the honey brown seemed to deepen with fear. "Was she hurt, Gareth? Did Lucien hurt her?" Panic rose in her voice at the thought of the bastard and his treatment of Lena.

"No, I don't think so," he said, shaking his head as his eyelids closed. "It was so dark in there I couldn't see much, but she seemed strong. She talked back to him, insulted him... feisty. Like you."

Marin chuckled softly at the apt comparison as his hands came down to squeeze Lindy's shoulders lovingly. "Lucien takes great pleasure from seeing others' revulsion. He thrives on terrorizing and intimidating those around him. I've rarely seen someone behave in this manner and can't imagine what happened to make him that way, but there's no time to worry about that now. We must find Sara and bring her back."

Lena scooped Notch into her arms and rose from the bed to stand beside Marin. She looked up at him, her jaw clenched with determination. "I'll help you, Marin, in any way that I can be of use to you. I'd like nothing better than to see that animal destroyed."

He smiled but shook his head. "I appreciate your support, but you've been through enough. You have Notch to take care of, as well as Mara's cub. This clan needs no more orphans. Besides, you took good care of me after I lost Terra, and I hope that you'll tend to Gareth while Lindy and I are gone."

Lena bowed her head in affirmation. "Of course, I'll care for him."

Marin bent down to bring himself closer to Gareth.

"Is there anything you can tell us that might help us find him?"

Gareth was silent as he turned his face toward the Guardian. The pain wracking his body was severe, but the pain in his heart when he looked at Marin was even worse. If he could only go back in time and undo the evil he had done to his friend, he gladly would, but there was no way to change the past now. All he could do was hope that someday Marin would forgive him. Unable to bear Marin's gaze any longer, he looked away and stared out the bedroom window.

"Gareth?" Lindy prompted, brushing her hand through his matted hair.

"He's fascinated with human things. Tools, personal items. That's where he got the chain and the stake to confine me in the cave. Attacking humans and stealing their things gives him a thrill. He has no fear of approaching their campsites; in fact, he spent a lot of time mapping out the buildings in forest home. I think he planned to check them out and see what else he could steal."

"What does he do with all the things he takes?" Lindy asked, mystified by the bear man's strange behavior.

"That's the weird thing," Gareth said, stopping again to shudder and force down the pain throbbing in his broken ribs. "He doesn't do anything with it. It's like he wants all this stuff and then doesn't know what to do with it. He acts like..."

Marin moved closer. "Like what?"

"Like he wants to be... human."

No one made a sound. The confusion, the bewilderment was almost palpable as they looked from one to the other.

Finally Lena clutched Notch closer to her breast and shook her head. "Why would anyone *want* to be human?"

Marin rose and turned to step away from the bed, bumping Lindy softly in the shoulder as he passed. The corners of his mouth were turned up in a sly smile. "Why indeed," he whispered to her, his eyes glowing.

She coughed into her hand, trying to hide the grin on her face. Then her expression quickly turned serious again as thoughts of Sara swarmed back into her mind. "We need to get going. I'll start packing." She left the room with Lena following her out.

"Marin," Gareth said.

He stopped in the doorway and looked back at Gareth without speaking.

Gareth forced himself to look Marin in the eyes. "I don't blame you for hating me, and I know that you want nothing to do with me now. Just know that I'm sorry for what I did to you, and I hope you find Lucien. I want you to kill him, Marin. Do it for our clan. Do it for me."

Marin stared at him, unable to overcome the memory of Gareth's betrayal. Finally, he turned and walked out without saying a word.

Chapter Twenty-Two

Jack swept the broom haphazardly around the floor of the trading post, missing half the dustballs and cobwebs that covered the dingy wood. Now that old age had stolen the vision from his one remaining eye, he knew that his housekeeping was sorely lacking, but the attempt at least made him feel useful. At ninety-two, there wasn't much in life anymore that made him feel that way. He banged the broom against a chair leg and cursed as the front door squeaked open. "Johnny?"

"Hey," the younger man said as he came in and closed the door behind him. Jack set the broom handle up against the wall and wandered to the faded chairs perched in the middle of the room. Feeling with his hands, he found the stuffed armchair that was his own and wearily sat down in it. A wisp of snow white hair drifted down across his wrinkled forehead while he tried to make himself comfortable. There wasn't a bone in his body that didn't ache anymore. "What happened?" he asked as he settled in.

Johnny hung his rifle in a rack on the wall and pulled a chair up alongside his uncle. "You shouldn't be sweeping, Old Man," he said, sitting down. "You might hurt yourself."

Jack snorted with a wave of his hand. "Pulling a muscle would be the highlight of my day. Now tell me what happened."

Smiling despite himself, Johnny leaned back and stretched his legs out before him. As much as it was a thrill to see the Bear People, it was always a relief to get safely home again. He exhaled loudly. "She was right, Uncle. The one they call Lucien couldn't be trusted to fight fair. Even though Marin issued a formal challenge, which other clan members are bound by honor

to observe only, Lucien called for his second in command to join him in the fight. If I hadn't been there, Marin would have been in trouble."

Jack nodded knowingly, his thin lips drawn into a tight grimace. "I thought as much. It's the same as happened when my Grandfather told the story."

"What story is that?"

"Don't you remember when the Guardian and Protector came here to ask about Lucien? I told them what I'd heard my Grandfather say about his dealings with a rogue when he was the clan's Protector."

"As I recall, you said that the clan dealt with him, but you didn't know how." Johnny grew quiet, his eyebrows raising suspiciously. "But you knew more than you told... you withheld information from them. And you told me that Marin was dangerous to Lindy. You want to tell me about that?"

Jack lowered his head and thought briefly, searching back over the years for the information that was of such importance now. After a long pause, he raised his head and nodded.

"I know what happened to turn that Bearwalker rogue. I heard my father and grandfather speak of it; but I couldn't tell Marin, not with so much stress on him right now. He must kill Lucien before he learns of this other."

Johnny leaned forward in his chair, his fingers resting on the knees of his jeans. "What is it? What turned the bear into a rogue?"

"When the Bearwalkers first withdrew into this forest, back in the day when there was no line between dreaming and waking, some of them felt great pain at separating from their human friends. Suddenly they were alone, isolated. They were torn between the necessities of keeping their kind safe and longing for companionship with those they had known for so long. Even though some humans tormented them, there were many others who still treated them kindly; and it was those that they missed. Once in a while, a human came into their forest, wandered into their territory, and as the Bearwalkers watched them they were reminded of what they had given up. From time to time, a Bear Person even saved a human who had fallen into some kind of trouble in the woods. Most of the Bear People handled these occasional run-ins with the humans well. But there was one who didn't."

Johnny sat motionless, spellbound by this long unspoken knowledge pouring from his Uncle's lips. "What happened?"

"That one... he was the one that turned rogue. Something happened to make him lose all reason. His mind snapped. He no longer obeyed the rules of his clan—no longer listened to the reasoning of his own people. It seemed that the only thing that mattered to him was getting what he wanted, and he let no one stand in his way. The clan tried to talk to him, convince him of his error, but he refused to listen. He became wild, uncontrollable, even killing some of his own kin. In the end, there was nothing they could do but kill him."

"I don't understand, Uncle. How could a run-in with a human cause such a turn in his behavior? Was he possessed by an evil spirit?"

"They called him 'the Bear with no Heart', the 'Devil Bear', but I think they were wrong. He did have a heart, but it led him astray when he fell in love with a human. She became his only concern, his whole world, much to the alarm of his clan. When she was taken from him, that was when his mind was lost and he went rogue."

"And that's why the clan didn't want Grandfather to help them destroy him, because it was a human that had started the whole mess?"

"Yes."

A rush of air came from the young man's mouth as he leaned back in the chair and swept his fingers through his long black hair. He was quiet for a moment before his forehead wrinkled with confusion again. "But what about Marin? Why did you say he was a danger to Lindy?"

Now Jack was the one who leaned forward, agitated and on edge. "Don't you see, boy? The story is replaying all over again."

Johnny shook his head in denial. "Because Marin is with a human woman you think that he'll lose his mind and turn rogue? Uncle, Lucien is the one who's crazy. *He's* the one we need to worry about."

"True, Lucien is a rogue. He must have had some dealings with a human that drove him to madness. But he isn't the *only* one we should fear. Marin has fallen in love with Lindy, isn't that obvious?"

"Yes, but he's no more a lunatic than I am. Why would loving her lead him to madness? He's the Guardian, he's strong."

"So was the rogue of my grandfather's day."

Johnny opened his mouth to speak and abruptly stopped as everything began to fall into place in his mind. "That rogue was a Guardian?"

Jack nodded, reluctant to speak further.

A fearful expression came over the younger man's face, but he had to know, had to be sure. "Tell me who it was, Uncle. Tell me the name of the rogue they killed."

Jack's voice quivered when at last he spoke. "It was Marowin. Marin's great-grandfather."

"Oh shit..." Johnny was stopped by a knock at the door. He rose and shuffled across the room, dragging his legs as though they were filled with lead. The shock of Jack's admission had taken the wind right out of him. Still shaking his head in disbelief, he opened the door and looked out at the tall man leaning casually against the doorjamb.

The man dipped his head in greeting and grinned.

"Evening, friend. Lucien has come calling."

Chapter Twenty-Three

Lindy laid out Marin's clothes on the bed, along with his heavy jacket and a cap. Next to these she placed a butcher knife, the meat cleaver and a pocket knife, though they seemed so inefficient for the job they had to do. *I should have bought another gun*, she admonished herself, remembering too well the strength and ferocity of the Bear People who had attacked them in her home.

Marin opened the door and walked in, his eyes immediately drawn to the items on the bed. His lips drew tighter in a grimace as he stopped next to Lindy and turned her to face him.

Tendrils of her golden hair had fallen free from the rubber band at the nape of her neck and begged for his hands to sweep them back from her lovely face. He touched one softly with the knuckle of his first finger and then lowered his hand to his side, afraid that if he touched her too much, he would delay their going. And that, they could not afford.

"Can you think of anything else we should bring?" she asked, smiling at his gentleness.

"Just bring your rifle and these weapons. I won't need the clothes."

Lindy uttered a soft snort. "I know you're a macho guy but it's about forty degrees out there, and I really don't think you want to be a Popsicle, do you? Haven't you had enough of that?"

"I'll be warm enough."

She opened her mouth to contradict him when his meaning hit her. A disappointed breath slipped from her throat. "You're going in bear form, aren't you?"

He nodded, bending to pick up one of the knives and finger it carefully as he tested the sharpness of the blade. "With these wounds, it's too great of a strain on my body to maintain human form. I can travel faster and conserve more energy as a bear than as a man. And you know as well as I do that I'll need every bit of strength possible when I encounter Lucien."

"I suppose you're right. I just hate not being able to communicate with you."

He nodded softly, forcing a smile to his tense face as he replaced the knife on the mattress. "Someday I'll teach you my language. But for now, just remember that I can still understand you when I'm in bear skin; and if I need to tell you something important, I'll shift for you. Ok?"

"Ok. What about the weapons?"

"You'll have to carry the knives in your backpack."

A protest came immediately to her mind. "But that leaves you with nothing."

"I wouldn't say that. I'll have the best Protector in the world by my side." Unable to stop himself, he swept his arms around her and pulled her tightly against him, ignoring the painful scrape of her clothes across his wounds. She lifted her head, and his mouth captured hers to kiss her lips with the passion that was still surprising to him. It amazed him how, after hating humans all these years, he could love this single one so dearly. But time was running short, and every minute wasted meant that Lucien and his captive were probably moving farther away. Reluctantly pushing her back, Marin turned and nodded toward the door. "Let's get going."

Darkness fell deeply over the wilderness on late autumn nights such as this. Even the light of moon and stars was obscured by a ceiling of heavy clouds that threatened to free a blanket of snow. Marin looked up and sniffed the biting, moisture-laden air, his black muzzle quivering at the scent of the coming snowfall. It was a bad omen and one he had hoped Mother Earth would postpone as long as possible. Over the long days he had spent in Lindy's company, sometimes wandering her house by himself when she left on an errand, he had wondered how she would react if hibernation sent him to sleep. The thought had been so painful he had tried not to think about it, but it was impossible. He and Lindy were a 'couple' now, sharing daily life in a routine that he had readily come to accept and which she obviously enjoyed. And though he felt more secure that she had accepted his bear nature and what it meant, he doubted that she had even considered the possibility that he might sleep through half of their time together.

Stop it, Marin, he warned himself. *This is not the time to burden your senses with thoughts like these.*

Lindy reached down and tangled her fingers in the thick, black fur of his shoulder. It felt so much like the heavy black hair that framed his masculine human face, reminded her of the many nights they had held each other and explored every part of the other's body in curious and loving fascination. It was impossible to mentally separate the man from the bear, because the two were so entwined. There was nothing about him that she didn't love and someday, she swore to herself, someday she would find the courage to tell him how much she loved him.

Marin swung his massive head to look up at her as she walked beside him, noticing how she struggled to keep up with his quick gait. He had to give her credit, she was every bit as tenacious and determined as he was, not to mention equally stubborn. He smiled to himself and turned his nose back toward the ground.

Lucien's trail was strong on the forest floor, mingling vividly with the scents of his accomplice Shara and the human woman they dragged with them. Marin's astute senses noted every scrape in the compacted carpet of dead needles where Sara had dug the toes of her shoes in, resisting as forcefully as she could. He could visualize her terror at being overwhelmed by a creature such as Lucien—it would be the same look he had seen on Lindy's face the first time he had attacked her that day in the forest. For a moment, a stab of remorse and guilt ached in his heart at the memory of the torment he'd put Lindy through. How on earth could she have forgiven him for such treatment? And yet she had, never once throwing it in his face that he had wanted to kill her on more than one occasion. Again, the capabilities of the human spirit amazed him. Had his great-grandmother been such a human? Would he have found her to be similar to the very woman he now loved?

Shaking his head, Marin growled at himself to keep his mind on task. Thinking it was perhaps time for a break, he stopped, arched his back and shifted silently into man skin.

Lindy paused beside him to watch the transformation, her blue eyes wide with wonder.

"That is so cool," she said, a huge smile lighting her face. "I could watch you do that a million times and never tire of it."

Marin laughed softly and pulled her to him for a quick hug. "Warm me, woman," he demanded playfully, snuggling her body against him. The temperature was rapidly dropping, and he only had minutes to remain in man skin before the cold would force him back into his fur.

"Are we getting close?" she asked, burrowing her chin in the valley between his shoulder and neck."

"Yes. They seem to be moving slower now... I think your sister is tiring and falling behind."

"Do you have any idea where they're going?"

"There are only a couple of buildings on this side of the forest. The path they're on could take them to either one, but right now it's impossible to predict which way they'll turn."

Lindy shuddered, not from the cold but from the thought of her little sister in the company of two creatures who had proven their complete lack of conscience. She and Marin had to find them before anything happened to Sara. "Here," she said, backing away. She reached into her backpack and withdrew a canteen. "Drink some water, and then we'll get going again."

Marin drank down a long draught before handing the canteen back to her. Goosebumps were beginning to mar his olive skin. "You're doing a good job keeping up with me, Lind." He shot her an affectionate smile.

"She's my sister. I can't let her down." She stashed the canteen away and watched Marin as he reversed the process and returned to bear form. He set off again, crashing heavily and quickly through the underbrush, while she followed close behind. His dark form merged so fully with the darkness of the forest that if she became separated from him, she knew she'd never find him again. She surged ahead and reclamped her fingers in his fur for security.

For hours they traveled the woods, picking their way cautiously over downed limbs and rotting logs. Lindy's legs ached so badly from the cold and strain that she couldn't imagine how Marin must be feeling with the wounds gaping in his chest. She could only pray that his strength held out until they could rescue Sara and end the clan's problem with Lucien and Shara once and for all. Then she would take Marin home, care for his injuries and resume their life together. Fate had indeed brought some strange twists into her life since the day she'd moved into the little log cabin and sworn off men forever.

Marin stopped abruptly and swerved to block her way. Lindy crashed awkwardly into his side, almost tumbling over his broad furry back. "Jeez, give me some warning next time," she groaned, readjusting the pack on her back.

A low rumble slipped from Marin's throat. The ominous sound of it made Lindy gaze down at him. His eyes were focused on something beyond them, his concentration so intense that he didn't even notice her looking at him. Following the path of his gaze, she peered ahead through the trees to search for the object of his interest. Yellow lights burned inside the windows of an old building just ahead.

He had found the place where Lucien had taken Sara.

"Oh no, not here," she whispered, her trembling hand again reaching down to Marin for support. "Not Jack's trading post."

Chapter Twenty-Four

Lucien held Johnny tightly around the throat with his good arm, the crook of his elbow pulling so snug that the younger man could only gasp in small breaths of air. Johnny flailed his arms, but Lucien was just too strong. "Calm down, human," Lucien smirked, watching Sara's reaction from the corner of his eye. "I don't plan to kill you... yet. Now hold still."

Johnny didn't have the strength to fight anymore. He had struggled with the bear man from the moment Lucien had forced his way into their home, with no success. Following Lucien's command, he went limp and still until the arm strangling him loosened just enough for him to gasp in a big breath. The feel of cool fresh air rushing into his lungs was one he was beginning to think he'd never experience again.

Sara saw the look of fear in the young man's eyes and wondered if he knew what he was up against. During the time that she had been their prisoner, Lucien had made it a point to shift in front of her to watch her horrified reaction. Shara, too, had taken perverse pleasure in shifting to his bear form and then threatening her with snarls and snaps of his powerful jaws. She had thought Gareth a freak of nature when he had performed the same feat with his body, but now it was obvious that there were many more of these mysterious shape-shifting creatures. She could only guess who was human and who was not, but from the way the Indian man was being manhandled by Lucien, it appeared that he was not one of the bear creatures.

Once Johnny was motionless within his grasp, Lucien swept his gaze around the rundown building and sneered. "Is this all you've got? Some worthless furniture and one broken-down old man?" He turned his full attention on Jack, who sat paralyzed in his armchair.

"That's right. There's nothing here you'd want," Johnny said, forcing the words out of his aching throat.

"I don't know about that," Shara said. He nodded toward the wall behind him where Johnny's gun was secured in the wooden rack.

Lucien's eyes lit up. "Get it," he ordered.

Shara pushed Sara roughly to the floor and pulled the weapon out of the rack. He fingered it carefully like a precious treasure, then lifted it to his shoulder and aimed it squarely at Jack.

"NO!" Johnny cried. "He's a harmless old man. Leave him alone."

Jack forced himself forward in the chair, his gnarled hands clenching the tattered armrests. Though he couldn't see the attackers, he knew exactly who they were. "Get out, you Devil Bear. You don't belong here."

Lucien threw his head back in laughter. How dare this worthless human order him to do anything! "Since you have a death wish, let me help you on your way to the Happy Hunting Ground, Old Man." Tossing Johnny aside like a feather, he stalked over to Jack and yanked him to his feet. The man was so light he virtually flew out of the chair. Lucien peered down into the weathered face and poked curiously at the sightless eye. "Too bad you can't see me so you can take the memory of my face with you to your grave."

"You are such a *man*," Sara screamed. Though her wrists were bound behind her, she had struggled to her knees and crawled over to Johnny, who lay stunned beside the wall. She glared defiantly at Lucien, knowing that there was nothing to lose. He was going to kill her one way or the other. "Look at me, you stinking bear turd. Is this what makes you feel like a real man? Picking on defenseless humans and others of your own kind who are weaker than you? Stealing women from their campsites? You are pathetic, you know that?"

Lucien froze, dumbfounded by the audacity of the woman. His palms itched to take her scrawny neck and twist it with all the strength he had. Never had he ached to kill someone as much as he wanted to kill her right now. Pushing Jack away, he wheeled with a snarl and took two steps toward Sara, his dark eyes blazing with fury. Blood pulsed angrily through the thick veins in his neck as he yanked her to her feet and glared down into her frightened eyes.

Sara yearned to cry out, but she didn't. She wouldn't give him the satisfaction of seeing her terror. Closing her eyes, she said a mental good-bye to those she loved and prepared herself for the pain that was coming. Her heart thundered in her chest at the feel of his hot breath on her face.

"Lucien!" Shara called out a moment too late.

Johnny staggered to his knees and butted the huge man in the back of the legs. Lucien fell forward with a startled yell and clutched for Sara. She ducked out of his way as a gunshot echoed through the room. A man's voice cried out in pain, followed by a woman's scream.

Johnny? Jack felt his heart break as he flattened himself against the wall and quietly backed out of the room into his bedroom. He cursed his damned sightlessness and his inability to come to his nephew's aid, but maybe it wasn't too late to save him or the woman. Feeling his way through the tiny room, he opened the window and struggled to lift his arthritic legs over the sash. His body rebelled and every muscle ached but he willed himself to do it. It would only be a moment before they discovered he was gone, and then it would be too late to help anyone. Giving one last grunt of effort, he flung his torso through the opening and fell onto the hard ground outside.

Sara watched in horror as the force of the bullet slammed Johnny against the wall. A red stain seeped from the right side of his jean shirt where the bullet had penetrated between his ribs. Groaning with pain, Johnny clutched his side and lay against the wall in semi-consciousness.

"Nice shooting," Lucien applauded. "Finish him while I take care of the little girl. Then go find that old one. When you're done, search the building for anything that might be useful. And look for food—I'm starving."

Shara lowered the rifle and glared at Lucien, more pissed off than he'd ever been.

"What's your problem?" Lucien growled. Cradling his shattered arm, he squeezed Sara's arm and pulled her close against him.

"You promised me a turn with her, remember?"

Smiling wickedly, Lucien nodded in acquiescence. "I guess I did. Tell you what. You finish what I told you to do, and I'll save a little bit of her for you."

Shara wasn't happy about the arrangement, but he knew better than to challenge Lucien. If he wanted any piece of the woman at all, he'd better do as he was told. Laying the rifle down on the floor, he stalked across the room and knelt down on one knee beside the wounded man. As a bear, he could easily rip Johnny's throat out, but somehow that wouldn't be as satisfying as killing him as a man. Raising his hands in front of Johnny's face, he cracked his knuckles loudly in preparation for strangling him. Feeling the muscles crush beneath his fingers would definitely ease his anger.

Johnny's eyes refused to focus. He felt blood pouring from his body in a steady stream, smelled the odor of it saturating his shirt even as it drained the life out of him. Unable to remain upright, he slid lower down the wall and fell to the floor with a thump. He watched in terror as Shara raised his hands before him and leered.

A thundering crash echoed around him as the front door shattered and wood splinters flew across the room.

Lucien turned in time to see Marin hurtling at him, a snarling missile of ebony fur and gnashing teeth. Automatically reaching his arms to the floor, Lucien quickly shifted and rose up to meet Marin chest to chest as the great bruin lunged for his throat. Their powerful limbs entwined as they fell to the floor in a rolling blur of fur.

Lindy charged in behind Marin with the rifle at her shoulder. She looked quickly around, searching for Sara, and found her cowering at the wall behind the fighting bears. "Stay where you are," she called to her over the deafening growls. "I'm coming for you." Moving cautiously to skirt her way around the clashing bears, she worked her way closer until her breath caught in her throat and her heart skipped a beat.

Shara rose from the floor with Johnny clenched in his arm. He swiveled around to face Lindy and show her his prize. "Looks like the people you want are over here with me, Protector," he taunted. Holding Johnny firmly with one arm, he swept his other arm to the side and grabbed hold of Sara, too.

"Don't be stupid, Shara. Let them go."

"Put the gun down, and I'll think about it."

"No.

Shara shook his head, growing anxious for a kill. "You know you can't hit me. All I have to do is swing around and put one of these humans in front of me. Either one will make a good bullet shield."

"I'm not letting you leave here alive, Shara. Let them go."

He was silent for a moment while he thought. It was clear that she wasn't going to let him walk away, but he knew that he still had the advantage with both of the humans securely in his grasp. He squeezed their arms viciously, until Sara cried out in pain.

"I'll make you a deal, Protector. You shoot Marin, and I'll let both your sister and the Indian go. And you'd better decide quickly, because this one doesn't have much blood left in him."

Lindy's heart seemed to thud to a stop in her chest. Shoot Marin? How could she kill the man she loved, the Guardian of the clan she was sworn to protect? But Sara and Johnny faced certain death if she didn't do as he said. From the amount of blood staining Johnny's clothes, it was clear that he would bleed to death without immediate medical attention. And she knew from Lena and Gareth's testimonies that Shara was strong enough and mean enough to strangle his prisoners with one hand. She looked at her sister, at the expression of horror on her young face, and knew she didn't have a choice.

She turned slowly and aimed the gun at Marin. He and Lucien lay bloody and exhausted beside each other on the floor, just watching Shara and Lindy's standoff and awaiting her decision. Tears streamed down her cheeks as her finger tightened on the trigger. "I love you, Marin," she whispered, feeling her life about to change forever. Her finger trembled, refused to move. The gun shook in her grasp. She swallowed down the lump in her throat and sighted the rifle on Marin again. He lay completely still and looked at her with forgiveness in his dark eyes, urging her to do what she had to do.

Suddenly, something flew through the shattered doorway and hit the floor in front of her in a thundering explosion of fire and smoke. Lindy recoiled from the intense heat and lowered the rifle as she tried to protect her eyes from the acrid fumes. Flames shot up to the ceiling, engulfing the old wood in crackling torrents of heat.

"Marin! Sara!" Lindy cried, desperately trying to see through the billowing clouds of smoke pouring up from the floor. She urged herself ahead, only to be forced back by the intensity of the heat. Her eyes watered, fumes choked in her throat, denying her air. She waved her hands before her in an urgent attempt to clear the smoke from her view. Through the flames, a faint movement appeared, a human figure moving quickly through the fire toward the front door. She couldn't see who it was. She lifted the gun once more and waited.

Shara pushed his way toward her, one arm raised to shield his face. He coughed and stared at her through the smoke, ignoring the gun in her hands.

"Die, you bastard," Lindy wheezed as she pulled the trigger and sent the bullet deep into the bear man. He looked down at the ragged hole in his chest, his expression one of disbelief, then sank to the floor with his mouth open but speechless as his heart stopped beating. When she was sure he was dead, she scanned the room again. The smoke was now so thick that she could barely breathe, but she had to find the others. Pulling her shirt up over the lower half of her face as a mask, Lindy struggled across the room and kicked her foot along the floor, searching for bodies. She bumped into something soft and bent down to yank it up. It was Sara. "Come on!" she screamed.

Sara staggered a few steps and abruptly stopped. "Johnny's down here by my feet. Get him, please Lindy. Get him."

Lindy pushed her sister toward the door and bent to retrieve the man. He was so weak that she couldn't raise him to his feet. The blood continued to soak his clothes, his arms stained scarlet. "Johnny, help me," she cried. "I can't lift you by myself."

His dark eyes gazed up at her helplessly. "Leave me," he whispered.

Before she could respond, Johnny jerked up from the ground. Marin had him in a tight grip and dragged him out the door to safety. They stumbled together into the cold night and gasped in breaths of fresh, crisp air. Lindy flew to Sara's side and embraced her before freeing the rope from her wrists.

"Sara, honey, did they hurt you?" Lindy cried, her voice shaking so hard she could barely speak.

Sara shook her head while she held Lindy tight. She couldn't stop trembling. "I'm okay. Thank God you came when you did or I wouldn't have..." Her voice trailed off.

"It's ok, you're safe now." Even as she cuddled Sara's head to her chest, Lindy gazed at the ground nearby where Marin sprawled. Blood oozed in thick streaks from his chest and head, but he still had Johnny cradled safely in his arms.

"Marin..."

He shook his head to silence her. "Not now," he warned, too exhausted to do anything but lay back on the cold ground and breathe.

Chapter Twenty-Five

They huddled together on the freezing ground and watched the walls of the trading post collapse. The ceiling followed, crashing to the ground with a splintering of old wood that sent showers of fiery red sparks drifting upward into the darkness of night.

Marin couldn't help but notice how similar the glowing embers looked to the tips of Lucien's fur when the sunlight hit it just right. *Lucien.* Suddenly remembering his enemy, he staggered to his feet and moved closer to the smoldering debris of the building. He waved away the last tendrils of curling smoke with his hand and moved as close as he dared. The interior of the room had burned fast and hot, leaving piles of ashes behind where something had once stood. In the center of the room he could see the remains of three chairs. His eyes traveled thoroughly over each inch of the charred ruin, searching. Finally a long breath eased from his throat. There, next to the wall, lay the burned carcass of Lucien.

He lowered his head to his chest in silent thanks before turning to address the others. "I see his body. Lucien is dead."

Lindy rose and joined him at the edge of the ruin, her arm slipping around his back. She shivered at the feel of his bare flesh. "You're freezing, Marin. You need to shift. And we need to get Johnny to the hospital right now."

"How are we supposed to do that? I'm too weak to carry him."

She looked around the property and spotted Johnny's car parked in the driveway. "Let's see if the keys are in it." She ran to the vehicle and opened the door, crying out in surprise when she looked inside.

Marin's eyes flared wide in alarm. "What now?

Lindy reached inside the car and slowly withdrew something. She threw her arms around it with a scream of delight. It was Jack.

The old man clasped Lindy tightly to him and sank back into the car. "You made it," he cried, a single tear falling from his blind eye.

"How did you get out of the fire?" Lindy asked, but Jack raised a trembling hand to stop her. "Johnny... is he... ?"

"He's alive, but he needs to go to the hospital right now. Do you have the keys, Jack?"

He motioned to the ignition, where the silver keys hung. "Everyone come. Hurry."

Lindy motioned for Sara to get in the front seat with Jack while she and Marin carried Johnny between them and placed him gently into the back seat. A soon as they were piled in, she started the car and roared down the driveway. The nearest hospital was in Timberlake, a thirty minute drive, and she prayed that Johnny could hang on until then. Driving like a madwoman, she floored the old Buick and flew down the highway.

"You must leave me here," Marin groaned, his voice weary with pain and exhaustion. "You know I can't go to the hospital."

"You have to. You're in terrible shape, and you need stitches to close up those slashes in your chest, Marin."

He laid one hand on her shoulder and squeezed it firmly, asserting his authority. "Lindy." His voice grew stronger, more demanding. "If I shift in front of someone at the hospital, I'll expose our existence and endanger my clan. There are so few of us left now..." His voice cracked with emotion, and he grew silent.

Though she knew it had to be done, she didn't want

to leave him alone out here, injured and by himself. "I'll drop you off at my cabin, so Lena can look after you until I get back." She glanced in the rear view mirror trying to see his face. He looked beaten and worn down. "Tell me you'll be okay, Marin," she begged, torn between tending to his needs and Johnny's.

He looked up to catch her eyes watching him in the mirror and forced a smile. "I'll be fine."

She continued her wild flight down the dark highway, passing mile after mile of dark forest until finally the light from her back porch came into view. Swerving into her gravel driveway, she waited for Marin to extricate himself from the back seat and stumble up the porch steps before backing out and taking off down the highway again.

Marin watched the taillights disappear into the night. When everything was black, he pushed open the door and collapsed in the warmth of the cabin.

Chapter Twenty-Six

Lindy handed Jack an ice cold beer and plumped the cushion behind his back. He took a long swig and sank back into the softness of the couch, feeling relaxation come over him for the first time in days. "You ok, Jack?" she asked, patting his arm as she sat down beside him.

"Fine." The smile he flashed broke his face into a thousand wrinkles.

Marin waited patiently for the old man to settle before beginning his questions. It had been five days since they had rescued Sara and during that time, Jack had never left Johnny's side as he fought for his life in the hospital. But now that his nephew's condition had turned the corner and they knew he would recover, Marin couldn't wait to hear Jack's explanation of what had happened before he and Lindy had arrived at the trading post. Gareth, Lena, and Sara sat in chairs nearby, equally anxious.

He cleared his throat and leaned forward. "Old one?"

Jack's grin grew even bigger. "Guardian?"

"How is it that you survived the fire?"

Jack uttered a soft, knowing laugh that shook his fragile body. He shook one bony finger at Marin in reprimand. "I know you think I'm a helpless old man, but I have strengths, too."

Marin shook his head, his ebony hair moving softly around his face. "You're wrong. You are descended from a long line of Protectors. There is nothing about you that points to weakness."

Bowing his head at the compliment, Jack breathed deeply. "I would have enjoyed protecting your clan, Marin. I wish I'd had the chance. But I'm glad that I could save the lives of you and the women."

Every eyebrow shot up at his words. They made no sense. Jack had saved their lives?

He chuckled at the deafening silence and launched into an explanation of how Lucien and Shara had forced their way into his home. "When the gun went off and Johnny was shot, I knew I had to get help. I had to get him out of there. I crawled out the bedroom window figuring I'd flag a car down on the highway; but then I heard you, Marin, break the door down. I heard you fighting with Lucien. I figured we'd need a diversion to get Johnny out, so I went back to the shed and made a Molotov cocktail." He snorted loudly, pleased with himself. "Worked like a charm, too. Except that it burned my house down."

Lindy's jaw dropped. "*You*... made a Molotov cocktail?"

"Yes, ma'am. I'm afraid I was a bit of a hell-raiser in my time and some things you just never forget."

Lindy reached over and gave him a gentle hug. "Thank God for long memories," she laughed.

"Well, I am very relieved to have this over with," Marin sighed. "Once again I owe you and your kin my gratitude. I'm glad that he'll recover."

Jack didn't answer. He set his beer down on the coffee table and reached his shaky hands into the air in front of him, grasping for Marin.

Marin looked at Lindy, a puzzled look on his face. When she motioned for him to take Jack's hands, he leaned further forward and took the gnarled hands into his own strong ones. "Is something wrong, Elder?"

Jack cleared his throat and nodded, sending a snow white wisp of hair down over his forehead. "I'm afraid, Guardian, that your troubles aren't over yet."

"I don't understand."

Lena, Gareth and Sara all leaned forward in their chairs wanting to hear more.

"Do you know how some Bearwalkers turn rogue, Marin? Do you know anything about them?"

"I never even knew there was such a thing, until you told us about it."

Jack pursed his thin lips in concentration, reluctant to share what he knew and yet knowing that he must in order to protect Lindy's life. "When you and Lindy came to me that day and asked what I could tell you about Lucien, I didn't quite tell you *everything* I knew. But now that the Devil Bear has been destroyed and the threat to your clan removed, there is one last threat you'll need to deal with."

"And that is?" Marin cocked his head expectantly.

"Yourself."

There was silence for a moment before he responded. "What do you mean?"

Jack squeezed the strong hands that held his, knowing that it would probably be his last encounter with the creature he so greatly admired. "There's something you need to know, Marin. Something that may affect the outcome of your life."

Marin withdrew his hands and ran them through the thickness of his hair. "Tell me, Old One. I grow impatient."

"Marin, I told you about the other rogue that existed in my grandfather's day. What I didn't tell you was that he lost his sanity, because he fell in love... with a human woman. The clan tried to reason with him, but he was unstoppable in his desire to claim her. When he put his kin at risk because of her, they knew they had to stop him. The clan killed him."

"And this concerns me how?" There was an edge in his voice that bespoke his uneasiness.

"Because I know that you, too, love a human woman."

Marin stood up and walked to the living room window, shaking his head furiously. He stopped and stared at his reflection in the smooth glass. "I'm strong. I don't think I'm insane, or even headed that way." He turned and looked at the people seated around him. "Do any of you?"

Jack interrupted before anyone could respond. "That rogue was your great-grandfather, Marin. The Guardian of the clan. He was strong, too."

The silence was palpable as each person looked from one to the other in shock. They were familiar with the story of Marowin and Emma, the story that Dr. Dean had revealed during his capture of the Bearwalkers. But no one knew how the Guardian and his human lover became separated, or how life had ended for the great Marowin.

Marin lowered his head to stare at the rug beneath his feet. "I don't understand. Why wouldn't my sire have told me of this? Why has this information been hidden from me, from all of us, all of these years?" The shock and humiliation were clear in his softly spoken words.

"I suspect that it was a great embarrassment to the clan, seeing how one of their finest warriors could go mad because of a human, and a woman, at that. They wanted to forget about it, bury the past so that they would never be reminded of what had happened. I assume that they thought it would never happen again."

"But it happened to Lucien... and it will happen to me..." Marin's voice faded into silence.

Lindy rose from the couch and stood beside Marin. When he refused to look at her, she took his face gently in her hands and raised it up. "Marin, we don't know what caused Lucien to turn rogue, and we *certainly* can't say that the same thing will happen to you."

His dark eyes shimmered with moisture at the sight of her sweet face looking at him. "But it might. How can I put the clan... and you... in danger by taking that chance?"

"The clan needs you now more than ever, Marin," Lena said. "We number half of what we once were, and we won't survive without your guidance and leadership. We'll need to find another clan to help us rebuild our numbers, and we can't do that without you."

Gareth turned slowly around, holding his bandaged ribs, and stared hard at Marin. "Yeah, we need you around to keep idiots like me in line." He smiled at the feel of Sara's hand on his leg, giving him encouragement.

"Marowin was the rogue? I just can't believe it." He shook his head again and again as if unable to process the information. "What would you have me do, then, Old One? And what of my feelings for this woman?" His eyes darted over and settled on Lindy's face.

"I think," Jack said softly, "that you are the strongest man I have ever met. Each of us has a path to take in life, and sometimes that path splits and we must choose. Humans aren't so lucky... we have just one spirit to guide us through our life. But you, Marin, you have two. You have the wisdom of a man and the great heart of a bear. I'm confident that you'll choose your path wisely and find both love and sanity."

Marin looked at the old man, feeling sudden affection for him. He was a man of courage and integrity, of honesty. A spark of hope flared in his heart that if Jack thought he would be ok, then maybe he would. "So why have you told me this, if you think I'll be able to choose my own path?"

Jack smiled. "Because each man should have the knowledge he needs to face his own destiny. And since Lindy is part of your destiny, you must know the truth in order to protect her."

"I would never hurt her... or my clan," Marin said.

"And that is what separates you from Marowin," Jack smiled.

Chapter Twenty-Seven

Gareth and Sara sat side by side on the back porch steps. The cold autumn wind blew his cinnamon colored hair back from his face, exposing the bruises that were slowly healing. He shivered and pulled the jacket tighter around him. "It was here that your sister found me," he said, his voice soft with the memory that he wanted to share with her. "It's because of her that I'm alive."

Sara brushed the hair out of her eyes to look at him. He seemed so young and innocent, which made perfect sense now that she knew his secret. *So strange,* she thought, *how human he can be.* The corner of her mouth rose in a smile. "Yup, that's my sister. She never could refuse to help someone in need."

He reached down beside him and took Sara's hand in his own, wondering if she would pull away. She didn't. Instead, her fingers squeezed his reassuringly. "I'm sorry I didn't tell you, Sara. I really wanted to make a good impression, so you'd want to get to know me better. But I couldn't tell you the truth. I hope you understand."

"I do, Gareth. Even if you had told me, I wouldn't have believed you. I hardly believed it when you changed... turned... whatever you call it, right before my eyes in the cave. It was totally unreal."

He exhaled softly. "Yeah, it is shocking when you don't expect it. And what we do... it's called shifting."

"Shifting," she repeated. "I'll remember that. So hey, tell me something. After we met at the museum that day, were you ever going to call me?"

"Call you?"

"Yeah, were you going to call me and ask me out on a date? Or was the attraction between us just physical?"

His expression went sheepish. "I did want to see you again, but I had no way to contact you. Lindy said she would let me use her telephone, but then Lucien came and I never got the chance."

"So you would have asked me out?"

"Sure. Would you have said yes?"

"Of course."

He raised his head into the wind to sniff the clean forest scent, so homesick that he could hardly stand the confinement of the cabin for one more day. "Would you still say yes, knowing what I am now?" His honey brown eyes zeroed in on hers, searching for the truth.

Slipping her arm through his, Sara chewed her lower lip for a moment. This was all so frightening and new, learning of the existence of these creatures Lindy called Bearwalkers and needing to keep their secret safe from everyone she knew. And worst of all was not knowing how to treat a man who was also a bear—how to love such a man. But Lindy did it. There was no doubt that Lindy loved Marin deeply and would find a way to work things out with him to ensure their life together. If Lindy could do, couldn't she?

Gareth lowered his head, disheartened by her silence. *I must be crazy to think she could accept me.* Then he felt the soft kiss caress his cheek. He turned to look at her, his eyes wide.

"Yes, Gareth. My answer is yes. I want to get to know you better. Not that I want to rush into having sex, you know, 'cause that's still a little freaky to think about, you being a bear and all. But I do like you. A lot."

He turned his head to hide the blush on his cheeks. "I like you, too, Sara. A lot."

"Gareth, if I ask you something, will you tell me the

truth?"

He squeezed her arm in gentle reprimand. "I'll always tell you the truth. There will be no more secrets between us from now on. What do you want to know?"

A worried expression clouded her face. "Do you think Lindy is safe with Marin? I mean really safe? After what Jack said, I just get the willies thinking that he might become like Lucien some day." Shivers tremored down her spine at the thought of her brutal kidnapper.

Gareth pulled her arm tightly against him to comfort her. There was no doubt in his mind about Marin, and he had to make her believe in him, too. "Marin could never be like that. I've known him all my life and trust him more than anyone. He's saved my life so many times, and the lives of my kin, when he could've just walked away. He's protective, not violent."

"I thought Guardians *had* to do that. Isn't it their job?"

"Only because they choose to do it. Sure, Guardians inherit the position from their sires, but it's still a choice that they can refuse if they want to. Marin could've walked away from us at any time, but he didn't, even after we betrayed him. Even after I betrayed him."

"I've heard your friend Lena say how much she respects him, how much your whole clan respects him; but he's not in love with any of them like he is with my sister. And he's so strong, Gareth, I can't help worrying that maybe Lindy doesn't know what she's getting into."

Gareth nodded, understanding her concern. "I agree that Marin can be intimidating. In fact, that's exactly what Lindy thought of him when they first met. She hated him, did you know that?"

Sara's eyes widened at this information. "She did?"

"Oh yeah. The first time I brought her into forest home, Marin attacked her and practically killed her, thinking that she had held me captive..." He grew silent at the sight of the blood draining from her face. "Uhhh... this isn't helping any, is it?"

Sara just stared at him. Finally she shook her head and looked up into the sky. "My sister is nuts. It's not Marin's sanity I should be worrying about, but Lindy's. She's obviously lost it."

Gareth chuckled at her. "It's a long story that would be better heard from her than from me, I think. Just trust me when I say that they're a perfect match and that Marin would die for her. She couldn't be in safer hands than his."

"I guess you'd know, Gareth. Thanks. I feel better now. Sort of."

They were quiet for a moment, until Gareth cupped her hands in both of his. "I suppose you'll be going back to school now."

"Yeah. I have one more semester after this one, and then I'll be done. What about you? What are you going to do now?"

A quizzical expression crossed his face. "Winter's coming. I do what I always do... sleep."

"Sleep?" Her hand flew to her mouth in shock. "Oh my God, bears hibernate, don't they? Do you really sleep through the whole winter?"

He couldn't help smiling at her naivete. It was comforting that she was as ignorant of his world as he was of hers. "It's not a deep sleep. There are times when I can rouse myself, days when it's warm, and I wake up and go outside for a bit. But then it's back to sleep til spring."

"So I won't see you until next spring then?" Her voice lowered with sadness at the thought.

"I'm afraid so."

"Well then, I guess I better make the most of the time we have left." She scooted sideways to take his head in her hands and plant a firm, wet kiss on his mouth. Momentarily stunned, Gareth squirmed for a second and then returned her kiss with an equally passionate one of his own. The two tangled together in a blur of raging hormones.

Lindy lowered the curtain and turned away from the kitchen window to look at Marin, who sat in the chair watching her. "Looks like the kids have really hit it off," she said, smiling at their youthful enthusiasm. "Have you forgiven him yet?"

Marin grunted as he stood and closed the distance between them. Pulling her into his arms, he sniffed her neck to savor the sweet human scent he had come to love. How did she always make everything so right for him? Even when his pride made him cling stubbornly to his anger, his heart melted at the look on her face that let him know he was wrong. "Of course I've forgiven him," he purred into her ear while his lips swept over her cheek. "I'd never hear the end of it from you if I didn't."

She backed away, ready to retort in anger, when she saw the sly smile curve on his lips. "You are a tease," she laughed. Her hands slipped over the sleek muscles of his arms as they held her close, appreciating the incredible strength that held her so gently.

"Lena came back to visit while you were in town," Marin said, pulling her onto his lap as he sank on a kitchen chair.

"How's she doing? Has her sister's cub accepted his new mother?"

His eyes grew misty at the thought of the kin he had lost to Lucien's madness. "It will take time, but the boy will adjust. Lena is a fine mother."

"Did she tell you what the clan decided about your Guardianship?"

He laughed heartily as contentment replaced the sadness in his eyes. "She said they *begged* me to come back and be with them. It seems that they weren't as enthralled by Lucien's promises as they thought they would be. And they're scared, Lindy. Scared that there are so few of us now. My kin need to find mates to keep our bloodlines going."

"How are you going to do that?

"Next spring, I'll have to search for another clan and

ask them to join us. It's the only way to bring new blood into our circle."

"Yeah, well... just don't be bringing any new female blood into *our* circle, Mister!"

Eyebrows raising with amusement, Marin wrapped his arms around Lindy and snuggled her to his chest. "Is that jealousy I hear in your voice, Mrs. Anderson?"

"Damn right. I have no intention of sharing you with another woman... or bear." Her lips curled into a smile before crushing down on his.

The kitchen door opened as Gareth and Sara walked in. "Oh oh, sorry, Sis," Sara giggled. "Hate to interrupt the love fest, but it's starting to snow and we're freezing. Anyway, Gareth wanted to say good-bye before he leaves."

Lindy slid off Marin's lap and stood beside Gareth. "You're leaving so soon, Gar? You know you're welcome to stay as long as you like."

"I know, Lindy, and I appreciate the invitation, but I need to get back. I want to get my den ready for winter and get settled in before the snow gets heavy."

"Hibernation, you know," Sara added, proud of her new understanding.

Lindy cocked her head as though the word were foreign to her. "Hibernation?"

"Yeah. It's that time... you can't fight nature," Gareth said, shrugging his shoulders. "See you in the spring and thanks... *again*... for saving me." Then kissing her lightly on the cheek, he turned and hugged Sara. "Think of me over the winter, ok?"

"Sure bet, bear man. I'll be waiting for you when the snow melts."

When Gareth was gone, Sara stretched her arms lazily over her head and headed for the guestroom. "Night guys. I'm hitting the hay." The door shut softly behind her.

Marin knew before she even turned to face him that Lindy was crying.

"Why didn't you tell me?' she sobbed. "Couldn't you at

least have dropped a hint that you guys go missing for six months?" The tears fell fast and furious now, her shoulders trembling.

He could hardly speak; the guilt was so great. Watching her cry was worse than any injury a bear could inflict on him. He sat still, giving her time to grieve while his own heart broke. When she finally caught her breath and calmed her nerves, he pulled her onto his lap and rested his head softly against hers. "I thought I could fight it, Lind. When I learned that I was part human, I thought that I could summon up that part of me and just refuse to go to sleep. But the pull of nature is too strong... I've been feeling it for the last several weeks now. When we went after Sara, it wasn't so much my wounds that made me weak as the compulsion to sleep. You don't know how hard I've fought this, how much I want to stay awake and be with you. But this is one battle I can't win."

The tears rushed out again, followed by great heaving sobs as she struggled to cope with his news. "I don't want you to leave me, Marin. I love having you in my life every day, sharing my life with you. I don't want to lose you. It's so damn unfair."

"I know. Believe me, I would do anything to stay with you. But there is nothing we can do about it."

"So when will it happen?"

He exhaled deeply, hating to say it. "Since snow is already falling I can't wait long. Sara goes back to school in the morning, so tomorrow night will have to be our last together."

Her throat was so swollen that she could barely swallow. Tears still shimmered in her eyes at the realization that there was nothing she could do but face the fact that he would have to leave her. Sniffling softly, she swept the hair out of his face to gaze at his penetrating eyes. Oh, how she would miss seeing those eyes, that face that made her pulse race. She forced a smile and kissed him tenderly before laying her head down on his shoulder. "Then I guess we should make our last two nights together special."

He nodded, too sullen to answer, though a thought was already swirling in his mind. Was there a solution?

Chapter Twenty-Eight

Marin took Lindy by the hand and led her into the guest bedroom. She followed silently, puzzled by his action.

"Why are we coming in here and not our bedroom?" she asked while he slipped off his jeans and sat down on the edge of the bed.

"I'll explain later. For now, I just want to watch you undress for me."

Still perplexed, she began to unbutton the light blue shirt covering her, moving slowly and taking her time with each button. She loved his attention, craved the sight of his gaze riveted on her.

His eyes followed her movements hungrily, expressing his delight with her body. His pulse rose as she unsnapped her bra and freed her breasts before his widening eyes. Her hand lowered to the zipper of her jeans, played with the single button to tease him before sliding the tight pants down her slim legs. She kicked them free and lowered her silk panties slowly, then stood before him, waiting.

Marin growled with pleasure at the sight of her naked. She was gorgeous, from the golden hair on her head to the red polish on her toes. His heart thudded in his chest, his groin aching with desire. "Come to me," he demanded.

She stepped closer as he spread his legs to allow her between them. When she stood nestled between his knees, he slipped his large hands around her waist to pull her closer. His mouth found one breast and kissed it softly, suckling the rosy peak that was taut with arousal. Cupping her buttock with his other hand, he buried his face in the soft flesh of her breast.

Lindy felt her face flush with warmth at his touch and gazed silently down at him. How could it be that this gentle man was the same angry bear who had almost killed her? Was it the humanity in him that allowed him to behave with such tenderness, or was it that she had tamed the beast in him? Not that it mattered. He was hers, however it had happened, and she thanked God for it.

His face still nuzzling her breast, Lindy ran her hands across his broad, burnished shoulders. She still remembered the day he had sat in her bathtub for the first time to soak away muscle spasms. The steam had risen from the water and curled his jet hair ever so slightly, until she couldn't fight the compulsion to run her fingers through it. The water had dripped down his chest, leaving a tiny trail between his muscular pectorals. She had known then that she would always love him, and she was even more sure now. She swept her hand down his arm, across the bulging bicep and over the curve of his chest.

Grabbing her firmly by the hips, Marin rolled them both down onto the mattress until they lay face to face. He gazed into her blue eyes, loving the way they shimmered with her passion for him. Then raising up on one elbow, he ran his finger down her ribcage and across her hip, smiling when tiny goosebumps rose on her flesh.

"Are you cold or is it something else causing these bumps?" he chuckled softly.

"Honey, you give me more than goosebumps when you touch me, don't you know that?"

"Honey?" His eyebrows shot up. "Is that an affectionate term or are you just hungry?"

It was her turn to laugh. "I'm hungry all right, Marin. Hungry to feel you inside me."

It was all he needed to hear. Lowering his mouth to hers, he brushed his lips softly over her mouth, nipping gently on her lower lip while his hand moved lower to caress between her thighs. Lindy moaned at the feel of his fingers stroking her, preparing her to receive him. He was so gentle, so thoughtful a lover. It was even more amazing because this was all so new to him. He'd told her about Terra and how mating between bears went; she knew that there was no tenderness, no lingering to build up the excitement before the physical act of joining. He had learned well how to pleasure her, and he obviously enjoyed it. Low rolling noises slipped from his throat to match each groan of her pleasure.

Lindy slipped her hand down between them and cupped the length of him in her palm to knead and caress him. His growl became a roar as passion built within him. His eyes closed momentarily as he savored the feel of her touching him. Only when his fingers had taken her over the edge with a scream of ecstasy did he roll on top of her and plunge into her warm heat.

Marin steeled his gaze on her face, memorizing the fullness of her lips and the curl of her eyelashes as he stroked within her. Plunging into her again and again, his eyes riveted to her softly swaying breasts, he savored each moan of enjoyment quivering from her throat. There was nothing he wouldn't do for this woman. He would gladly give his life for her. He had never loved another this way.

She clutched at him, running her nails lightly across his broad back until he quivered. He thrust his full length inside her, passionately yet carefully keeping control of his incredible strength. He had worried about taming his power enough to keep from hurting her, and he had accomplished it so well that he knew the moans coming from deep in her throat were cries of passion instead of pain.

Lindy grabbed his head to smother his mouth with hers. His dark hair tumbled down around his face, marring her view until she swept it back with the caress of her fingers. His body was shaking now, quivering on the verge of explosion. With one great cry, they came together in a moment of complete ecstasy.

His body sated, Marin rolled over and buried his arm beneath her head to hold her close. Drops of sweat beaded on his olive skin and rolled slowly down across his chest. Lindy turned toward him, still full of passion, and swept her tongue across his hardened nipple. She loved the feel of him, the taste of him. She would never have her fill of him.

When they were rested, Marin gazed over at her with a curious expression on his face. "I've been meaning to ask you something."

She traced her finger along the line of his jaw. It was angular, so bear-like and yet so humanly handsome. "Ask anything."

"Would you have shot me to save Johnny and your sister from Shara?"

The corner of her mouth upturned in a vague smile. "Do you really need to ask that? Don't you know that I could never hurt you?"

He shook his head as if in doubt. "I saw the look on your face, Lind. And anyway, I would have understood. A good Protector does what must be done."

"A good Protector saves her people, even if the one needing saving is the Guardian." She leaned over to kiss him. "I told you that you'd always be safe with me, and I meant it."

Marin smiled and swept his gaze across the room to drink in his surroundings. "It's funny how uncomfortable I was when I first came here. Now it feels like home."

His words made her heart ache with the thought of being separated from him. Slipping her arm around his waist, she nestled her head against his chest and sighed. "What's going to happen with us, Marin? How can this ever really work out between us when your world is out there in the wilderness and mine is here?"

He was quiet for a moment while he pulled her tighter against him. When he finally answered, his voice was low and serene. "I don't know the answer to that, Lindy. But I do know that I never want to be without you in my life. Nothing that I do for the clan can give me the joy, the completeness, that I feel when I share life with you. I'm just thankful that you've accepted what I am and have learned to deal with it so well. I'm afraid that very few women would tolerate a bear in their bed." He smiled but it quickly turned into a tired yawn.

She laughed softly, amused by his words. "I've only had a bear in my bed one time and that was the night you were wounded and shifted in your sleep."

When he turned his head to look at her, his eyes twinkled with happiness. "I know of a way we can be together during the winter."

Her lips parted slowly in wonder. "How can that be? You told me that you can't fight nature to overcome hibernation."

"I can't. But that doesn't mean I have to hibernate at forest home."

It suddenly dawned on her what he was proposing. "You can hibernate *here*?"

"I'll be asleep, but at least I'll be near you. And if you need me, you'll know right where I am. You can just wake me."

"So that's why you wanted to make love in this bedroom instead of ours. When you fall asleep tonight, you can shift and just stay here until spring."

"That, and I want your scent around me to give me sweet dreams while I sleep."

She kissed him again, this time more passionately. "I love the idea. You'll be safely hidden in here if someone comes to visit, yet I can see you anytime I want."

Marin closed his eyes and yawned again. "It's coming on me so strong I can't resist anymore, Lind. I can't keep my eyes open despite how much I'd like to right now. Forgive me for leaving you."

"Don't ask my forgiveness for being what you are, Marin. You're a bear and a man, and I love you either way. I just... love you." She lowered her eyes and looked away.

He tightened his arms around her for one last hug. "I love you, too, Mrs. Anderson. I've never said that to anyone before, but I can't sleep without telling you how I feel. You are my friend, my lover, my precious Protector. I will always be yours, as you will always be mine. And somehow, we'll work through things until we find a way to make a life together. But for now, just knowing that you're here near me while I sleep is all I need."

Lindy swiped at a tear falling from the corner of her eye. "I'll watch over you and keep you safe, Marin. I promise."

He rolled from the bed and stretched his arms down to the floor, never once letting his eyes waver from the sight of Lindy. Fur thrust out from his body in thick ebony strands to hide the olive skin he had worn for her. His human ears shifted to the top of his head while a long black muzzle thrust from his face. Claws appeared on the end of his fingers, now paws. Grunting as the shift completed, Marin sank back down on the mattress and rolled his small black eyes to look at the woman he loved one more time. Then his eyes closed, and he drifted into the sleep of bears.

Lindy touched the soft thick fur before pulling the blanket up over him. She kissed his muzzle gently. "Sleep well, my love. Keep me in your dreams."

Then she rose and closed the door quietly behind her, leaving him in deep slumber.

About the Author

Being followed by a black bear in Wisconsin's Northwoods was the inspiration behind Lori Johnson's fascination with the lore and natural history of these beautiful creatures, and the impetus behind her first book, People of the Bear.

After earning a Biology degree from Valparaiso University, she combined her love of nature and writing to publish numerous nonfiction articles in local and national magazines. She lives in Illinois with her husband, daughter and a menagerie of pets.

Explore Lori's world of black bears at www.lori-johnson.com

Printed in the United States
154583LV00001B/15/P

9 781594 261169